Dedicated to the
Appalachian Trail Thru-Hiker Class of 2022

... for the memories of a lifetime ...

******

In remembrance of Daddy
Bill Lonsbury, Jr. // October 6, 1952 – November 24, 2002

... I hope I make you proud ...

PREFACE

Zoby is a real dog who actually did hike the Appalachian Trail with his human mommy in 2022. They started the trail in March at Springer Mountain, Georgia, walking together through 14 states to arrive at Baxter State Park in Maine in September.

The length of the trail changes annually due to restoration and re-routing; in 2022 the length was 2,194.3 miles. Statistics show that approximately 20-25% percent of humans who begin the trail actually walk each mile within 12 months to complete a thru-hike.

The percentage for dogs is even lower. Especially small dogs.

After nearly dying from a dog attack in 2018, Zoby displayed such amazing courage and strength to not only survive, but thrive in the days and months following, his mommy promised her adventure-loving furry best friend she would give him his best dog life ever. Selling everything and moving into an RV in 2021, she began to fulfill that promise, so it was only natural they take the opportunity to do the im-paw-sible together:

Thru-hike the entire Appalachian Trail.
Small dog. Big Courage. Bigger Adventures.

Author's Note:
While the majority of events in this book are based in reality of life on the trail and true encounters, many are embellished for drama and storyline purposes, and a few are entirely fictional. Dogs outside of service animals are not allowed in Great Smoky Mountains National Park or Baxter State Park in Maine, wherein lies Katahdin and the northern terminus of the AT. In real life, Zoby was kenneled, or as he knew it, "stayed at the doggie spa" through the Smokies. A celebration for his "summit" and his completion of the miles he was able to hike was held at Abol Bridge, the border to Baxter State Park. Overall, Zoby still hiked over 2,000 miles, therefore he relaxed and enjoyed time in Millinocket, Maine while his Mommy completed her thru-hike atop Katahdin.

Zoby is indeed trained as a Medical Alert /Therapy Dog to assist Mommy with an anxiety disorder and resulting anxiety/panic attacks. Therefore, he *is* actually a Service Animal. However, his Mommy had previously experienced problems with Rangers and business establishments not recognizing Therapy Dogs as Service Animals, therefore made a difficult decision to follow rules for "normal" dogs to avoid potential logistic issues with their thru-hike.

The facts and story surrounding his attack by a dog, surgery and recovery in 2018 are true.

GLOSSARY OF THRU-HIKER TERMS

Nobo vs Sobo: Northbound (GA to ME) hikers versus Southbound (ME to GA) hikers

Flip-flop: Starting in the middle of the trail, going one direction to its terminus, then back to the middle and going the other direction to the other terminus

Section Hiker: A hiker doing a section of the trail, could be a couple days, weeks or months

Shakedown Hikes: Practice hikes to test gear and to remove unnecessary weight from packs

Zero / Nero: Hiking zero miles, a rest day / hiking "near zero" miles, a partial rest day

Trail Angel / Trail Magic: A person who provides services to hikers for no cost. These services are trail magic – which may be anything from providing a bottle of water to setting up a grill and tables full of food at road crossings on trail, to even hosting hikers in their own home providing showers, hot meals, a warm bed and shuttle services or slackpacking (see below).

Slackpacking: When a hiker is able to leave the majority of their gear with someone else and essentially just do a day hike with minimal gear. Getting the weight off their backs enables them to hike faster and do more miles, plus may allow for an injury to heal but the hiker still gets miles logged. Usually hostels offer these services, or trail angels may assist.

Tramily: Mashup of "trail" + "family" – a tramily is hikers who typically meet on trail and begin hiking together, share rooms on zeros, split expenses, and basically become family on trail.

Trail Name: A nickname usually given to a hiker by their fellow hikers on trail. Many times hikers do not know one another's legal, real names.

Blue blazing: The AT is marked by white blazes, so hiking it is referred to as "whiteblazing," but when a hiker skips miles of the AT by taking side trails instead, it's called blueblazing. (Many of the side trails are marked with blue blazes.)

Yellow blazing: Similar to above, but skipping sections by driving further ahead on the trail.

Platinum blazing: Spending a lot of money, like a platinum card, on days in town, hotels and hostels, hot meals, shuttles, slackpacking, getting off trail to go into nearby cities, etc.

Yogi-ing: The art of begging for food from fellow hikers (like Yogi Bear)

Camel Up: To either consume or carry water when the trail is dry of water sources.

PROLOGUE

May 30, 2018

The pain searing through the jagged rip in his belly had somehow managed to dull, but through the fog of medicine, Zoby was still aware of his surroundings. The doctors had worked quickly to stop the bleeding and get him what they called "stabilized," but he was smart and alert; he heard the undertones of fear and concern in their voices.

He understood what surgery was – his Mommy had to have those a couple times, and he'd helped her recover afterward. They made Mommy feel better, so he knew if he had surgery, the pain would stop and he would be able to continue living the life of adventure he loved with Mommy, and more important, continue to take care of her like he had been trained.

"This poor baby. Have you ever seen so much blood from an attack on a small dog like this? His chances aren't good, but it's a miracle he's even still with us now," Zoby heard one of the doctors say through the fog threatening to envelop him, as she stroked his ears.

"Such a brave little fighter. So they're doing the surgery then?" came the reply.

"They're talking to his Mommy right now. I'm not sure she understands that it's likely he won't make it through surgery, or how expensive it could be. Especially if he has complications or he is disabled or paralyzed after. I hate to say it, but they're trying to make her see it might be best to say good-bye and let him go."

WHAT?! Suddenly alert, Zoby started shaking. Trying to lift his head up or make his legs cooperate so he could stand up – he instead struggled with the effort. Why couldn't he make his body move?! He *had* to tell the doctor he was okay! He *needed* the surgery – they *had* to let Mommy know that, they *had* to let him tell her to give him the chance!

"Oh sweet boy, you're shaking again. Stay still, I know it hurts, just lie still. Let's get you another blanket," the doctor stroking his ears said. While the other technician got a blanket, she inserted something clear into the tube running into him, something that made the fuzzy edges of his vision and hearing quickly become fuzzier.

NO! No, no, no, I need to tell Mommy! I need to tell her to fight for me! I need her to know I'm going to be ok and I need the surgery! I need. I need...

Zoby's world went dark.

CHAPTER 1

March 3, 2022 – The Journey Begins

"Zoby! It's here, it's here! It's our Start Date! Oh my goodness, I can't believe it's finally here! This is going to be the greatest adventure!" Mommy was bubbling over with excitement. "Wait. Oh my goodness, what am thinking? What *on earth* am I thinking, Zoby?! How are we going to actually do this? I mean, *walk* from Georgia to Maine? In snow and cold, and heat and bugs, and, and…"

Recognizing the pitch of her voice and the look on her face, Zoby went from being amused by Mommy's mood swinging all morning from excitement to fear and back again, to jumping into action. Anxiety was hitting, and he had to calm her down.

Leaping into her lap, putting his paws on her chest, Zoby began kissing Mommy's face. Closing her eyes, she put her hands on his paws and stroked his little body while she concentrated on taking deep, even breaths.

Feeling the constrictions in her chest ease up, and the gray edges of her vision clear, she held Zoby tight. "You are the best dog ever. You know that, little man? This is exactly why we are doing this thing together." Holding him face to face, she looked Zoby in the eye. "You are the bravest dog. Even braver than most humans I know. You constantly inspire me."

With a huge smile, tongue hanging out and tail wagging, Zoby gave Mommy one more big kiss then began his happy dance and yip-yips he knew always made her laugh and smile. Mommy was calmed down, so it was time to get excited about their big adventure!

One of Zoby's favorite activities was hiking with Mommy. He loved the smells everywhere, the interesting animals he met and sometimes had a chance to talk to on trails, and most of all the time with Mommy, especially on breaks with beautiful mountain views or waterfalls.

At ten years old, he had hiked hundreds of miles with Mommy, as she began taking him on hikes when they moved from Florida to Tennessee when he was only two. He had hiked all over the southeast with her, and after they moved into the RV, he was as blown away by the beautiful, rugged terrain out west as Mommy was. He was proud to add to his own hiking resume ´ bucket list locations in Montana, Wyoming, Utah and especially Colorado – because Mommy had been so proud of him hiking what she called "14ers" out there. He just thought they were really fun, as he loved rock scrambling most of all.

No actually, most of all, he liked proving people wrong.

He couldn't understand why whenever they passed another human on trail they would ask Mommy if he had "hiked the whole thing" with her? Or why they asked if she carried him, especially over rocks? And some of the mean, bigger dogs he met on trails would scoff at him and say things about how small dogs can't hike big mountains.

Whatever.
He not only hiked big mountains, he hiked big miles!

But ... then again, he had never hiked the kind of miles Mommy was telling him they were about to do. 15-20 mile days, day after day, for six months.

Sometimes doubts would creep in, when he seriously meditated on it. He intensely disliked going over rushing rivers, or up and down ladders or grated steps. He got cold easily and wasn't crazy about snow and ice. And storms. He shuddered. Zoby *really* despised storms.

Catching a glimpse of himself in the mirror while Mommy was on the phone with someone she called their shuttle driver, he puffed up his chest as he gazed at the special hiking outfit Mommy had bought for him that he was proudly wearing. Glancing over to the backpack full of gear and the tent that would be their home for the next six months, he thought about all the preparation Mommy had done. Test hikes together in a variety of weather, changing out gear, buying more special items just for him – he even had his own sleeping bag and a special puffy winter coat! He had really enjoyed their shakedown backpacking trips in Georgia the past month ... even if some silly big dogs at their campsite one night had about rolled down the hill with their laughter when Zoby told them he was preparing to thru-hike the Appalachian Trail.

"Small dog on a big hike? Yeah, right! You won't get out of Georgia!"
More laughter.

With the memory of their mocking ringing in his mind, determination set in as Zoby looked at Mommy and back into the mirror at his own face.

He was walking from Georgia to Maine. He'd prove them all wrong.

"So are you planning to bring your dog with you on the whole trail?"
Michelle, their shuttle driver asked.

Bracing herself against the question she'd already been asked dozens of times and had been the cause of her receiving some nasty messages and comments online, Mommy responded with cautious but determined cheer, "sure am! My little man is an amazing hiker. I'll carry him when I need to, but he has hiked all over the country with me, and can scramble like a boss!"

Lifting his head in pride, Zoby looked at Michelle defiantly.

"That's awesome!" she replied. "I love that he's going with you. I hope you two make it all the way to Maine together!"

Mommy and Zoby looked at one another and smiled.

Michelle continued, "you said you used to live here in Georgia, and have hiked around here, have you done much of the AT in Georgia then?"

"Oh, we've actually done *all* of the AT in Georgia! But it was day hikes and several years ago," Mommy replied, "We're excited to do it again, together, backpacking the whole section this time. We've also done the Approach Trail and visited Amicalola Falls about five times before this," she said with a laugh. "We went there a few nights ago to register and get our photo at the infamous arch, but decided to start at Springer Mountain."

Zoby grinned. He loved hiking around Amicalola Falls State Park, but hated those grated steps and how loud the Falls were. He wasn't sad to be skipping that part – besides, Mommy said the Approach Trail miles don't count anyway.

Putting his paws up on the edge of the window and looking out in anticipation, Zoby felt excitement coursing through him. He was looking forward to starting at Springer Mountain because he hadn't been with Mommy when she hiked it before. But he had done most of the rest of the AT in Georgia with her – he had even hiked Blood Mountain a *few* times!

And then, just like that, they were there!

Jumping out of the Jeep, Zoby ran over to say hello and sniff other hikers gathering in the Springer parking lot. Mommy had arranged to meet some online friends starting there at the same time, and their shuttle had just arrived as well. Mommy was laughing and hugging people, making Zoby's heart happy. New friends!

"Hey!"

Zoby heard the high-pitched, almost squeaky voice through the chatter of humans and looked around seeking its source.

"Little white fluffball, over here," the voice giggled, "you're barely larger than I am."

Whipping his head around and already feeling defensive, Zoby spied the source of the voice. A chipmunk standing on a downed branch beside a nearby tree, hands on his hips with a somehow disarming and friendly smile on his face.

Cautiously, and still feeling defensive, Zoby approached him. "Who are you, the welcoming committee with tiny insults to match your size and voice?"

That comment made the chipmunk squeal with glee and about fall off the branch with laughter. "I like you, kid. Good personality along with good looks, hahahaha!"

"Ohhh-kay," Zoby began to back away, "well, you enjoy your day. I have a trail to hike."

"Wait kid. Seriously, sorry we got off on the wrong foot. Or paw, as the case may be. I'm Chip." He continued, rolling his eyes when he saw Zoby's smirk, "yeah, I know my parents were super original. It's a family name, what can I say?"

Zoby said nothing, just continued smiling in amusement at Chip the Chipmunk.

"OK, so this is where you tell me *your* name," Chip declared.

"Alright. I'm Zoby."

Gleeful laughter again had Chip about rolling off the branch. "And what kind of name is Zoby?!"

Indignant, Zoby puffed his chest out. "One that is named after a World Series MVP, Ben Zobrist. See, Zobrist ... Zoby? I'm named after a champion. Not some stupid family name with no creativity, Chip the Chipmunk!" Zoby turned on his paws and began marching away.

"Ok, ok, you're right, kid. I'm sorry, that actually *is* a cool name. I just had to give you a hard time." With exaggerated arm motions, he blocked Zoby's getaway, gesturing to himself. "It's what I do – I joke with others out of my own insecurity. My therapist reminds me frequently not everyone finds my jokes and personality as charming and hysterical as I do." Chip stated, comically mocking his own self.

"That's for sure," Zoby agreed. Then chuckled as Chip fell back into his gleeful laughter.

"You're an interesting one, Chip. But uh, like I said, I've got a trail to hike." Zoby saw Mommy had introduced herself to everyone and was looking over at him. Time to go.

"Wait, so you're with one of those humans over there? They're all thru-hikers. Are you really hiking the entire Appalachian Trail?" Chip looked at Zoby with interest. "I spend a lot of time in the Springer lot here this time of year. I like following the nobo thru-hikers through Georgia, North Carolina and Tennessee, and a few I've even hiked with all the way to Maine. But I've never met a dog as small as you attempting this. I'm intrigued, kid."

"Ok, first, my name is Zoby, not 'kid,' and second, yes, I am hiking the whole trail. I have hiked *all over* with Mommy – why does everyone have such a hard time believing that?!"

"First, I only call the people I like 'kid' – kid," Chip said with a wink. "It makes me feel bigger than you, ok? Therapist says that needs work, too. And second, I'm not disbelieving it. To the contrary, I am intrigued. I think you may benefit by befriending me, kid. I know this trail inside out and have connections the whole way to Maine. If you play your cards right, you just may have me and Blaze as friends and trail angels to help you actually do this thing."

"Blaze? Who is Blaze?"

"That's me." Out of nowhere, a beautiful red cardinal dropped out of the tree above them, landing on a branch beak-to-nose with Zoby.

"Blaze is the better-looking one of our duo. All that crimson flash and attention," Chip laughed, "but he's actually pretty chill, and does *not* have a bird brain, contrary to popular belief."

"I prefer to think of myself as not only the better-looking one, but the smarter one as well," Blaze stated matter-of-factly, never taking his eyes off Zoby. "We'll see about this one, Chip. But I too, am intrigued."

Zoby returned Blaze's stare. Coolly and intently he stated, "I need neither your approval nor your help to hike this trail. But either way, you can," Zoby leaned in and bit off each word, "Just. Watch. Me."

That earned a smile and nod from Blaze. "I like it. You're gonna need that bravery on this trail."

"Zoby!!" Mommy called. "Zoby, come on buddy, we're gonna go, let's do this thing!"

Turning away but with a look back over his shoulder, Zoby called out,

"Chip, Blaze – it's been, um, interesting. I guess I'll see you on the trail!"

As he ran over to Mommy, Chip and Blaze looked at one another and smiled.

"Oh this is gonna be a fun thru-hiker season with this one," Chip said, "Kid has a lot of guts, I'll hand it to him. He has no idea the grief the woodland chain is going to give him. Especially the Squirrel Mafia. Whaddya say to helping the kid out?"

"I say we follow him a bit these first few days. The squirrels will start in on him in no time, they'll have their orders on that for sure. See how he does before getting attached and offering our services." Blaze playfully poked Chip with his wing, adding "what is it with you and latching on to these types so quickly anyway?"

"I don't latch."
"You do."
"Do not."

And on it went as Zoby and Mommy made their way past their first white blazes of thousands to come.

Out of sight high in a tree, two squirrels exchanged a menacing look.

"We need to tell Jezebel."

"She's not gonna like this. Not one little bit."

Later that night, Zoby lay awake in the tent with Mommy curled up beside him, thinking about their first day on trail, and the encounter with Chip and Blaze. Despite himself, he liked Chip. Odd sense of humor, therapist quotes and all. Blaze, he wasn't sure about, but could sense a deeper, quieter counterpart to Chip's quirky, loud personality. What did they mean about "benefitting" from their friendship, and that comment about how he would "need that bravery" … did these two know something Zoby didn't?

Tossing those thoughts aside, he reflected on their hike that first day. Abnormally warm for the first week of March, it had been beautiful hiking weather. Upon reaching the summit of Springer Mountain, signing the register, taking photos with the plaque and first official white blaze, they then had a rest stop at a beautiful waterfall. Zoby knew where they stopped for camp was a mile short of where Mommy had planned, but the women they had met up with needed to stop early, and she was enjoying hiking with them.

Yet it was already nagging at him, on the very first night, that the day may come Mommy had to split from this group and hike alone. Her anxiety tended to run high when she let perceived loneliness bother her.

Although, she was never alone. Zoby was with her. And like Mommy always said, God was with them both.

With that thought, Zoby yawned, snuggled into Mommy's side, and drifted off to sleep.

CHAPTER 2

Georgia, Squirrels and Tramily

Zoby hated mornings.

He knew it amused Mommy, the way he would refuse to wake up, barely open his eyes, yawn and pretend not to hear her perky "good morning!" telling him it was time to get up.

But *he* did not find it amusing. At all.

After what felt like the hundredth time Mommy poked at him, he finally growled and opened his eyes to glare at her. Seriously, it was barely even light out! Let a sleeping dog lie!

She merely laughed at his growl.

Giving up, with a yawn and a stretch, he decided to go outside the tent.

Where he came face-to-face with a fiercely angry squirrel glaring at him.

Startled, and still sleepy enough to feel crabby, Zoby barked, "Excuuuse me! Do you have a problem with mornings too, or is this nasty vibe radiating off you personal?"

Glare intensifying, the squirrel simply replied, "personal," before disappearing as suddenly as she had appeared.

What on earth? Zoby wondered. Shaking his head, he went about his morning routine and wondered what Mommy had for breakfast.

Returning to the tent, he heard Mommy talking to the other women about the trail in Georgia. "78 miles that includes Springer (check!), Sassafras, Blood, Cowrock and Trey Mountains, lots of ups and downs and pretty streams – let's attack this state, ladies! Sassafras awaits us today!"

Spirits up considerably, Zoby agreed. Angry squirrels, quirky chipmunks and sage cardinals could take a backseat – he had a trail to hike with Mommy!

Three days later, Mommy was limping down Blood Mountain - appropriately named as her feet were bloody - into Mountain Crossings, the outfitter and gift shop at Neel Gap, while Zoby was wondering if he was going crazy or if there really were angry squirrels glaring at him around every bend of the trail. He couldn't shake the feeling he was being watched, and it was throwing off his hike.

Relieved to see the familiar building come into sight, as he and Mommy had spent a lot of time at Mountain Crossings during their hikes in Georgia, while Mommy talked to their friends who worked there about her feet, he laid by the picnic tables taking in the view and did a gut check.

Was he imagining this squirrel thing, after that first angry glare that morning? What did she mean by, "it's personal," anyway ... and to where had Chip and Blaze disappeared? And why was he letting all this bother him so? He realized despite their brief encounter, he oddly missed the nutty chipmunk and had been hoping to run into him and his brightly-colored feathered friend again.

And as if he could have summoned them with his thoughts, there they were.

"Hey kid!" The almost-squeaky voice made Zoby smile. "You're really doing this thing so far! Four days and 31 miles down. A lot of humans hang it up right here, ya know. Literally." Gesturing to the large tree out front with about a hundred pairs of shoes from hikers calling an end to their hike dangling off it, he laughed, "the most fun tree for a chipmunk and bird to hang out in, in all of Georgia!"

Zoby laughed and did his happy dance. "Hey, it's good to see you. I wondered where you guys have been!"

Chip scampered over and climbed up on Zoby's back, throwing his little arms around his neck. "Missed us, huh kid?"

Blaze chuckled and rolled his eyes at Chip. "No, you don't latch on quickly, not at all." Turning to Zoby, "oh we've been around. You're the talk of the trail, Zoby."

Surprised, Zoby sat up, sending Chip tumbling to the ground. "What do you mean?"

"Have you felt like you're being watched ..." Chip started but Blaze cut in, "what he means," with a side glare to Chip, "is that not many small dogs attempt to thru-hike this trail. Especially little white fluffy ones. The woodland chain is curious to see how you do, that's all."

"The woodland chain?" Zoby asked.

Chip jumped in, gesturing wildly. "C'mon kid, you've hiked before! You talk to animals you meet on trail, and you're not surprised when another animal further up the trail says hello and they heard you were on trail, right?" Zoby nodded. "Well here along the AT in Georgia, thru-hiker season is like our Super Bowl! Trail Talk is at an all-time high! We place bets on the human hikers, but our favorite is betting on the canine hikers, or the "domestics" as some refer to them. Ooooh boy do we love to watch how the cushy lives in homes for those dogs transfer to life in the wild. Some of us get really excited and into the hikes of these dogs, becoming trail angels to help them and their human counterpart on their journey. But others..." he cast a sidelong glance to Blaze, "others are not so thrilled domestics think they have a place out here with us."

"So let me get this straight," Zoby began, "you're telling me that wild animals are betting on me? And some don't like me being out here simply because I have a Mommy and an actual home, what they call a 'domestic,' so that somehow makes me less able to hike this trail? So most bets are against me finishing?"

"That, and you're small." Chip stated. Zoby winced, there it was again.

"Chip!" Blaze admonished him.

"Oops, sorry kid. Therapist says I'm too blunt, especially when I'm excited and babbling. Didn't mean to hurt your feelings." Chip threw himself in an embrace around Zoby's front paws.

Exasperated but chuckling, Zoby looked over at Blaze. "It's fine, I'm used to it. Even here on trail these first few days, humans and other dogs we meet can't believe I'm planning to hike the whole trail." Zoby paused, then asked, "by any chance are the squirrels in particular unhappy a domestic is on their trail?"

Blaze gazed knowingly at Zoby. "Keep an eye on the squirrels."

That night, Mommy and the ladies – Zoby learned they were called tramily, or "trail family" – decided to rent a cabin just off the trail. Mommy needed her foot medication to take effect and the other ladies had various injuries. Since it had started to rain, Zoby was more than fine with a comfortable bed in a warm, dry cabin for the night.

Chip and Blaze had stayed outside Mountain Crossings with Zoby, laughing and telling him tales of other dogs on trail from past years, and funny human stories as well. He saw them through the window of the cabin as Mommy and other hikers celebrated a birthday and enjoyed a hot dinner (from which he happily got a full belly as well), but he knew they planned to spend the night in the hiker boots tree at Neel Gap. It was good to have friends nearby.

Yet as he curled up between Mommy and "Auntie Lisa," the hiker they had both grown attached to the first few days, he felt there was more to the story with the squirrels. Why was it "personal" to them that he be on the trail? Zoby pondered this as he fell into a deep sleep.

****

Through the misty fog around the bend in the trail, he could make out a shadowy figure. Was that another dog? Happy, he bounded toward it to say hello. But as he approached, the shadow seemed to morph in the fog. Larger, smaller, then larger again. Well, he just wanted to say hi and he was excited to see another dog … or… at least he *thought* it was a dog. Shadows shifting became a large dog shape, then smaller dog shape, then … was that a large squirrel? As Zoby finished running up to it, eyes flashed toward him, glowing yellow then a dark, inky black. Suddenly out of the shadow shiny teeth glared and all Zoby saw was red as the pain roared through him…

"Zoby! Zoby! Hey baby, it's ok. It's ok. Mommy's here, Mommy's here. You're ok baby boy."

Through the red haze of pain, Zoby heard Mommy's voice, and woke up to her holding him, and Auntie Lisa sitting up with a look of concern on her face. "Is he ok?" she asked, reaching over to stroke his ears.

Zoby licked her hand, then back to Mommy's again. It was a dream. Just a bad dream.

"He's ok," he heard Mommy say as he snuggled into her arms, "he started having these nightmares after the dog attack a few years ago. Sorry we woke you."

"It's ok… poor baby. What a brave little guy to live through that and be out here now."

Mommy held Zoby tighter to her. "Yes," she agreed, "he is."

Deep in the wintery March forests of Maine, within a large hidden cave made of boulders and wrapped in fairy-tale size roots around its exterior, an intimidating but beautiful squirrel narrowed her eyes into dangerous slits as she balled her paws into fists. The news she had just received was *maddening*. Around her the squirrels fell silent, nervously anticipating her next moves.

Slowly turning from her informant, she looked out over her subjects in disdain.

"It seems we have a certain domestic to keep an eye on. It is our job to get *all* domestic threats off *our* trail, sending them scurrying back to their comfortable suburban lives. I shouldn't have any need to reiterate the danger a certain breed brings to us." Pausing for effect, seeing the nods of agreement, feeling empowered and fueled by her own anger, she bellowed into the shadows of the cave, "For our homes, for our families, for our lives … do *NOT* let this domestic get to Maine!"

Squirrels erupted in cheers all around her, as Jezebel stood silent taking it in, with an evil grin on her face and wicked glint in her eyes.

CHAPTER 3

A Wild Encounter at the GA/NC Border

The first snow fell 10 days into the hike, the day they were supposed to cross the state line from Georgia into North Carolina.

Snuggled up in a blanket on Mommy's lap in the cozy lounge area of Hostel Around the Bend, Zoby relished their unplanned zero day, a warm and crackling fire in the fireplace, hearing the laughter from Mommy and his tramily of "Aunties" filling the air.

The last few days had been fun, mostly hiking with Auntie Lisa, who now had the trail name of "Potato Chip" but in the last two days they had added his Aunties "Brazil" and "StickyBuns" to their tramily. All the ladies adored him (and fed him!), but most of all they made Mommy smile and laugh a lot, and that was what mattered.

Additionally, it had been entertaining seeing Chip and Blaze regularly at camp each morning and night. They kept Zoby updated with stories of other dogs (or "domestics" as he was getting used to hearing), some already off trail for good, as well as some others that were ahead of him on trail. Many of those dogs he had met and wondered how the squirrels were treating them. Now only six miles away from entering North Carolina, Zoby was rather proud when Chip informed him a lot of animals were about to lose their bets that he wouldn't get out of Georgia.

"Oh, look at that beautiful bright red cardinal through the window!" exclaimed Auntie StickyBuns, "I've got to get a picture of it in the snow!"

Turning, Zoby saw Blaze, that glorious crimson framed by the freshly fallen white snow. Blaze gestured with his head clearly meaning, "come out here" … now what on earth could be so important for Zoby to give up the warm comforts of the hostel to go outside in the cold snow?!

But Mommy was getting up to go outside with Auntie StickyBuns, saying she wanted photos of the snow on the daffodils, so resigned to the impending cold, Zoby did his "potty dance" to let Mommy know he wanted outside, too.

"OK, come on buddy, let's go outside then," Mommy said as she put his puffy coat on him and led them out the door.

"Hey kid! Over here!" The unmistakable pitch of Chip's voice came from around the corner of the porch.

"Did you not see how nice and warm and cozy I was – in *there*," Zoby gestured, "not out *here*, where we don't have to be today?"

"Keep that talk up and you're going to earn being called a domestic, kid," Chip laughed, "it's just a little snow. It'll be gone tomorrow. You gotta toughen up."

Zoby glared at Chip. "You have no idea how tough I am." But he swore he wouldn't show them again when he was acting "domestic" either. "Now what is so important you drug me out into this white stuff?"

Blaze landed beside Zoby. "You've been doing great, Zoby. You're about to get the first state behind you. That has the Trail Talk talking. Some folks are not real happy about that."

"Yeah, yeah so I cost them a bet. Tell them to get over it." Zoby tried not to show he was shivering. "Is that all, seriously?"

Blaze and Chip looked at each other. Walking over and putting his little arms around Zoby's front paws, Chip stood between them, looked up at Zoby and said, "I think it's time to tell you about Jezebel."

"Chip!" Blaze snapped.

"What?! If what they're planning tomorrow isn't just a rumor, it's only fair Zoby knows what he is up against, and why! My therapist may say my bluntness needs work, but hey, at least I'm honest!"

"Stop!" Zoby came between the chipmunk and cardinal, "you two can fight it out later, but right now you're going to tell me what you had me come out here to tell me. Who is Jezebel and what is being planned for tomorrow?!"

"Sorry kid, my emotions get the best of me. I care about you, you know. You've kinda got me all up in the feels," Chip pounded his chest over his heart, "so Blaze and I here, we're going all gangsta trail angel on you tomorrow."

"What? I'm lost."

Blaze landed on Zoby's shoulder. "Please, allow me to do the talking now," he said with a chuckle, then sobered up looking at Zoby. "Jezebel, for lack of a formal title, is the "Queen" of the Squirrel Mafia, as we like to call them. They are a large community, running from Georgia to Maine along the Appalachian Trail, who have taken a particular dislike to domestics thru-hiking the AT, and in particular, small white dogs." At that, Zoby's eyes narrowed. "There's history there, but right now you need to know that Jezebel is formidable and influential. Her gang of squirrels has friends – of all shapes and sizes along the trail. Sometimes it isn't too hard to convince an animal in the wild that a domestic has no place in their home, and trust me, she uses that to her advantage. "

"Wait," Zoby interrupted, "What about 'in particular, small, white dogs' do they dislike?"

"Because Jezebel witnessed…" Chip started before Blaze flung his wing in front of him.

"I told you there's history there. You'll learn it as needed. For now, you only need to know you have a bigger target on your back than the other domestics still on trail past Georgia."

With a deep sigh, and shaking off feeling irritated, Zoby decided to focus only on the information being presented at the moment. "Ok then, so what do I need to know going forward? What is this rumor about tomorrow?"

"The Squirrel Mafia sees it as their job to get a domestic off-trail," Blaze continued, "and they don't hesitate to use their, um, 'resources' when necessary. As most domestics don't make it much past Georgia, the tactics are usually pretty mild. That is, until you start making it through state lines, and then more state lines, and then their tactics get more aggressive…"

"Wild hogs. Coyotes. A bear. Something will be on trail tomorrow, one of their resources who will attempt to scare you off trail before the North Carolina border." Blaze paused, seeing Zoby's eyes widening. "Most won't actually physically harm you, just scare you … but … well, there have been incidents in the past."

Chip jumped up onto Zoby's back. "Hey kid, don't worry! We trail angels have our gangsta 'resources' too! We've got your back. Literally, hahaha!" Chip exclaimed as he rolled around in laughter on Zoby's back.

Rolling his eyes at Chip's antics, Zoby looked at Blaze. "Is that true? You two are really watching out for me, and plan to help me out like this?"

Blaze nodded and smiled. "We wouldn't be here right now having this conversation otherwise."

"Get used to it kid, we kinda like you!" Chip danced around, and leaping off Zoby, grabbed his face and pulled him down to stare him in the eye. "We're going to make sure nothing happens to you, and furthermore, we're going to get you to Katahdin in Maine."

Touched, and with a triumphant grin, Zoby saw Mommy coming around the corner of the house looking for him. "Thanks guys. Really. Now not to sound too domestic, but I'm heading back in where it's warm and curling up with Mommy on that couch again!"

"Oh, the cardinal!" Mommy exclaimed, grabbing her phone.

With a look at Zoby, Blaze rolled his eyes but obligingly posed for photos, making Mommy's day.

"Why don't they ever get excited about pictures of me?" Chip muttered as he scampered away.

Laughing, Zoby headed inside to warmth and a good night's sleep to prepare for whatever tomorrow may bring.

The day dawned with sapphire skies and golden sunshine, which when combined with a warmup already occurring overnight, had most of the snow melting before they even got back on trail around mid-morning.

Mommy was excited to be crossing the first of 14 states off the list, and enjoying the tramily of ladies she was hiking with. This next section of four days would take them past their first 100-mile marker and into Franklin, NC where she had friends and plans to stay at their rental cabin. Spirits high, she found herself laughing at Zoby's antics that morning. He seemed a little more animated than usual.

"Little man, I guess a zero did you some good, huh? You are certainly full of energy this morning. Ready to get back on trail?"

What Mommy didn't know was it was nervous energy that had him running around, but he loved the attention and laughs it was bringing, so he poured more into it. Mommy had a way of bolstering his confidence too, and he needed it today. Full of ambitious self-assurance, he headed off onto the trail.

"Look at you, kid, what's up with that attitude today? Loving it, loving it, work it... work it!" Chip pretended to snap away on a camera like paparazzi.

Hamming it up, Zoby pranced along. "Coyotes? Wild hogs? Bears? Bring it! I'm ZOBY, King of the AT!"

"Hahahaa, love it! You go, kid! We're right here and have your back!"

Chip scampered off as quickly as he had appeared.

****

Enjoying the animated conversation flowing between Mommy and his Aunties as they hiked, Zoby almost missed seeing Chip sitting on a rock near a river crossing.

As the group slowed down to rock hop over the river, Zoby looked over at the chipmunk with curiosity, as his typical silly antics on display were absent and he was abnormally quiet.

"Not too far from the border," Zoby said quietly. Chip nodded and darted off.

And with that, just ahead he heard Aunties Brazil and StickyBuns stop and yell. "Wild boar!"
Mommy quickly scooped Zoby up into her arms. "Stay quiet, buddy. He will ignore us if we ignore him."

Not quite, Zoby thought. But stayed quiet.

"If he acts aggressive and seems like he may charge, you're supposed to climb a tree if possible. Six feet off the ground," Mommy said to the others.

Looking up, the large boar with tusks easily six inches long honed in on Zoby in Mommy's arms. His lips curled up in an ugly sneer. "Hello little domestic. Hiding in your human's arms, I see? Oh my, aren't we a brave one?" he mocked.

Zoby growled. He couldn't help it.

"Zoby," came the stern warning from Mommy.

The boar advanced a step toward them, sending Mommy and the Aunties all scurrying backwards while keeping an eye on it.

"Leave me alone," Zoby said, and gathering his courage added, "and go tell Jezebel I'm coming for her in Maine."

The boar stopped for a moment, then chuckled. "So the pipsqueak chipmunk and his feathered friend have told you about Jezebel. Interesting. Well," he stopped and, raising his tusks to glint in the morning sun, continued, "then you know it's my job to get you off trail. *Even* when you're in your human's arms," he finished, aiming his tusks directly toward Mommy.

Everything seemed to happen at once. Forgetting he was still leashed, Zoby growled ferociously and jumped out of Mommy's arms to charge the boar and protect Mommy. The Aunties were backing up while

Mommy lunged forward to grab Zoby.

And then the black bear appeared out of nowhere, stepping in between Zoby and the boar.

"Oh my God!" Mommy and the Aunties yelled. "Don't run! Just keep backing up slowly. Oh my God..." Mommy yanked the leash hard, pulling Zoby back up into her arms, where she stuffed him into her coat and zipped it up.

Ugh! Now he couldn't see, and couldn't protect Mommy from the boar, and now the bear! And – how humiliating to be stuffed in her coat when he needed to look brave and courageous!

Facing the boar, the bear rose up and spoke two words in a lethal tone.

"Leave. NOW."

After a moment, in disgust, the boar turned around, yelling out, "watch your back, domestic. This isn't over."

Zoby had managed to get his head out of the coat, so when the bear turned and looked directly at him, he was able to see the look sent his way. Not friendly but also not unfriendly, the bear simply said, "that's because I owe one to Blaze. Undecided on you so far. Make me a fan." And with that, he lumbered off into the woods.

"Did that really just happen?!" Mommy and the others exclaimed, breathing deep sighs of relief. "Wow, did anyone get any of that on film?!" "No one is going to believe us!" ...

Back on the ground, Zoby looked up at a flutter in the tree above him. Seeing Chip and Blaze, he nodded and mouthed, "thank you," as he, Mommy and the tramily continued down the trail, to the celebration awaiting them at the North Carolina border.

The next morning, a few miles into North Carolina, a half-asleep and cranky Zoby stumbled out of the tent to another face-to-face encounter with the same angry squirrel from his first morning on trail in Georgia.

"We have got to stop meeting like this," Zoby said grumpily.

"Agreed. Why don't you leave then, and we won't have this problem," she spit out at him.

"What is your problem with me? Huh? I'm a domestic, I'm small and white, and Jezebel doesn't like me, so you don't just because of her?"

Zoby paused. "Or are *you* Jezebel?"

Glaring at him and approaching him slowly, menacingly, she leaned into his face. "No. I'm her daughter. Ariana. *NOT* a pleasure to meet you."

Turning, she tossed over her shoulder, "welcome to North Carolina. You're gonna *love* it." And with a malicious laugh, vanished into the morning mountain mist.

CHAPTER 4

Franklin and Fontana

"Zoby, you are seriously the worst morning dog ever," Mommy laughed as Zoby managed to pop one eye open to look at her. "I think I need to manufacture some sort of doggie coffee for pups like you!"

Whatever it takes, Zoby thought as he stretched and yawned. Thankfully they were arriving in Franklin that day, which meant a warm, cozy bed that night – and probably some table scraps from the town food Mommy and the tramily would be feasting on.

Perked up by that thought, Zoby headed outside the tent, where he quickly saw Chip on a low branch of the tree he knew the chipmunk and Blaze had spent the night in.

Since the boar incident at the border and the encounter with Ariana the following morning, things had been rather quiet on the squirrel front, allowing Zoby to soak in the days with Mommy on trail and enjoy stories and laughter with Chip and Blaze around camp.

The day before they had hit the 100-mile mark on trail at Albert Mountain, a fun rock scramble Zoby had really enjoyed. Chip and Blaze had been impressed, and he knew them well enough now to know praise from Blaze was a gift he carefully handed out.

So it touched him when he got closer to the tree and saw a small "1-0-0" on the ground, made from nuts and seeds.

"Surprise! Congrats, kid! We're so proud of you!" Bubbling over with excitement, Chip bounded down the trunk of the tree and flung himself around Zoby's neck. Laughing and looking up, Zoby saw Blaze smiling at the antics as he fluttered down to land beside them.

"Yes, seriously, congratulations on the first 100 miles! Many domestics either don't make it here to this first milestone with their human counterpart, or their human has decided to send them home and continue on without them."

"Thanks guys, I'm touched. Now only about 2,100 miles to go," Zoby laughed. "I'll show the Squirrel Mafia, the mean big dogs on trail – everyone! I've got this!"

At that, the trio of friends looked up to the cackles of laughter coming high up from the tree over. A pair of squirrels dropped to the ground beside them, and began circling.

"Well hello, domestic. Sorry to barge in on your little celebration here, but we just couldn't help overhearing your declarations, and felt the need to give you a reality check," one taunted.

Puffing his chest up and standing on his hind legs, Chip marched over to him. "Oh go back to your nuts, you nut, and leave him be."
The second squirrel, a quite large and bulked-up one, silently came up behind Chip. Tapping him on the shoulder, Chip turned to look at him with eyes reaching only chest level. The beefy squirrel waited only a moment before putting a finger under Chip's chin to raise his head up, then easily threw the chipmunk aside with such force he went flying into the tree trunk.

"Hey!" Zoby yelled, growling and baring his teeth. "There's no need for that!" Indignation for Chip fueling him, Zoby air-nipped at the squirrel, only to receive a direct punch to his nose that made his eyes water. Startled, and more than a little angry, Zoby growled deeply and was about to move in when Blaze flung a wing between dog and squirrel.

"That's enough." Looking at the first squirrel, he warned, "you know this will end badly for you if you antagonize him into going after you." Looking at Zoby, he continued, "This is exactly what Jezebel wants. If you injure or God forbid, kill a squirrel, she will use that to stoke the fires of rage within the Squirrel Mafia, putting all their resources to work against you. Don't give her what she wants."

Nose still stinging, Zoby looked at Blaze, then over at Chip rubbing his head on the ground by the tree trunk. "If they go after either of you again, she just may get the fight she's looking for." Glaring at the beefy squirrel, he stated in a low voice, "*no one* hurts my friends."

Walking back toward the tent and Mommy, Zoby glared over his shoulder at both squirrels, "tell Ariana that I've survived way worse than a measly punch in the nose from a squirrel on steroids, and that oh, she's right – North Carolina is a *blast* so far, can't wait for Tennessee."

Franklin was just the break Zoby and the Aunties needed. With a beautiful rental cabin all to themselves, Mommy's friend's car to borrow, and a storm moving in, they decided to zero and spend the day in the hiker-friendly town. That meant photo ops at the town's sign strung with "welcome hikers" banners, shopping in the stores, a stop at the trail-famous outfitters, Outdoor 76 – where Mommy got new shoes – seeing some hiker friends in town (including another dog he had met several times on trail, Scout!), lots of laughter ... and even more food!

"You've been such a good little thru-hiker dog, you deserve your own burger," Mommy said, as she rubbed his ears and gave him – yes, indeed – an entire cheeseburger all his own!

In absolute adoration, Zoby licked Mommy's hand ... then dove into the burger, causing all the Aunties to laugh.

"It needs to be a specific butterfly, I think," StickyBuns was saying, continuing their conversation regarding Mommy's trail name, "you're so attracted to flowers and you speak in butterfly metaphors, but 'Butterfly' just doesn't feel right."

"Do you have a favorite butterfly?" PotatoChip asked.
"I do, but 'Blue Morpho' doesn't make a great trail name," Mommy laughed, then jumped up when some hiker friends entered, "Oh hey guys, good to see you..."

"You're so social," StickyBuns laughed, "maybe it should be 'social butterfly.'"

"Is there a butterfly that is more social, like one that flies in groups?" Brazil asked.

"A monarch," Mommy replied, then her eyes got wide. "Actually, monarchs are the only butterflies that travel long distances in large groups! Actually, around 2,000 miles! That's it!"

Zoby looked up from the last of his burger in approval. Yes, "Monarch" was a good fit for Mommy. Four paws up!

"Well, now we just need one for Zoby," PotatoChip laughed. "I still say 'Tootsie' because his poop is the size of Tootsie Rolls." All the Aunties laughed.

Zoby rolled his eyes and tried to shake his head toward Mommy. NO. He was not going to get a trail name after his poop. And one that sounded like a sissy, to boot!

Mommy just laughed, "we'll see."

After dinner and watching sunset from their deck, Zoby decided zero days in town with burgers, warm, cozy beds and plentiful laughter with the Aunties and Mommy were the best part about thru-hiking the Appalachian Trail.

The next week on trail took them through Wayah Bald, Nantahala Outdoor Center, (where they stayed one night in a bunk and had another delicious dinner on the river), then camping at Cheoah Bald where Zoby and Mommy loved sitting on a rock watching sunset together. From there they made their way toward Fontana Dam and Fontana Village, where Nate, one of Mommy's high school youth group friends, had gifted them all with two nights in a cabin, to prepare for the Smokies.

In that week, aside from more angry glares coming from squirrels, the only incident Zoby could really count as negative actually came from another dog. At NOC, a black lab decided it was his mission to mock Zoby, the typical snide, "small dog, get off the trail, what are you thinking," kind of jeering from a bully. While it still hurt, Zoby was getting used to it, and used it to fuel his fire to get to Maine. And – he couldn't help but smirk and bury his laughter when a certain red bird "accidentally" pooped on the black lab. Ooops.

Another special surprise awaited them as they neared Fontana – StickyBuns' dad, "Bouncer," who had thru-hiked the previous year, was waiting for them at a road crossing with his dog, Aussie! Zoby and Aussie had met and were buddies, so Zoby was excited to hike alongside her for a couple days. Introducing Aussie to Chip and Blaze, they made their way up the trail with the three of them relaying stories to Zoby of sites and places along the trail yet to come.

"You're already good at rock scrambling, so you'll love New Hampshire and Maine," Aussie said, "the only problem will be the ladders and rebar, but your Mommy can help you with those."

"I'm more concerned about the Squirrel Mafia as I get closer to Maine," Zoby said, "what were they like with you?"

"Annoying, but not threatening. I wasn't top on their list of targets that year. They're particularly bad in Maine, though – very loud, practically screaming through the trees with their chatter, and they will throw nuts at you and your human on the trail."

Chip laughed from where he was lounging on the back of Aussie's neck. "Oh I almost forgot they do that! I throw 'em right back! Take that, take that! Hi-yah!" Chip's karate kick had him tumbling off Aussie onto the ground.

Laughing, Zoby nudged Chip back upright and patted him on the head. "Remind me to hire an actual black belt when I get up there."

"Don't worry, kid. Black belt or not, I've got your back." Chip threw himself at Zoby. "But let's worry about that when we get there. First, we have fun in Fontana before your Mommy kennels you in the Smokies!"

Zoby pulled up short. The sudden stop had all three looking at him in surprise.

"What did you say? About a kennel? Mommy has *never* kenneled me! We're hiking this trail together, why on earth would you say that?!"

Blaze, Chip and Aussie cast sidelong looks at one another. "I'm thinking he doesn't know," Chip pretended to whisper behind his hand to the others, "do you think we should tell him?"

Rolling his eyes at Chip, Blaze fluttered over to Zoby. "Has your Mommy really not said anything? I mean, we have heard her talk about it with the tramily, how she has a set number of days to get through the Smokies to get you back out of the kennel. That they're picking you up in Fontana…." Blaze trailed off as Zoby's white face got whiter and big eyes got bigger.

"I… I… She… She told me about visiting a dog spa. That it would be after Fontana. She's putting me in a *kennel?* She's hiking *without me?!*" Zoby fought back tears. How could Mommy do this?

"Hey kid, I'm sorry." Chip jumped up and wrapped his arms around Zoby's neck in a big hug. "All dogs have to do this through the Smokies, the Rangers in the National Park have rules about dogs." Chip sighed as a single tear escaped from Zoby's eye. "It's ok, it'll be ok. The place you're going really is like a dog spa. You know your Mommy wouldn't send you there if it wasn't."
"It's true," Aussie interjected. "Me and all the other dogs had to do it too. It's really like a nice vacation from the trail."

"But how can I watch over Mommy and help her, protect her from the Squirrel Mafia and their resources … or what if she has a panic attack? Or gets hurt?" Zoby wondered if dogs could have panic attacks, because he was about to, if so.

"Hey, tell you what kiddo." Jumping from his back, Chip went around and grabbed Zoby's floppy ears, pulling him face-to-face. "Me and Blaze, we've got your back, right? You trust us?" Zoby nodded. "We will watch your Mommy for you. Report to you every night. We'll keep her safe from the Mafia. OK? You believe me?"

Raising his eyes to look at Blaze over Chip's head, he saw the nod the cardinal gave him, and the look of compassion coming from Aussie. Returning his gaze to Chip's eager and sincere face, Zoby nodded, "OK. I trust you."

"Good," Chip hugged him then danced away, "because we are almost to Fontana Dam, which is the end of the trail before the Smokies, and that means you get a night in a cabin!"

That night in the cabin, Zoby overhead discussion between Mommy and the Aunties about miles per day and how many days it would take to get through the Smokies. He wasn't sure, but it sounded like Mommy was very stressed and maybe arguing a bit with the tramily. And then he heard it.

"Guys, I have to be done before that, I have to get Zoby out of the kennel by then."

So it was true. He felt Aussie's gaze on him but pretended to sleep. Not that he doubted Chip, Blaze and Aussie, but he'd been hoping they were wrong. Now, the stress he heard in Mommy's voice had him worried. He just had a bad feeling something was going to happen to her in the Smokies and he wouldn't be there to help.

He just had to trust Chip and Blaze to be there for her while he was … shudder … in a *kennel*.

CHAPTER 5

The Smokies, Part I

"I am going to miss you so much," Mommy cried, "you have to be good, so good, such a good boy, and make Mommy proud, ok?" Burying her head in his face, Zoby felt her tears falling onto his fur. Pushing back, he licked the tears and fought back his own.

"I've never kenneled him before. We've never been apart this long," she was saying to the lady picking him up. Jerica, he remembered.

"Give me something that smells like you, something he can sleep with," she replied. Mommy handed her a bag – his bag, he recognized – and said she had that in there, with some food, treats, and a toy.

Burying his head back in Mommy's shoulder, Zoby clung to her neck. How could he let her go hike all those days alone? That day the tension in the cabin was thicker, he could tell there was something wrong between Mommy and the tramily of Aunties. He couldn't be apart from her now.

"Oh baby boy," Mommy said, dropping her face down to his, snuggled in her neck. "I don't want to say good-bye either. But, look at me." She pulled Zoby's face to her own. "I am going to hike through these miles with a mission to get back to you at the other end of the National Park. I am not going to stop and get off trail until you're in my arms again, you hear me? And you are going to be a good boy and have fun with the other doggies and Miss Jerica here, ok? Can you promise me that? That you'll be a good boy, and have fun?"

Zoby looked sorrowfully into Mommy's eyes. He knew she was trying not to cry again. Kissing her nose and face, Zoby promised.

And as Mommy stood in the driveway waving good-bye while he drove away with Miss Jerica, he saw the flutter of red wings landing in the tree above her, and prayed his friends would be true to their word and keep her safe.

Aussie was right, the kennel was more like a doggie spa than what his mind feared when he heard "kennel." The other dogs were nice, but he was more interested in the humans and trying to overhear when any of them talked about hearing from Mommy, who was checking in daily with them. And of course, whenever he went outside he was looking for the scarlet feathers and the indelible animated voices of his friends.

Finally, on his last visit outside for the night, he heard it. "Hey kid!"

Looking around, Zoby saw Chip just inside the edge of the far corner of the fence. Racing over there, Zoby breathlessly asked, "how is she? Is she ok?"

Chip laughed. "Relax, it's only been a day, kid. Blaze stayed back at the campsite while I came to report to you. She's ok, but it's extremely cold in the Smoky Mountains this week." Zoby nodded and shivered, it was getting colder as the sun began to set behind the mountains, even as they spoke. "It's going to be brutally cold this week up there for them. The tramily had a rough time with the cold today, and are talking about getting off trail for a break from the weather in a couple days at Newfound Gap. Also, they are all dealing with injuries right now – and your Mommy isn't. I'm just warning you kid, I've seen this before. I think the tramily may be breaking up in the next few days. Your Mommy is tough, plus she is driven to get back to you, so she'll keep going. But she may be alone."

This was exactly what had Zoby worried. Sometimes Mommy would feel lonely and start crying, and sometimes that would lead to anxiety attacks. This was what Zoby was there to help her through. He looked at Chip. "You *have* to promise me to tell me the truth. How she is doing, if she is upset and lonely. And if the Squirrel Mafia has any plans – you've *got* to be on top of Trail Talk. You *have* to help me, Chip. I'm counting on you and Blaze."

"You have my solemn word, kid." Looking up, Chip saw the kennel workers collecting the dogs to head inside. "Gotta run…" he yelled as he scrambled into the evening gray.

Inside her tent, in the bitter cold, Mommy struggled to keep her thoughts under control. She knew the others were not doing well, between the cold and the injuries, but she was determined to keep this group together… somehow. Moreover, worries about Zoby in the kennel had kept her breathing shallow all day as she fought the anxiety centered in her chest. Vivid flashes of her baby lying on the ground covered in blood, his little body ripped open, kept invading her vision. They had promised to keep him in the small dog group, but what if a big dog decided it didn't like Zoby? It had happened in a split second last time … what if it happened again and she wasn't there? What if he didn't make it this time, and she wasn't there? What if he was crying for her and she wasn't answering him and he thought she had abandoned him? What if, what if?...

Feeling the pressure in her chest tighten and her breathing begin to get shallower and raspier, she clawed at the strings keeping her sleeping bag closed around her head. The mittens she wore against the cold prevented her fingers from functioning to undo the strings so she could get free. Feeling as though the air was being sucked from her mummy bag and the walls of the tent closing in around her, she fell into a full-blown panic attack. Pulling off the mittens, desperately clawing at the strings, they finally gave way and she burst forth from her bag, into the inky blackness and utter silence of her tent in the middle of the night. Gulping the icy air and adjusting her eyes, slowly... slowly... the gray edges of her vision cleared and her gasping began to even out. Still breathing shallow and still feeling pain in her chest, she decided to crack open one vestibule of her tent to allow more fresh air in. As she unzipped and pushed her head out for just that one minute, what she didn't see were the eyes of a chipmunk and cardinal popping open, alert at her movements.

Looking at one another in the freezing night, Chip and Blaze wondered what was happening in the tent below them. Watching, they saw Mommy zip it back up, never getting out, nor making any sounds. Odd, they thought.

"Needed a bathroom break, but decided against it." Chip declared and curled back up under his layers of pine bough blankets. Yawning, he shrugged and fell back asleep.

Blaze, on the other hand, wasn't so sure. But for the moment, she was ok, and it was over.

Two days later, as the setting sun was streaking fiery colors across the mountains, it happened. The tramily had a heartfelt conversation, and decided it was best to split up. Due to injuries, the others needed to slow their pace and total miles, and all wanted to get off trail at Newfound Gap until it warmed up a bit. Mommy had no injuries and needed to continue on to be reunited with Zoby from the kennel within a certain timeframe. With a lot of sad tears, the decision was made that Mommy would continue on with the bigger miles the next day, alone.

Mommy's heart was filled with sadness. She had seen it coming, but tried to prevent it. While she didn't mind hiking alone during the day, she enjoyed having a tramily at camp in the morning and night, and to plan zeros with. She loved these women and had grown close to them over the past nearly 200 miles now. The loneliness of doing this hike without tramily, and even momentarily without Zoby, was hitting her hard that night. Despite the cold, she walked away from the shelter and camping area into a nearby clearing on the side of a mountain and gazed out over the shimmering last colors of sunset.

Talking out loud to herself and to God, she lamented the end of this time with her tramily of ladies and prayed for strength to carry on alone. She fought back her fears of rejection and loneliness, and worries about Zoby, all trying to overwhelm her in that moment. She just let the tears fall and gave in to the moment of sadness.

Nearby, Chip and Blaze exchanged a look. They decided they needed to go together to tell Zoby.

In another tree nearby, Ariana slowly grinned. She too, had been watching Mommy. Getting her alone on trail now may be just the break she'd been waiting for.

Tap. Tap. Tap tap tap tap tap.
Zoby woke in his little "room" of a cubicle space in the kennel, disoriented at first, then taking in his surroundings, saw Blaze through the small round window near him. Relieved, as he hadn't heard from his friends that day, Zoby went over to the window.

Chip's face suddenly appeared in the little window too, startling Zoby but making him question what was going on, as only one or the other had come to report to him thus far.

"What's up guys?" Zoby tried to whisper loud enough to be heard through the window.

"Hey kid!" Chip yelled, loud enough to not only be heard through the window, but loud enough to have some other heads around Zoby's space popping up.

"Chip!" Zoby whispered, "keep it down!" Looking around, he saw curious eyes still on him from the Yorkie beside him.

"Sorry kid," Chip said, quieter but still not quiet. "We have some news."

"Ssshh! Geez Chip!" Zoby hushed him. "Blaze, you gotta help me out here."

Pushing Chip away, the cardinal put his face as close to the window as he could, and matter-of-factly stated, "it happened tonight. The tramily broke up. Your Mommy will be continuing on without your Aunties tomorrow."

Crestfallen, with tears hitting his eyes, Zoby sank back down on the floor away from the window. Looking up at Blaze, he asked, "she's really upset, isn't she?"

Head popping back into the window, Chip attempted to whisper, "yeah kid, she's struggling. We had to tell you. But she is strong, she'll push through and come get you."

Blaze nodded in agreement. "It's going to get bitter cold tonight. Between the frigid temperatures and it being her first day on trail alone tomorrow, she might break down. We've seen it before with other humans. We will watch her for you and let you know if anything happens."

Heart heavy and feeling helpless, Zoby hung his head. "I should be there." Looking up, he asked, "have you heard any Trail Talk, anything from the squirrels?"

"Nothing to worry about there. Try not to feel guilty, kid, it's not your fault you're in *here* while she's out *there*."

"Chip!" Blaze admonished. "What he means is, this will be a test of her strength, and she'll get through it and be even stronger in the end. You get some sleep and don't worry – we'll be back tomorrow with an update."

Turning from the window, Zoby caught the Yorkie next to him laying back down, pretending to be asleep. Knowing she had overheard everything, he started to say something, then decided to let it go. He didn't need to explain his situation to nosy neighbors.

Lying back down, Zoby knew he wouldn't fall asleep quickly. And Chip was right, there was truth within his usual bluntness – Zoby *did* feel guilty. Here he was in a warm bed getting spoiled in the lap of luxury, while Mommy was dealing with freezing temperatures outside all day and all night, hiking over tough terrain, losing her circle of friends she held so dear, and doing all this without him. She had promised him his best doggie life after surviving the attack, but he had also promised in return to be the best doggie for her, and always make her happy when she was sad. He couldn't do that for her now.

After a long, long time, Zoby finally fell into a fitful sleep full of nightmares.
*

****

"Hey! Hey Zoby!" The unfamiliar voice was cutting through the haze. "Zoby, wake up!"

Finally breaking free from the depths of his dreams, Zoby realized the voice belonged to the Yorkie next to him. What was her name again?...

"There you are," she said. "That was a bad one, huh? I get them too – the bad dreams. Had a pretty rough puppyhood, some bad humans back then. Sometimes they come back in my dreams. But I have great ones now, the best! Sounds like you have a great Mommy too, I heard the bird and chipmunk earlier. You have bad dreams because of humans before her too, or bad dreams tonight because of not being with her?" The mile-a-minute talk and swiftly changing topics had Zoby's sleepy head spinning and couldn't keep up.

"Huh?" he mumbled.

Giggling, she walked back over to her bed from their divider. "Sorry, I ramble. Go back to sleep, I just wanted to wake you from your bad dreams. I'm Tinkerbell, by the way."

That was it. He knew it was something *super* girly.

"Alright, well, um, thanks Tinkerbell. Sorry to wake you, and good night." A little mortified he'd been caught having a nightmare, now that he was awake Zoby tried to clear his mind from worries about Mommy or past promises born out of a horrific event, before he drifted off to sleep again.

CHAPTER 6

The Smokies, Part II

"Kid, hey kid! Over here!" Surprised, Zoby saw Chip at the far corner of the fencing area in the afternoon the next day.

Racing over, Zoby anxiously called out, "what's going on, Chip?" He had been worried about Mommy all day.

Reaching the corner of the yard, Blaze dropped down to the fence post beside Chip. "It's not so good, Zoby. I'm gonna be straight with you. She got up earlier than normal this morning, before everyone else and left camp quickly so there weren't any drawn-out, sad goodbyes. It was bitter cold this morning - single digits - and she was crying, except her tears were freezing, so she made herself stop. She hiked quickly to try to stay warm, and we followed her up to Clingman's Dome."

"That was really cool though, kid!" Chip interjected. "She got pretty emotional hitting 200 miles there at Clingmans Dome, but was missing you and the tramily to celebrate that milestone." Jumping up and down, he exclaimed, "But Blaze and I here celebrated with her for you! Not that she knew we were there," he laughed, "but we got our party on."

"You're never one to miss an opportunity to celebrate, Chip." Sad to have missed that, but knowing there had to be more, Zoby anxiously looked at Blaze, "OK, so what happened after that?"

Taking a deep breath, Blaze continued. "She hiked fast today, and got to her campsite early. First one there, which I think contributed to her … well … to her breakdown. She set up her tent, and with no one around, it being so cold out, and her tramily not there … she had a panic attack. She cried a lot and questioned what she was doing out there, alone."

Paws up on the fence post, Zoby looked from Blaze to Chip and back again. "But what is she doing now then? Is she still there? Is she trying to get off trail? She can't quit! I've got to get to her, you've got to help me get to her!" Zoby's voice rose in passionate pleas.

"Whoa kid, slow down." Chip looked at Blaze. With a nod from the bird, he continued, "we thought you might react this way. We left her in the tent, she's not trying to get off trail. She was shivering in the cold and crying, real heartbreaking." Chip sighed, rubbing his chest over his heart. "Gotta think clearly though – Jerica and the kennel workers let you be outside in this area until dark. After that, they'll notice you're gone. We can't have that. And if your Mommy actually sees you coming to her in the Smokies? She'll freak out, and things will go downhill fast."

"But I've gotta see her!" Zoby emphatically yelled. "Please, please just get me near her. She'll calm down just having me near, I know she will. I can't let her be alone out there right now!"

Blaze smiled. "You're right. Which is why we recruited Eli."

Zoby's eyes widened as a massive elk emerged from the nearby woods.

"Eli, meet Zoby. Think you can get him there and back before dark?" Blaze glanced at the sun getting lower in the sky.

"Oh! Don't worry about that," came a feminine voice from behind Zoby, causing all to turn and look. "YES!" Tinkerbell shouted in excitement, "*This* is where *I* get to come in on the scene! My humans are directors of action and adventure movies, and oh, isn't this fun and exciting?! I'll totally create a distraction in the kennel at dark to help you sneak back in! I get the temporary sidekick role then, right? How fun! I can't wait, I'll think of something clever – go, go, get to your Mommy! I'll have them chasing their own tails here while you're gone!" Tinkerbell's mile-a-minute chatter had the quartet of other animals grinning in entertainment.

"Well, let's do it then!" Eli exclaimed, as he lowered his head with its mighty display of thick antlers over the fence to Zoby's level. "Climb aboard, and hold on tight!"

Doing as asked, Zoby shouted in fearful glee as the graceful elk took off lightfooted and sure, speeding into the woods. He heard Chip call out, "I'll catch up!" as he saw Blaze's blur of red through the trees beside him.

After a few minutes of breathless fear and excitement, Zoby took in the scenery flying by him. The sun was just beginning to streak some colors across the sky as it began its descent behind the layers of blue-purple mountains, and as they gained elevation, the winter cold started turning everything into an icy wonderland that sparkled in the golden rays of the sun. He was wearing his hiking base layer Mommy had left with Jerica, but the chill was definitely seeping in, and Zoby shivered.

"You ok up there, Zoby?" Eli asked. "Sorry for the cold and the wind."

"It's ok," Zoby responded, not wanting to sound too domestic and remembering something he had overhead Mommy and hikers say, he added, "when it's this cold, we 'embrace the suck,' right?"

Chuckling, Eli replied, "something like that. Almost there."

Seemingly out of nowhere, a tall, swirling tower reaching up into the sky appeared in a clearing amidst the forest. Zoby recognized it; he had been there with Mommy when they lived in the Smokies – Clingmans Dome. He noticed the "2-0-0" made out of stones on the ground underneath it as they sped past, and was thankful he got to be there and see that mile marker, even if he wasn't actually with Mommy.

Just a few minutes later, he spotted their yellow tent through the trees set up just down from a shelter. Other hikers were there now, various colors of tents dotting the scene around where Mommy had set up earlier.

"Better stop here," he heard Blaze say as he landed on the antlers beside him. "Any closer, the humans will get overly excited about an elk sighting, particularly one with a small white dog riding in its antlers," he chuckled.

Eli lowered his head. "Go ahead, Zoby. Her tent is pretty sheltered by trees, you can get there without being noticed, especially as it's getting darker under the canopy now. I have something else to attend to real quick, but I'll be back in a little bit."

Zoby climbed down, and standing beside Blaze, marveled at how quietly and gracefully the elk quickly took off. "He's kind of a shuttle driver of animals," Blaze answered the questioning look in Zoby's eyes. "Someone else probably needs his services at the moment. Don't worry, he'll be back, and we'll get you back to the kennel."

Zoby nodded, and focused on the yellow tent through the trees in front of him. Coming from inside it, he swore he could physically feel Mommy's anxiety and sadness inside his own chest. "How close do you think I can get?" he asked Blaze.

"The way it's situated, you could go right up to this side of it, staying nearly under tree and brush cover the whole time. Just be as quiet as possible."

Slowly making his way there, Zoby focused all his energy on sending good vibes and praying Mommy felt his presence in some way and would be able to calm her anxiety, loneliness and sadness. This is what he was *trained* for – he *had* to be successful at it.

Reaching the side of the tent, he decided to risk sticking his head under the rain fly, just enough to see inside the mesh of the tent itself and check on Mommy. He knew it was a risk, that she might actually see him, but he couldn't deny the pull to do so.

Quietly, gently sticking his nose under the flap and pushing more of his head in, he was relieved to see Mommy lying in her sleeping bag with her eyes closed, but he knew she was not asleep. Still some scent in the air, he assumed she had only recently finished dinner and crawled back into the bag, as she was slightly shivering. But what broke him were the tear tracks he could see on her face and shimmering in her lashes still, and the pervasive sadness that clung to the air like the scent of her dinner. Closing his eyes, he mentally began kissing her tears, snuggling up to her chest, wrapping his paws around her neck, all the things he knew calmed her down. Sending all his love he felt in every ounce of his tiny body through the mesh of the tent and into her bag and her heart, he prayed it was working to calm her down.

And he felt it. The sadness lifting, peace coming into her, and the tears stopping. The shivering ceased, and he heard her breathing even out. She was calm now, warm, and beginning to fall asleep. Tears of relief hit Zoby's eyes – he had done his job.

Backing up and pulling his head out from under the tent, Zoby turned around to head back into the woods.

Only to be confronted by a lineup of a dozen angry squirrels.

Eyes quickly darting back into the woods and all around, Zoby didn't see a sign of Blaze, Chip or even Eli. He was alone against the mob. And Mommy was safe and asleep right beside him – he could *not* wake her up and let her see him out there.

Making a snap decision, Zoby bolted off in the other direction from the woods in which he came. Running down the trail, he glanced up fast enough to see a blue blaze, and from their time on trail already, he knew running in the other direction from the shelter would lead him out to the white blazes of the AT, and hopefully back toward Clingmans Dome where maybe Eli would be able to find him.

It took a second for the squirrels to realize Zoby wasn't going to engage in a battle right there, but it was only a matter of moments before they were chasing after him. Zoby knew he could take one squirrel, maybe two... but 12? They'd be all over him. Where was Blaze? And Chip? And Eli?

Suddenly, Zoby came to the intersection with the AT. Pausing a moment, he read the sign which mercifully pointed the direction to Clingmans Dome. He didn't know why, but was sure if he could get there, he'd find safety. Turning that direction, he realized his momentary pause had allowed the squirrels to catch up.

One jumped on his back while another came at him from the front. Sliding on ice and rolling into a large branch, he shook them off and leaped over the branch while another came at him.

Suddenly, Chip appeared, flying through the air and intersecting the squirrel mid-air before it could land on Zoby. "Hey kid!" Zoby heard as Chip went at it with the squirrel, then catching his balance on the ice, Zoby turned and faced off with yet another one coming at him, with more just behind.

"We're outnumbered!" Zoby yelled back.

"No you're not," Zoby heard a chorus of voices similar to Chip's suddenly saying. An army of chipmunks appeared from the mossy, ice-covered depths of the forest, springing into action. Icicles became swords and weapons between squirrel and chipmunks, scattering across the trail. With the assistance of Chip, Zoby got the last squirrel off him, and looking around, saw the other chipmunks were hard at battle with the rest. "Come on, kid, let's go, they've got this!" Chip jumped onto Zoby's back, and grabbing his collar, kicked him in the sides to propel Zoby forward on the trail.

Running as fast he could away from the squirrel and chipmunk scene, Zoby yelled up at Chip, "where did Blaze go?!" To which came the reply, "to find Eli and get you out of here! I got there just as the squirrels were lining up, and sounded the alarm to my extended Trail Angel family. I had a feeling it was going to get ugly."

"How could they have known I would be there? I'm supposed to be in the kennel!" Zoby shouted as he ran, "it doesn't make sense!"

"I dunno, kid. We'll put our ears to the Trail Talk to find out."

With a swoop of red feathers, Blaze appeared, flying ahead of them. "Eli is on his way! He's meeting us at Clingmans Dome. Great job shaking off the squirrels, guys. We're going to get you back by dark still, Zoby!"

With a triumphant grin, Zoby put on another burst of speed and in a few minutes came flying out into the clearing with Clingmans Dome towering over them and flaming sunset colors painting the sky.

But they weren't alone.

"Park Ranger!!" Blaze and Chip cried in unison.

"Keep running, Zoby!" Chip kicked his ribs again, "He'll catch you and take you to the pound! Dogs aren't allowed in the National Park, and without your Mommy, he's going to think you're a lost stray!"

Out of breath and unaccustomed to fearing a human, Zoby stopped long enough for it to take a minute for what Chip was saying to sink in. In that minute, the Ranger saw him and started toward them.

"Zoby! RUN!" Chip kicked harder.

Zoby took off on the paved trail leading from Clingmans Dome down to a parking lot. Humans coming to watch sunset packed the trail. Racing around children and people in wheelchairs, Zoby put those and other obstacles between him and the oh-so-close Ranger.

"What are you doing?" Chip hollered, "there's going to be more Rangers at the Visitor Center and parking lot!" he yelled as both began to come into view.

"You just said, 'RUN,' not *where* to run!" Zoby bellowed in reply.

Then he came to an abrupt stop as they neared the parking lot and two more Rangers were there greeting tourists.

Jumping off the trail and racing toward a pile of boulders, Zoby narrowly dodged the Ranger behind him grabbing him, and now that first Ranger had gotten the attention of the others.

Reaching the boulders, Zoby realized he had boxed himself in. Eyes looking around wildly, he saw all the Rangers approaching him, and no escape. "Chip," his voice trembling, "now what?"

"Now *this!*" Eli bellowed as he jumped over the boulders and landed in between Zoby and the approaching Rangers.

Shocked, all three Rangers quickly backed up as Eli lowered his rack, pretending to prepare to charge them.

"Zoby, over here!" Looking sideways along the base of the boulders, he saw Blaze gesturing to a small opening between that grouping and the next. With Eli distracting the Rangers, Zoby and Chip hurriedly disappeared through the opening and out the backside of the pile of boulders, bordering the forest, into which they quickly dashed.

Barely able to catch his breath, Zoby looked at his friends with his eyes full of gratitude as well as a touch of humor. "Thanks guys. This has been beyond crazy, huh?"

Chip laughed, "Trail Angel life. We get *all* the excitement on trail this way!" Blaze shot a look at Chip and said, "well, maybe not *this* much excitement usually, but it's nice to get all the Angels working together along the trail again this way."

Eli returned then, smirking with not-so-hidden glee. "That was fun. I can't say I make a practice of terrifying humans, but gotta admit, doing it once in a while for the greater good is rather entertaining!" Putting his head down toward Zoby, he said, "climb aboard, let's get you back, it's getting dark!"

Giving Chip a hug, Zoby thanked him, then did as told. As Blaze flew alongside them in the blur of deepening twilight in the forest, Zoby said a prayer of thanks for Mommy's safety and well-being, thanks for his woodland Trail Angel friends, and glancing at the darkening skies around him, hoped Tinkerbell had indeed been able to create a distraction at the kennel.

As they arrived, it was clear she had.

"What did she *do*?" Zoby laughed as the cacophony of barking reached them well before the kennel came into sight.

Quietly reaching the far side of the fence, Eli lowered his head and Zoby jumped off, then saw Tinkerbell racing toward them.

"Who let the DOGS out? Who, who, who, who?" she sang. "AND who let the CATS out, who, who, who who? ME, me, me me!" she answered herself in song. Giggling hysterically, she continued, "I let the cats out! AND the dogs! All together with no separators, doors and kennels open, oh it's a madhouse in there! 'Who, who, who who? Me, me, me, me!'" She sang again. "Come on Zoby, let's get in there, they'll never know you weren't here!"

Laughing, he looked back at Eli and Blaze, "thank you. Thank you for everything. Really." And singing along with Tinkerbell, they headed back into the kennel. "Who, who, who who?!"

CHAPTER 7

A New Start, A Snowstorm and A Tornado

Mommy! There she is! Tail wagging, happy dancing, grinning from ear-to-ear, Zoby nearly jumped out the window of Jerica's car as they approached the AT parking lot at Davenport Gap where Mommy was waiting, just as excited as Zoby.

Running to the car, Mommy grabbed Zoby through the open window and swung him around in circles, then smothered him in kisses. "Baby boy! My baby boy, my little man, oh I've missed you! I've *missed* you!" Smothering her right back in doggie kisses, Zoby gave round after round of the happy yip-yips he knew Mommy loved.

Laughing, she set him down for a moment to talk to Jerica. Looking up, Zoby saw Chip, Blaze and Eli at the edge of the woods near the trailhead. Through Trail Talk, they had discovered Ariana had ordered the Squirrel Mafia to wreak havoc on Mommy that night. They were to tear her tent and gear, get in her tent while sleeping and terrorize her ... basically attempt to get her off trail, and therefore Zoby off trail. Had it not been for his friends breaking him out of the kennel and getting him there, unintentionally foiling their plans, the Squirrel Mafia may have succeeded that night.

Smiling widely, he yelled over, "thanks for everything guys! See you back on trail!" They shouted goodbyes for now, and turned back into the forest.

Mommy picked him back up, and as he gave her more kisses, she said, "Now we're gonna hike *together* again ... all the way to Maine!"

****

After a zero, Mommy and Zoby headed out on trail again, just the two of them for the first time on this journey.

Surprisingly, Mommy felt total peace, even excitement, about this fresh start on the trail. Ever since that first night away from the tramily when she had a breakdown in her tent over it all, she had dug deep and found a renewed sense of purpose, and an overall sense of harmony within and without. She enjoyed meeting new friends on trail at camp and on breaks, and finished the Smokies in two days after that, hiking her longest days yet, even a 21-mile day. Now she was looking forward to seeing what she and Zoby could do together.

That night, they camped upon a bald with 360-degree views of the rolling mountains in all directions. Mommy held Zoby while watching sunset from one side of their tent, then cuddled with him in the cold morning while they watched sunrise from the other side of their tent. Alone, just the two of them, they both felt it was the perfect way to re-start their journey together.

The days on trail were flying by, and Zoby was loving his time alone with Mommy. He did miss the Aunties and was sad he never got to say good-bye, but the blessing in disguise from the tramily break-up was the quality time with Mommy and their growth together on trail.

Remaining cautious of Ariana and/or Jezebel sending orders to the Squirrel Mafia, Zoby checked in daily with Blaze and Chip. Nothing happening according to Trail Talk, so Zoby ignored the hateful glares and comments he received daily from squirrels they passed on trail, and was instead determined to enjoy time with his friends as well as Mommy.

One memorable day came when Mommy's friend Jake drove from Atlanta to meet them on trail and do his unique form of Trail Magic – even Chip and Blaze said they had never seen anything like it – and oh yes, both chipmunk and cardinal enjoyed it as well! Jake had an actual inflatable sectional couch set up under a huge awning at a trail intersection, along with chairs, a grill, an enormous roaring fire and, get this – a movie screen, projector and disco lights! After filling their bellies with food from the grill (Zoby got his own sausage!), Mommy and Zoby slept under the stars cuddled up by the fire on the couch that night, along with their friend Marina whom they had hiked with a bit, and watched a movie in the wilderness with Jake and other hikers! Blaze and Chip enjoyed the popcorn and movie as well, and Zoby *might* have snuck them some graham crackers from the S'mores Mommy made too!

After stopping for an overnight and resupply in Hot Springs, North Carolina, Zoby was happily prancing along the AT-logo'd sidewalk that marked the trail through town as they headed out to climb up Lover's Leap, when he heard Blaze and Chip singing along to the song Mommy sang to him while hiking. Mommy was humming and singing, overjoyed that spring flowers were beginning to burst forth everywhere and kept stopping for photos. His heart full, he looked up at his friends flying and scampering along beside them singing with Mommy, at colorful flowers blooming, at the mountains ahead of them and the river they had just crossed beside him, and thought things couldn't get much better than this.

He was right. Those idyllic days were about to hit some obstacles from both Mother Nature and the Squirrel Mafia.

****

On April 9, five weeks into their thru-hike, a winter storm hit, covering the mountains along the Tennessee and North Carolina border where the AT meandered for 200 miles with a blanket of cold, white snow. Mommy made the decision for them to get off trail and zero out the storm, but the next day they returned to the trail.

A white, winter wonderland of a trail.

Wearing his puffy coat, Zoby was transfixed by the beauty of it, and then laughing, he ran and dove in the drifts, jumping around and shaking off the snow, then doing it again. Mommy laughed at his antics, which spurred him on to continue playing with more silliness along the trail for several miles.

"Hey kid! Isn't this great?" While Zoby waited for Mommy to gather water, Chip dove into a snowdrift, disappearing into it, then flying out again, sending snow flying in Zoby's face.

"Oh that's how it is, huh?! You asked for it!" Zoby struck at a drift, sending a chunk of snow smack into the chipmunk's belly.

Falling over with laughter, Zoby missed seeing Blaze overhead as the bird dropped bombs of snow on him, then landed beside Chip, the two friends' gleeful laughter ringing through the forest as Zoby shook off the snow Blaze had deposited upon him.

"Alright, that's it!" Zoby went after them and the three began a snow-flinging romp through the drifts.

As their energy and laughter died down, Zoby lied on his back, squirming around to get the snow off him, in what Mommy referred to as his "roly poly" act. What he didn't realize was the thick black mud puddle he had rolled himself into now made him soaking wet and filthy.

"Oh.my.goodness!" Mommy exclaimed, her eyes wide, when she saw him. "What did you do?! Ooooh Zooooby," laughing in exasperation, she examined him, "*what* did you *do?!*"

Wet, shivering and muddy, Zoby ignored the hoots of laughter coming from behind him as Chip and Blaze found the situation highly amusing.

"My little man," Mommy said while pulling out a towel, "sometimes you are such a *boy*," she laughed while attempting to remove some mud and get him a bit drier, "today was definitely *not* the day to get wet and muddy. Now you're gonna be cold, and we still have about five miles before getting to camp!"

Cold and shivering herself, she wrapped Zoby in the towel and set off carrying him, hoping her body heat would help warm him a bit through the damp towel to his little, wet body. The sun was dipping lower with late afternoon shadows making the day suddenly feel significantly cooler. Mommy was exhausted from sludging through knee-high snowdrifts and slipping around in slush and mud all day. Five more miles to get to the campsite just past Big Bald felt like a marathon, plus they had a significant elevation gain to get up and over the mountain.

Three miles later, Mommy hit the wall. Sitting on a boulder on the edge of the trail, she gave in to her fatigue and the urge to cry. Zoby was cold, she was cold, the trail was slippery or covered in thick snowdrifts and slow-going. She'd been looking around for potential campsites to stop early, but the trail was cut into the side of the mountain on a ridge in this section, sharp angles to each side, plus large boulders covering the terrain.

Zoby shivered in Mommy's arms but couldn't stand seeing her cry. Reaching his head up to cover her face in kisses, he saw Blaze and Chip emerging from the shadows of the forest, with an elderly man slowly walking toward them.

The man walked over to Mommy and asked, "can I help?"

Sniffling, she answered, "no, I'm sorry, I just needed a moment to break down. We're thru-hiking and today has been cold and miserable, and I'm so exhausted. We have two more miles to go before camp, and I'm fighting every step."

"It's my pleasure to help thru-hikers. I live just over the ridge there, and I hike up to Big Bald nightly to watch sunset. Why don't I just lead the way? I'm slow, but you can have some company and simply focus on one step at a time." Reaching over to pet Zoby's head, he continued, "has your little friend here been hiking the whole trail too? How many miles did you do through the snow today?"

"Yes, and almost 14 so far. It will be about 16 when we finish."

"16? On a day like today? Well, you and your little one here have my respect. If you've slogged out 14 today, you can get through 2 more. Let's go, we've got this." At that, Zoby jumped down eagerly, looked at Mommy, and willed her up and forward back on trail. As they started hiking again, Zoby saw Chip and Blaze bopping along from tree-to-tree above them.

"I don't know where you found this guy, but thank you," Zoby called out to them.

"His name is Taylor," Blaze responded, "he is a wonderful human Trail Angel here in the area, and when we saw your Mommy beginning to struggle, we hoped we'd find him on his daily sunset hike and be able to get him to you."

Looking back at Mommy he saw she was doing better, obviously still tired, but following Taylor's lead and making her way up Big Bald. As they got above treeline, Taylor motioned for her to turn around. Doing so, she gasped at the layers of rolling hills spread out all around them, the golden sunset playing with the colors, shadow and light as far they could see.

"Oh, it's stunning. And just what I needed for a boost and refresher to get to camp." Mommy and Taylor stood at the top of the Bald for a moment and talked, then she turned to Zoby, "alright little man. Less than a mile to camp now. Somehow we made it through this cold, snowy day together. Let's finish it."

Saying goodbye and thank you to Taylor, they set off and found the campsite, a sweet little cove tucked into the evergreens just off trail, with a large pile of boulders and the trees blocking the wind blowing across the Bald. Set up in their tent, changed into dry clothes and cuddled in their sleeping bags together, Mommy told Zoby just how proud she was of him, and of their day together. Pushing through the physical and mental obstacles, she felt confident they had what it takes to make it all the way.

"And Taylor. What a blessing at just the right moment." Mommy observed.

With a grin, Zoby sent a silent thank you to his furry and feathered friends he knew were tucked into a tree just outside their tent, then snuggled in to sleep.

Indeed, that day bolstered their confidence to continue right through the next stretch, getting them to the other side of Roan Highlands, where their next break awaited them with a stay at Mountain Harbour Bed & Breakfast, known for the best breakfast on the trail (and it was!). It was also Easter weekend, which had Mommy in high spirits as she listened and sang along to worship music while hiking.

Easter Sunday itself was a particularly memorable day on trail, as it was warm and sunny, flowers were blooming with butterflies dancing across them, and they hiked past 3 waterfalls and lots of cascading streams. Additionally, they hit the 400-mile mark that day, which made Mommy proud of them for hiking just as far alone as they had with the tramily. Zoby loved that day on trail with her in the warm sun, taking lots of pictures in the fields of flowers and beside waterfalls, celebrating Easter in God's Creation together.

As they set out for the last stretch of days in Tennessee before hitting the Virginia border, Zoby saw Chip the first two days out on trail, but no sign of Blaze. Enjoying laughter and the company of his chipmunk friend, he did wonder where the other was. Odd, he thought, as the trio had stayed together lately. But he shrugged it off as Mommy enjoyed walking around Lake Watauga on another blue sky, warm sunny day and had Zoby posing for pictures.

As they gained elevation the next day after leaving the Lake, the wind was picking up and thunder rumbled in the distance. Zoby hated storms, and Mommy was hurrying him along when he caught sight of the red bird on a small shrub ahead of them.

He could tell Blaze had news.

"What's going on?" Zoby asked him as the bird flew alongside them through the trees and shrubs.

"Ariana. I heard some rumbling through Trail Talk. They're not happy you're still out here and about to enter Virginia. She's betting on the weather getting bad for you up here on the mountain tonight, and she has something planned. I can't seem to find out from anyone what that is, though, it's pretty concealed."

Nodding, Zoby looked at his friends. "Ok, well we know, and that's important."

"Right. We'll be prepared. Whoaa!" Blaze yelled as the roaring wind kicked up and blew him off course from the branch he had been aiming toward.

"Weather isn't looking good, kid, that may or may not work in our favor, actually. See you tonight, I've got some favors to call in!" Chip yelled into the howling wind as he ran off.

Pushing against the raging wind uphill toward the shelter they were aiming to camp at, the distant thunder getting closer, Mommy unexpectedly stopped when they came to a stealth site surrounded by rocks, with enough room for one tent. "Hmmm," she said to Zoby, "we're only two-tenths of a mile from the shelter, which I think is going to be more exposed at the top of this ridge, and not a good idea in this wind. Let's check this out." Walking over behind the boulder pile she exclaimed, "oh! Look at this view back here! This will be sunrise. With the wind protection from the rocks and this view? Sold!" She laughed as

Zoby happy-danced for her, and, throwing her pack down, she pulled out the tent and went about setting up camp.

And none too soon was it up and they were inside it, as the storm hit with scary ferocity. Lightning lit up the sky above like fireworks while thunder literally shook the ground below. The wind tossed heavy sheets of rain against them while it whistled and blew sharply against their tent, tugging at its stakes and poles.

Zoby *hated* storms. And this one was the *worst*.

Mommy held him while he shook in her arms, and he could tell she wasn't exactly calm, either. Then suddenly a loud crack and a flash of bright light struck right beside them, then the boom accompanied by his and Mommy's astonished shrieks rang through the forest as a tree fell not 20 yards from their tent. In addition, he heard the scrambles and yells of what he thought must be animals fighting near their tent.

"Zoby!" he heard Chip yell. "You ok in there?!"

"Define 'ok!'" Zoby yelled back, "what is going on out there?"

"Lightning hit a dead tree, but let's just say it got some help from squirrels! Just stay inside the tent, we're going into combat!" Chip yelled as he jumped on the back of a squirrel chewing a limb hanging precariously close to the tent.

No problem, Zoby thought, *I'm* not heading out there. Outside the tent, he heard the raging storm as well as the eruptions here and there of the squirrel battle. Saying a prayer of safety over his friends, he felt a combination of guilty and blessed while he listened to it all.
And then ... the entire scene was swept into the deafening vacuum of what sounded like a freight train roaring through the forest. Almost simultaneously came the shrill sound of sirens rising up onto the mountain ridge from the valley below.

"Oh my God!" Mommy yelled, eyes wild, "those are tornado sirens coming from town!"

Barely able to hear her through the train-sounding roar and the sirens, Zoby sank deeper into her arms as the wild wind beating against the tent threatened to collapse it around them, while small twigs and other debris slapped against it.

Then, just as abruptly, it stopped.

The roar was replaced with a silence so empty it somehow seemed just as loud.

Exhaling loudly and making herself breathe evenly, Mommy said, "I think we're ok now, buddy. Storm's over. We're gonna be ok."

Giving Mommy kisses, Zoby then cautiously walked to the edge of the tent. "Chip? Blaze?" Zoby called out. "Are you there, are things ok?"

Chip popped his head under the rain fly of the tent and grinned widely at Zoby. "Another check in the 'W' column for the good guys, kid. That tornado sent everyone running. Good thing you stopped here instead, because they had chewed through branches and dead trees all around the shelter, hoping the storm would blow them down and scare you away from the trail."

"Scare us away?!" Zoby looked back at Mommy re-organizing the tent and pulling out food for the dinner they had skipped. "That could have *killed* us!" he hissed in anger.

"They're getting bolder, kid," Chip said, then moved over as Blaze bumped his way into the tent's vestibule, too. "Will only increase as you get closer to Maine," Blaze added, "But we've got your back. Get some dinner and a good night's sleep now, the storm has passed."

****

The next day as they passed the shelter, Zoby noted in anger the downed trees and limbs littering the campsites around it, and sent the nastiest looks he could to the small gathering of squirrels nearby. A few hours later as Mommy literally did cartwheels and a kickline dance across the Tennessee / Virginia state line, he spotted a large squirrel he recognized watching them from the trees above.

In an ominous tone, he snarled up at her, "gonna have to do better, Ariana. Jezebel must be furious with you for failing to get me off trail, huh?" At that, her eyes narrowed angrily. Zoby grinned. "Oh, and thanks for all the *fun* in North Carolina and Tennessee. I know I'm just gonna *love* Virginia." And with that, ignoring her glare and the nuts she hurled at him, he walked with Mommy into Damascus.

CHAPTER 8

Damascus, Ponies and a Man Named Stan

Deep in the recesses of the cave-like tunnel maze under house-sized boulders in Maine, Jezebel stood with her back to her daughter and informant.

Speaking slowly to control her anger, enunciating each word, she started, "I thought I made it *very* clear that domestic was not to make it out of *Georg-ia*," drawing out the state name and slowly turning to face them, she continued, "so why am I hearing he is in," pausing to suck in her temper, "*VIRGINIA*?" she spit out, her eyes tapered into dangerous slits.

Marcus, the informant stepped forward, nervously wringing his paws, and stuttered, "M-Miss Jez-Jezebel, our efforts were, they were, you know, g-greatly c-c-compromised. The b-bear and then elk, and tt-t-tornado..."

Losing patience, she snapped at him, "do I look like I want to hear *excuses*?" Voice rising, she slapped Marcus aside as she finished, then spun and placed her finger under her daughter's chin, lifting her face to meet her eyes.

"You have 550 miles in this state to get it right. This domestic doesn't Make. It. Out. OF. VIRGINIA." She bit off each word in barely contained rage.

"If I hear of him past the border and in Harper's Ferry..." her eyes gleamed with malice and fury into her daughter's eyes, "...then I will be *extremely* upset. We don't want *that*, now do we?"

Zoby fell in love with Damascus. Nicknamed "Trail Town USA," the Virginia Creeper Trail and the AT intersected right through the middle of town. Everyone was so friendly and welcoming to thru-hikers, including their dogs. Mommy had only booked an overnight there, not a zero, but they took all evening and the next morning to explore the town together, and he even got an entire bacon cheeseburger and some ice cream! Trail town stops were the *best*! Mommy said she would like to come back with the RV, ride bikes on the Creeper Trail, and be there for the Trail Days festival the following year. Zoby thought that sounded like so much fun. All the past AT thru-hikers together in one place at the same time, with lots of food?! Um, yes please!

Their time in Damascus came to an end, and as they hiked out of town that afternoon and continued northward into Virginia, they experienced their first truly warm days on trail. The calendar was about to flip to May, and in the warm sunshine, the trail was bursting forth with spring flowers. A little addicted to the colorful blooms, Mommy stopped frequently for pictures, as well as around the rushing streams full of cascades.

Reaching Grayson Highlands, Zoby was full of excitement. He had hiked this area before with Mommy, and remembered the wild ponies who lived in the area. They had been friendly to Zoby and one southern belle in particular had been extra cordial, taking a fixin' to him.

He wondered if any of the usually sociable ponies were hidden "resources" to the Squirrel Mafia. He hadn't forgotten the anger he had felt radiating off Ariana at the state line.

Voicing this to his friends at camp the morning they were heading in to Grayson Highlands, he was assured the ponies loved hikers – both human and domestics – and that neither had heard anything through the Trail Talk grapevine. Blaze added he heard Ariana had returned home to Maine, with the unenviable task of facing the wrath of her mother.

"That must have been an interesting scene," Chip declared, then changing the subject, "hey kid, you just cost more animals their bets, by making it past Damascus," he whooped.

Defiantly, Zoby stuck his head up and puffed out his chest. "Small dog, big adventures!" Laughing, Chip and Blaze agreed.

That day they passed the 500-mile mark, and Mommy sang a funny song about walking 500 miles and 500 more while they hiked. As it approached late afternoon, they finally saw the infamous ponies on trail. They called out a greeting to Zoby, knowing who he was from Trail Talk, and told him they were all cheering him on, which made Zoby's heart full.

That evening, Mommy was setting up camp on a grassy clearing in one of the highest parts of the Highlands when four ponies wandered into their campsite ... and instantly Zoby recognized one as his sweet friend from their last visit!

"Well bless yer heart, y'all it's *Zoby*!" Shelby called out as she trotted over. "Well I'll be happy as a hog in mud! We were fixin' to walk all night 'til we found y'all!"

Instantly feeling at ease with the gracious southern pony and her funny sayings, Zoby greeted her nose to nose. "Hey Shelby, it's so good to see you again!"

"Now sweet pea, let me take a look at ya," she said, backing up. "As I recall, you were day hikin' here last time. Now look at ya – a courageous *thru-hiker* dog gettin' them squirrels all in a dither!" She winked, "I reckon Jezebel is madder than a wet hen right about now."

Jumping up on the tip of Shelby's nose, Chip wrapped his arms around her muzzle and kissed her between the eyes. As he gave the pony a wink in return, he cheerfully sang out, "You know it! We're making sure of that." Then laughing, climbed over to her mane and curled up in it. "Hey Shelbs, always a pleasure to see you."

Landing beside Zoby, Blaze agreed with Chip. "One of our trail favorites, Miss Shelby here."

"Well heavens to Betsy! I'm tickled pink y'all." If possible for a horse to blush, Shelby accomplished it. "Me and the crew, we're proud as all get out of our friend Zoby here! Everyone's talkin' about y'all dodgin' and foilin' those nasty squirrels and their nastier accomplices! Why, if I had my druthers, I'd march right on up there to Maine and tell that Jezebel to ... "

"Now Shelby, hush your mouth," another of the ponies admonished as he nuzzled up to the agitated Shelby's side, "gettin' worked up and pitchin' a hissy fit over what you can't control doesn't help Zoby. Or help Chip and Blaze help Zoby."

Sheepishly, Shelby agreed. "Mind my manners y'all, I do apologize. The Squirrel Mafia gets me under my duck feathers, ya know? There's just no need for their nastiness and shenanigans on trail." Looking at Zoby, she said, "I want you to know, I'm a key link in the Trail Talk chain and I've never been hankerin' so badly to help a domestic no bigger than a minnow in a fishin' pond get to Maine. Jezebel has her reasons for detesting domestics, particularly your size and color, and God bless her dearly departed, but that ain't no reason for hatin' on *all* the way she does." Shaking her head sadly, Shelby proclaimed, "She's sittin' on a bitter stick and someone needs to remove it!"

As Chip, Blaze and the other ponies chuckled in response, Zoby cocked his head in interest. He still hadn't heard the background story as to why Jezebel, Ariana and the Squirrel Mafia in general took a particular dislike to small, white dogs. "Dearly departed?" he repeated.

Blaze quickly responded, "Let's get you through Virginia. No need to burden you with stories that have been exaggerated and manipulated up and down the trail until it's necessary." Casting a quick look to Shelby, he continued, "the important thing to focus on is simply continuing, day after day, mile after mile. And let us handle the squirrels. Shelby here is not only one of our favorites, but as she stated, a key link for us. And we love her for it!"

"Zoby!" Mommy called from the freshly set campsite, "time for dinner buddy, let's eat!"

"We'll be right over yonder tonight," Shelby gestured with her head toward the edge of the grassy clearing where a small cluster of trees provided some shelter. "I reckon we'll be seeing you off in the morning. You've got gumption, Zoby. We like that 'round here."

The next morning, Mommy spent some time on her phone responding to text messages from some fellow thru-hikers near them on the trail, and googling reasons why her feet were hurting in the now persistent way they were each day. Fearing it was more than just aches from hiking long miles, she realized while looking back through her saved daily routes in her FarOut app trail guide that they hadn't taken an actual zero since the snowstorm nearly three weeks and about 250 miles ago.

"Well, no wonder my feet hurt," Mommy said to Zoby. "We've taken neros, but I think we're due for a full day off. What do you say, buddy?" Looking ahead, she figured it was two more days before reaching an easy way off trail into a town. "OK, we can do two more days, right little man?"

A full day off sounded good to Zoby, too. Plus – town food! Jumping around excitedly, he loved making Mommy smile and forget her foot pain while she finished packing up and they got on trail. Passing by the cove of trees, Zoby called out a good-bye to Shelby and her pony friends, chuckling at the, "y'all come back now, ya hear?" that came in response.

Only a few miles later as they reached a dirt road crossing, Zoby heard Mommy exclaim in happy surprise, "trail magic!"

Indeed, a gentleman was sitting on the tailgate of a truck stocked full of food and drinks for thru-hikers, with a circle of camp chairs set up around him.

"Well now, you're my first for the morning! I'm Jimmy," he said, extending his hand, "Would you like a Gatorade or Coke? And how about the pup?"

Jumping up and doing his dance that always resulted in treats, Zoby ecstatically received some goodies he took under the truck in the shade to enjoy, while Mommy settled into a chair.

"Jimmy?" he heard Mommy ask, "are you the Jimmy that is slackpacking my friend Stan these past few days? He was texting me this morning that he's nearly caught up to us."

"You know Stan?" Jimmy exclaimed, "Yes, I am that Jimmy, and I'll be picking Stan up later, then I'm taking him back to Damascus where he's zeroing to resupply and rest before I drop him off to continue on."

"Oh wow, we've been talking for a few weeks about Stan catching me and hiking together. This could work … I wonder… would you be willing to take me back to Damascus with Stan? I just realized this morning I'm overdue for a zero, and my feet are killing me..." Zoby listened as Mommy and this man named Jimmy discussed and made arrangements.

Getting up with renewed vigor, Mommy called out to Zoby, "come on buddy, we're gonna get a break! We only have eight more miles to hike together, then our new friend Jimmy here is going to pick us up, and we're gonna go back to Damascus and meet up with another new friend named Stan!"

The "back to Damascus" part of that sounded great – more burgers and ice cream! The "Stan" part of that he wasn't so sure about. He enjoyed meeting other hikers, and he had loved hiking with the Aunties … but … he had been relishing his alone time with Mommy. Plus, he knew Chip and Blaze could protect him and Mommy, but how much more difficult would it be if they were hiking with someone else, too? Or, would that slow down the Squirrel Mafia's attempts at getting him off trail? He needed to consult with Chip and Blaze about this. They had hung back to visit with Shelby and the ponies this morning, so he hoped they would show up on trail soon to discuss these latest developments with them.

****

Eight miles later, he was lying curled up in the grass beside Mommy, enjoying the warm afternoon sun while waiting to be picked up by Jimmy and Stan. Still no sign of Blaze or Chip had him anxious his friends would lose him on trail with the unexpected return to Damascus and a zero the following day.

As the truck pulled in and Mommy greeted the men and introduced them to Zoby, there was still no trace of his furry and feathered friends. Sighing deeply, Zoby found himself in the backseat with Mommy heading back to Damascus, hoping his friends would be able to figure it out and find him.

****

Hidden in the shadows of a tree high above, Ariana had watched the day progress. Overhearing the domestic's human discussing her foot pain, the need for a zero, and them going 50 miles backwards on trail to Damascus was going to work in her favor.

Still seeing the fury in her mother's eyes and smarting from the brutal tongue-lashing, her return trek down the trail from Maine had been one full of subtle humiliation. Trail Talk, she knew, was full of conversation about both her failure, and how her mother would react. She felt the gleeful glances from those she passed on trail who enjoyed her failure and subsequent punishment, as well as the scornful looks from fellow Squirrel Mafia upset she hadn't done her job, and feeling she should be relieved of this particular responsibility.

Neither scenario sat well with her, to say the least.

She sighed in disgust. Virginia of all states, to have a short leash put on her to get this done. The Mafia was a bit dry on resources in this stretch, those ridiculous wild ponies controlling the woodland animal chain for most of southern Virginia. She was going to need a little time to come up with a plan, and gather resources.

First things first. That despicable duo of the bird and chipmunk were unaware the domestic had been picked up and returned to Damascus. She would use that to her advantage to get the Trail Talk "misinforming" them of their domestic's whereabouts.

Within a Damascus B&B, Zoby was falling head over heels in love. Stan had immediately offered Zoby beef jerky in the truck, then offered him some of his burger even though Mommy had gotten Zoby chicken when they ate in town. Then when Mommy couldn't find a room for them, Stan offered to share his, which had two beds, and when arriving he let Zoby curl up on his pillow then went about petting and massaging him. With a full belly, he fell into total blissed-out mode, forgetting completely any trail troubles or angry squirrels.

Amused, Mommy looked at Stan and Zoby, "I think you've stolen my dog."

"Well, he's a good one to steal," Stan laughed.

Yeah, this Stan guy was alright, Zoby thought as he drifted off to peaceful sleep.

CHAPTER 9

Alpacas, Coyotes and Foxes, Oh My!

On their zero in Damascus, Mommy and Zoby never left the B&B. Already resupplied for a few more days since they weren't expecting to get off trail, Stan ran out for his own food resupply, and returned with take-out for lunch and dinner. (Including an entire burger for Zoby, and Stan shared his ice cream with him, too. This guy could stick around, Zoby thought.) Mommy wanted to stay off her feet, icing, soaking and elevating them. She had come to the conclusion she was developing plantar fasciitis, which Zoby thought sounded terrible, so he was doing all he could to help Mommy feel better.

Inside, he kept hoping to hear a rapping on the window and see red feathers flutter by, but his friends never came. A gnawing pit in his stomach warned him something was amiss, but stuck inside with Mommy's injury and not on trail, he was helpless to learn what Trail Talk was saying.

Nevertheless, he enjoyed the zero, and hearing Mommy's laughter and conversation with someone again. Sure, he had savored their alone time on trail, but he knew both he and Mommy had grown in confidence and abilities on their own, and he had to admit, it was more enjoyable to share the trail and its experiences making memories with others.

Speaking of others ... that nagging feeling something was wrong just wouldn't go away as the day passed into night, and night into morning, with no sign of Chip and Blaze.

"You're going to stay here with Jimmy today, buddy, you get an extra zero!" Mommy exclaimed as she stroked his ears in the truck's backseat. Looking back and forth between Mommy and "Uncle Stan" as he was being dubbed, Zoby was on high alert and confused.

"That's right baby boy, Jimmy's gonna help out some other hikers while he slackpacks us today. You get an extra day off, so be a good boy for Jimmy, ok? We'll see you tonight, he has a site at a *real* campground we're going stay at!" Mommy jumped out of the car with Uncle Stan, and with a last kiss on his head, she disappeared onto the trail.

What. Just. Happened?!

Jimmy started the truck while Zoby looked around in bewilderment. This would be the third day he hadn't seen Chip and Blaze, not since the morning they left Shelby and the ponies. Did they think he was off trail? Were they looking for him? He hoped they would spot Mommy, but she was using a different pack and was with Stan, whom they didn't know, and without Zoby. And tonight they were staying at a campground instead of on trail?

This was not good.

Back in Grayson Highlands, Chip and Blaze reconvened with Shelby.

"I just don't understand it," Chip chattered as he paced about, flinging his arms wildly as he talked, "we've gone up and down the trail from here to what could be as much as three to four days ahead. There's no sign of them. No word that anyone has seen them. How could they have just vanished, just gone poof, just disappear, just ..."

"Chip!" Blaze flung his wings in the chipmunk's path to stop him. "Stop! Zoby and his Mommy didn't disappear. Shelby is *trying* to get your attention if you'd shush for a minute." Looking at the pony, Blaze stated, "you've heard something."

"Well I do declare! That may be the right truth, I *do* know something, but that ain't mean it isn't foolery. And y'all that is what I'm thinkin'. It's foolery alright. It doesn't amount to a hill of beans considering I've tracked the source to that rotten beast of a squirrel daughter, bless her heart." Shelby stopped her rambling to take a breath and realized Chip and Blaze were staring at her impatiently. "Sorry ya'll, mind my manners. Here it is. That Ariana, she has started up runnin' a rumor that Zoby's momma got off trail with an injury, so - and I quote, 'the domestic has failed in his quest to conquer this trail and terrorize its inhabitants.'" Blood boiling again, Shelby started in, "Why I *never*..."

"Shelby, you are the queen of all things Trail Talk." Blaze interrupted her next rampage of southern-coated indignation against the squirrel. "Now why on earth would she say that Mommy got hurt? We would have heard, I'm positive, if she did. Is there any report - anywhere, other than from Ariana - of her actually getting injured?" Shelby shook her head.

"OK, we've got to think. Figure this out. They weren't at the camp Zoby said they were stopping at the night they left here. We went forward several miles that night in case they hiked further. Nothing. We've covered the trail extensively from here north the last two days. No sign of them since breaking camp here."

"I hate to say this Blaze, but maybe she did get hurt. Maybe she got a ride off trail that day and they're done. Maybe Ariana is right … not about Zoby terrorizing the trail," Chip rolled his eyes in anger at that, "but saying he is off trail. Then following it up with that nonsense stirs the pot. Reminds animals on the fence with their feelings about domestics on trail that they are a danger, like the Squirrel Mafia wants everyone to believe."

"Hush your mouth!" Shelby admonished Chip. "We ponies pride ourselves in making this trail a safe place for all, including humans and domestics, so don't be all thinkin' that squirrel is highfalutin' enough to change minds 'round here!"

"Hold on," Blaze stopped them, and continued thoughtfully, "Chip, you said 'maybe she got a ride off trail that day' … I think you're on to something. What if Zoby's Mommy actually *is* sick or slightly injured, and they are off trail zeroing it out? What if Ariana saw them leave, and is spinning it to her advantage?"
"Well if it had been a snake, it would've bit me," Shelby shook her mane back and laughed. "I do reckon you're right on that, Blaze. And I say we put out our own counter-rumor stating just exactly that. Ariana has to know soon as Zoby's back on trail again the animals 'round here will find her even less credible. But then again … common sense ain't a flower that grows in everyone's garden."

Chip laughed, and jumping up on Shelby's muzzle, gave her a hug and smooch between the eyes. "Love ya, Shelbs. Go do your thing with Trail Talk. We're gonna keep trying to find them."

Not only did Jimmy slackpack Mommy and Uncle Stan that day and stay at the campground off trail, but he did the same the next day as well. Jimmy offered to take Zoby around with him while he did trail magic shuttling hikers and picking up his wife, as they were heading back home together the following day. He knew his wife would love some time with Zoby. All this meant Zoby hadn't been on trail in three days, and it had been four days since leaving the ponies and seeing Chip and Blaze.

On the morning of what would be the fifth day since seeing his friends, Zoby excitedly jumped around while Mommy laughed and clipped him onto his leash tethered to her. "Oh little man, you know what? I've missed you too. It hasn't been the same hiking the last couple days without you. You ready to get back out there?" Zoby yipped and jumped in agreement. "Yeah I bet you are! Let's go!"

Racing ahead of Mommy, he pulled on the leash, sniffing and looking everywhere all at once, hoping to see his friends. But alas, as the miles went by, he didn't see them. Matter of fact, that stretch of trail seemed strangely absent of most animals he was accustomed to seeing. That pit he'd had in his stomach for days tightened into a knot. Something was off.

That night Mommy had made reservations for them at a hostel on an alpaca farm. Zoby wasn't sure what an alpaca was, but Mommy was sure excited to see them. As they ended their hike that day and turned into the driveway leading to the farm, Zoby caught his first glimpses of them. A body kind of like a baby pony, but covered in shaggy hair, then these crazy long necks and small heads with enormous eyes, and long, thick eyelashes Mommy said made her jealous. As they approached the fence, he marveled at how they all seemed to move as one. A wave of heads and bodies moving together, up to look at Mommy and Uncle Stan, and then down to the ground to examine Zoby as they reached the fence.

Silently curious, each of the alpacas were at the fence line, moving with their choreographed fluidity together, when suddenly one of them pulled forward and out of alignment with the others. Sticking her nose right up to Zoby's through the fence, she cocked her head, batted her lashes, then said, "are you Zoby?"

Surprised, Zoby's eyes widened. "Yes! I am! How do you know that? Are Chip and Blaze ok? Are they still around here?" Eagerly, Zoby stepped forward and stuck his head through the fence.

"Hey y'all, it's *Zoby*!" The alpaca who questioned him yelled to the others. All coming forward, they began talking at once. "Shelby is gonna be so happy!" "They've been looking for you!" "So you're *not* off trail!" "Is your Mommy ok?" "We need to get the word out!"

"Whoa, whoa, slow down!" Zoby said, "you know Shelby? And Chip and Blaze then, right?"

"Yes," the original alpaca responded. With a friendly bumping nose-to-nose with Zoby, she said, "I'm Allie. Shelby is my best friend. Chip and Blaze I've met before, but mostly communicate with them through Shelby and the Trail Talk. They've been looking for you, for *days*! Ariana tried getting everyone to believe you were off trail but Shelby said it was only temporary. Because I'm her bestie, I knew they were looking for you. What *happened* to you?"

Filled with relief his friends were still there and still looking out for him on the trail, he filled Allie in on the last several days.

"Well, we are certainly happy to see you, and to have you staying here with us. We will get the word out you've been found. I expect a visit from Chip and Blaze soon!"

Happy, he momentarily forgot about the knot he'd had in his stomach and how quiet the last couple miles of trail had seemed. Mommy and Uncle Stan had been enamored with the alpacas but were ready to check in … and he heard them talking about a Mexican restaurant nearby. Fajitas and a reunion with his friends? Could it get any better?!

The next morning, after Uncle Stan gave Zoby his leftover fajita meat for breakfast, (seriously, this guy was the best!), Mommy called for Uncle Stan to come outside. Following him out, Zoby was tempted to go after the snooty cat Mommy and Uncle Stan were giggling over, as she would rub up against them, then start hissing and howling if they attempted to pet her. Stupid cats, Zoby thought and rolled his eyes, then jumped up in excitement when he spotted Chip bounding across the farm with Blaze flying just above him.

"Chip, Blaze!" Zoby yelled in excited greeting.

"Boy are we glad to see you, kid!" Chip raced the final yards to the porch and jumped up, right onto Zoby's back and gave him an enormous hug.

"Zoby!" Blaze yelled. Thinking his friend was calling out in greeting, Zoby happily started to respond, only to be interrupted by the bird divebombing him in an almost panic. "Get inside, get inside!" Blaze hollered. "Coyotes and foxes, they're coming, almost here!"

Just as he said it, they appeared. A pack of coyotes and several foxes accompanying them rushed the farmyard, sending alpacas, chickens, roosters and cats scattering in sudden chaos.

Mommy and Uncle Stan were yelling for the owners, and other hikers were rushing out from the hostel, blocking the entry for Zoby to run back inside as Blaze kept commanding him to do.

Then he saw it. A coyote lunged at Allie.

"Nooooo!!" Jumping off the porch and racing toward the alpaca fence, Zoby could only see his friend, terrified, with a cut on her side.

"Zoby!" Uncle Stan and Mommy screamed, jumping after him. Pulled from his focus on Allie, Zoby realized fox and coyote were all around him, going after the farm animals – but one fox and one coyote in particular seemed to have their eyes on *him*. Uncle Stan managed to come between Zoby and the fox, shoving back at the fox with a stick, just in the nick of time. Mommy was able to reach down and snatch Zoby up just as he saw across the pen the coyote that had attacked Allie and was eyeing him, had started to charge.

Bang, bang, bang, bang!!!

Shots rang out, breaking the chaos and creating a brief moment of silence. Looking over Mommy's shoulder, Zoby saw the owners and their farmhands racing out of the house with hunting rifles. "Get inside!" they yelled to Mommy, Uncle Stan and the other hikers.

As they dashed back to the hostel, Zoby could see the coyotes and foxes already retreating and heading back toward the woods lining the edge of the farm. Catching Blaze's eye just before Mommy got inside with him, he hollered, "Allie! Check on Allie!" Then the door slammed shut.

That evening as Mommy and Uncle Stan set up camp, Zoby sat beside a stream catching up with Chip and Blaze from the past few days, then discussion turned to the events from that morning. Blaze had been able to learn Allie was going to be ok, but had a serious wound that would take a while to heal. Another alpaca was also wounded, and one of the older ones hadn't survived the attack. Nor had a number of chickens.

"Was that a coincidence I was there, or was that an intentional attack on me as part of something else?" Zoby's gut told him the latter, and as a result felt an enormous amount of guilt the farm animals suffered because of him staying there. Zoby laid on the ground with his head between his paws, unable to hide his sadness.

Seeing that, Chip leaned up against him and grabbed his face. "Hey kid. This isn't your fault, ok? You didn't make those coyotes and foxes do what they did. It was their own choice, and it's part of natural predator and prey cycles out here in the wild. Don't get all domestic on me with this, got it? This is *not* your fault," he reiterated.

Nodding, Zoby looked at him, and then at Blaze. "So what was that then, this morning?"

Blaze came over beside the two and sighed deeply. "The foxes have been a problem there already. A nuisance with a few of them going after the chickens pretty regularly. The coyote pack – that was new. They run in the area, but not this close to the trail, and they've never attacked the alpaca farm, although they have reportedly been terrorizing other farms nearby. While I can't confirm this just yet, Trail Talk has it that Ariana got the two packs together and organized the attack on the alpaca farm to coincide with your being there. But only the coyote leader of the pack and fox leader of their pack knew to target *you*. The rest were there for the chickens, roosters and alpacas."

Remembering the close call with the fox and the stare of the coyote's eyes upon him, he asked, "how did they know I was there?" Then it became clear to him. "Allie. She activated the Trail Talk to get word to Shelby and the two of you." With a sigh, Zoby raised his head and looked at his friends, "that's why she was targeted by the coyote leader."

Tears in his eyes, Zoby looked at his friends intensely. "Guys, that was scary. I could have been killed. Mommy. Uncle Stan, one of the other hikers, anyone could have been hurt. Seriously."

Getting up, he walked toward the tent Mommy had ready. "I think I need to just lie down, process this, and try to get some sleep before morning. Night guys, I'm glad you're here."

Watching him walk away, Chip threw his arms around Blaze and sighed. "She's being more aggressive than normal. Jezebel must have really ripped into her in Maine."

Agreeing, Blaze said, "no more letting him out of our sight. We need to have all our resources alert and ready all the way up the trail from here to Katahdin now."

CHAPTER 10

The Virginia Triple Crown

The night of the incident at the alpaca farm, Zoby was tormented by nightmares. Claws and fangs coming at him, the excruciating pain of his body being ripped open, the fear in Mommy's eyes and her tears, the doctors trying to save him … and then begging Mommy to have the surgery. Even as Mommy woke him up time after time from dream after dream, they came, until finally in the wee hours of the morning, he slept.

The following morning, he heard Uncle Stan asking Mommy about Zoby's nightmares. Zoby looked over at Chip and Blaze on a low branch nearby, hanging on their every word. He sighed. So far he had managed to avoid talking about his attack to his friends.

Getting up, he walked over to where they were. Maybe it was lack of sleep, maybe some stress left over from the previous morning, but he snapped up at them, "*you* haven't told me about Jezebel's history. *I* don't need to tell you about *my* history then, either."

Chip and Blaze looked at each other as Zoby marched back into the tent. "Time will tell all," Blaze said quietly.

The following weeks went by quickly and without incident from the Squirrel Mafia. Now May, spring was in full bloom in the mountains, and Uncle Stan was much like Mommy in his enjoyment of wildflowers and appreciating views and waterfalls. They were joined on trail for two nights by a man named "KrizAkoni" who was section hiking. Zoby had fun with him, especially because he managed to yogi food from him quite a bit more than other hikers. Well, except Uncle Stan. He actually bought human food specifically to feed Zoby on breaks!

Passing the 600-mile marker, Mommy's feet were beginning to hurt again, so they decided to take advantage of a stretch of trail where hostels were every 15-20 miles and offered slackpacking services from one hostel to the next up the trail. Not only did this get the extra weight off Mommy's feet to help her heal a bit, but that meant every night for several nights Zoby got to yogi table scraps of hot meals from Mommy and Uncle Stan, plus a warm, comfy bed to sleep in! His favorite was

Woods Hole Hostel, where the food was amazing, plus he and Mommy woke up early to watch sunrise over the mountains while Mommy drank coffee from a AT logo mug handmade by Neville, the owner, which she wound up buying and shipping home.

And the best part was Blaze and Chip never left his side. Every day the chipmunk and bird were alongside him, making him laugh with their antics, trail stories and even their light bickering with one another. Every night Zoby would play with them while Mommy and Uncle Stan set up camp, and sometimes they even brought additional trail friends around to meet Zoby. The weather was beautiful, mountain views were plentiful, spring filled the air with its floral scent, and the Trail Talk seemed to believe that Ariana had perhaps been called back to Maine again.

Chip and Blaze warned Zoby against believing that one. They were fully convinced Ariana was still in the area, only having difficulty getting recruits, hence the seeming silence.

Nonetheless, Zoby soaked in these peaceful and beautiful days on trail. In what seemed like no time, they were reaching 700 miles, and entering the Virginia Triple Crown area. He had hiked each of the three jewels of the Triple Crown – Dragon's Tooth, MacAfee Knob and Tinker Cliffs - with Mommy before, as day hikes. They were all looking extra forward to this section because Stan's daughter, Carissa, was joining them for an overnight on trail and sunrise on MacAfee Knob. As they approached Dragon's Tooth toward the end of a long day of hiking, they were passing views of a stunning ridgeline that had Mommy and Uncle Stan ooh-ing and ahh-ing, then happily reaching the first jewel of their Triple Crown.

Climbing up onto the giant building-sized boulder with a tall appendage on one side resembling, well, a Dragon's Tooth, Mommy leaned back against the rock to take in the expansive views, but was clearly exhausted. Putting his paws on her chest, Zoby began kissing her face and snuggling up against her.

"Feet are killing me today," Mommy said to Uncle Stan, "but I'll push through it. Right now, I just wish we could stay right here and take in this view all evening."

"Agreed," Uncle Stan replied.

Agreed, Zoby thought, and seeing the red wings and striped fur of his friends in the tree above them, he put that sweet, sun-drenched late afternoon moment in his memory bank.

The next day was a short one, as they were meeting Carissa in a nearby town for lunch. As they hiked along a river with waterfalls for a few miles, Zoby chatted with Blaze and Chip about the Trail Talk and their plans for sunrise at MacAfee Knob.

"It's the most iconic spot on the trail," Chip said enthusiastically, "the most photographed, the most visited, everything! There's a lot of excitement about you reaching this point, Zoby! Many in the woodland animal chain are going to show up tomorrow morning to witness it, and help you celebrate. Shelby sends her congrats, as does Eli, and oh, Allie is healing nicely and sends her love, too! Everyone is on your side, kid! This is a big deal!"

Much as he wanted to believe Chip, he also knew everyone wasn't on his side. He'd been enjoying the time without incidents, but he knew if this was a "significant" moment on trail, there would be repercussions for reaching that milestone with the Squirrel Mafia.

As if reading his mind, Blaze chimed in, "Zoby, we have an even closer ear to the ground with the Trail Talk than ever. There's been no sign of Ariana, or talk of any plans. Enjoy this time with no worries. We've got you."

Reaching the parking lot and trailhead for MacAfee Knob, where Mommy and Uncle Stan had made arrangements for a shuttle to take them into town to meet up with Carissa, Zoby saw a dog sitting beside the back end of a car near them in the lot. Not recognizing him as fellow thru-hiker dog (which were becoming fewer and fewer as they continued north), he assumed he was day- or section-hiking with his humans. Always eager to make friends with fellow canines, he called out a friendly hello.

Then, to his surprise, popping out from behind the wheel of the car beside them, a face he recognized – Tinkerbell!

"Zoby?!" she exclaimed, "is that you?! Oh, I hoped we might run into you! Hey Cody," she gestured to the golden retriever beside her, "this is Zoby, the one I told you about from the kennel in the Smokies!"

"Tinkerbell! Wow, you're here?!" Zoby couldn't believe it!

Fascinated by the stories he had heard, the other dog and Tinkerbell came over to Zoby, all talking at once. Through the excited chatter, Zoby learned their humans were section hikers doing the Virginia Triple Crown – along with their dogs. Joining the group, Zoby introduced them to Chip and Blaze, whom Tinkerbell recognized and of course Chip threw himself at her in a hug and cuddled up in her soft yorkie hair.

Cody, the laid-back golden retriever wearing a tie-dye bandana, had hiked many sections with his humans and, knowing how rough the trail could get, looked at Zoby with respect. "Stoked to meet you! When

Tinkerbell told us about you dude, I have to be honest, I took you as a poser and assumed you probably had gotten off trail sometime after the Smokies. So wrong about you dude, and happy to be! This is a sketchy trail to thru-hike for any dog, especially a small dog that's a newb. It's sick you've made it this far, mad props! High paw!"

Laughing and returning the high pay, Zoby said, "um, thanks I think?"

Chip and Blaze chuckled and in reply to Cody, Blaze said, "Zoby's the real deal. Otherwise, the Squirrel Mafia wouldn't be working so hard to knock him off trail."

"Yeah, that Jezebel chick sounds like a real drag," Cody stated in his chill manner.

In stark contrast came Tinkerbell's mile-a-minute prattle, "you have to fill me in on everything – and I mean *everything!* – that has happened since the Smokies. And how is your Mommy? That's her right there, talking to mine, right? And is that guy with her hiking with you now too? Where are you camping tonight and maybe we can make sure our humans are together. Ours are planning to hike to MacAfee Knob for sunrise, are yours?" Continuing on without pausing for answers, she babbled, "there are a couple more meeting us soon, and you can meet their dogs, too! Oh this is so fun, so awesome to be here with you, I'm so excited!" While she was bouncing around with excitement, Chip fell off her back, and hitting the ground, he looked up at her while rubbing his head.

"Woman, settle! Wow, and I thought *I* talked fast," he hooted in amusement.

Looking up as a car drove in and stopped beside them, Zoby saw Mommy and Uncle Stan starting to load their gear in it. "Must be our shuttle," Zoby stated, and looking in amusement at Tinkerbell said, "to answer your rapid-fire questions, yes that is Mommy, and the guy is Uncle Stan – he's awesome! – and we are planning to be at MacAfee for sunrise. Right now, we are meeting Uncle Stan's daughter, Carissa, in town, but we'll be back tonight. Mommy said they're stopping at the Catawba Mountain shelter, so get your humans to stay there too!" And with that, Zoby ran to Mommy and waved goodbye to his friends, old and new, as they drove off into Daleville to meet Carissa.

Uuuuuugggh, Zoby thought as they returned to the trail at the MacAfee trailhead with Carissa in tow, why did he eat *so much* at lunch? The pulled pork Mommy had bought him at Three Little Pigs in Daleville was *so* good, he just couldn't stop eating. But now it was sitting heavy in his belly while they were climbing steeply uphill over the natural rock steps built into the trail.

Stopping at an intersection in the trail for a quick break to catch their breath, Zoby laid down and rolled over on his back, moaning over his full belly. Looking up into the tree above him, he caught Chip and Blaze in hysterics over his state of gluttony. "Ha ha ha," he dryly muttered up at them, then groaned again as Mommy told him it was time to get going, only causing them to laugh harder.

"You know, we'd stop making of fun of you if you'd thought to share some with us," Chip snickered jokingly. "Good thing you're only going a couple miles … but too bad it's all uphill!" That sent the bird and chipmunk into bursts of gleeful laughter again.

Rolling his eyes and focusing on putting one paw in front of the other, after another mile, he immediately perked up as he caught the voices of Tinkerbell, Cody and other thru-hiker human friends he knew gathered around the shelter.

After rounds of hugs and hellos between humans and canines alike, Tinkerbell and Cody sided with Chip and Blaze on not feeling sorry for Zoby's bellyache. As he settled in to accepting more rounds of joking at his expense, it was at that moment Mommy and Carissa pulled out a couple large takeout boxes from their packs, and announced they were still too full from lunch to eat what they had packed out for dinner. Laughing, Zoby looked over at Blaze and Chip, and then at Tinkerbell and Cody, who were bug-eyed and salivating at the scent of the BBQ pork and chicken coming from the boxes. Bounding over to Mommy and Uncle Stan, Zoby did his dance that always resulted in treats, then took the spoils to his friends. Seeing the dogs' exuberant enjoyment, Mommy made a separate dish for them, enamoring Cody to her with his declaration of undying love for all eternity. With all animals and humans now stuffed, and laughter dancing through the air as twilight fell, it was determined an early bedtime was on tap for all, as alarms would be ringing at 3:30 am for the night hike up to sunrise at MacAfee Knob.

Zoby hated mornings.

And Zoby *especially* hated mornings that started *before morning*.

And Zoby especially hated perky little yorkies that yip-yapped cheeky, wide-awake chatter in his ear in the darkness that was not morning.

They had slept their first night in a shelter, as mommy preferred their tent to a shelter. Tinkerbell's chipper, "good morning! Time to get up Zoby!" right in his face, along with Mommy and Carissa's giggles over his grumpy attitude, and Mommy poking at him to get up, and the chilly night air seeping into the shelter … all of this did *not* make him a happy camper. What did they not understand about the low growls and stink-eye looks he was giving them?! What *time* was it, anyway, for Pete's sake?!

"Zoby, come on buddy, seriously, time to go," Mommy reached in and snatched him out of his sleeping bag before he could even fully wake up.

Snarling, he grumpily looked around. The humans were wearing red lights on their heads as they packed up, making everything glow funny, it was cold enough to see your breath, and Tinkerbell was *way* too chipper for this time of night. Yawning, stretching and heaving a deep sigh, he glared at Tinkerbell. "What on earth are you on, to be awake, and *happy* about it?!"

Bubbly as ever, Tinkerbell just giggled, "Oh Zoby, you really are the worst morning dog! C'mon, this is going to be so fun! We get to night hike together and then everyone – *everyone*! – is going to be at MacAfee! We'll watch sunrise, take the photos from the ledge, have coffee and breakfast, share trail stories and celebrate the beauty all around us!"

Cody rolled his eyes at Zoby as he came over. "Chill chick, slow down on the caffeine intake or something," yawning and rolling his shoulders, Cody stated he agreed with Zoby it was too darn early for chipper.

And cold, Zoby thought, shivering. What were they waiting for? Looking around, he saw all the hikers and dogs ready … except Uncle Stan. He heard Mommy laughing with Carissa over how that was normal. Grinning, Zoby thought, yup it sure is.

Zoby had never night hiked before. With the light from Mommy and the other hiker's head lamps shining on the trail, he found it a somewhat eerie experience. Walking through the woods with only a small light in front of you and complete darkness around you … he wondered if Ariana was hiding in that darkness. It was like he could *feel* her watching him.

They only had about a mile and half to hike, so even in the darkness it went quickly. They reached the large rock outcropping just as light was glowing on the edge of the horizon where mountains met the sky, the last stars still twinkling before giving over to day. Zoby took in the spectacular sight and suddenly wasn't the least bit upset they'd had to awaken at o-dark-thirty to see it.

And Tinkerbell was right – everyone was there. A couple dozen thru-hiker friends Zoby knew, whom Mommy and Uncle Stan were laughing and talking with, Tinkerbell and Cody's humans and their friends as well as two other dogs with them Zoby had met the night before. And looking into the tree next to where Mommy had set her pack and was boiling water for coffee and breakfast on the far ledge, Zoby saw Blaze and Chip.

Heart full, he walked over to his friends. "Hey guys, good morning!" he sang out.

Laughing, Chip responded, "did I just hear you say 'good morning?' Blaze, it's a miracle! A mir-a-cle!" The chipmunk pretended to drop to his knees in worship while Blaze spread his wings as a mock angel in reverence. Chuckling, Zoby admitted to them the early wake-up call was worth it.

The not-yet-risen sun was sending glowing fingers of orange and red into the sky above the layered mountains of Catawba Valley. Hikers lined up for their iconic photo, ready to pose at the edge of the infamous sliver of rock protruding off the larger rock outcropping of MacAfee Knob. This particular ledge that when photographed from the angle of a different ledge, gives the appearance of standing on a thin slice of rock extending over the rolling layers of mountains far below, particularly stunning when standing in silhouette against the rising sun.

Putting her coffee cup down, Mommy grabbed Uncle Stan and Carissa and said, "come on, the light is perfect right now!" Picking up Zoby, she got in line with him first for their photo, while Uncle Stan and Carissa went to the other ledge where hikers gathered to take the photos of those posing on the iconic outcropping.

When it was their turn, Uncle Stan had Mommy's camera ready on the other ledge. Zoby heard the cheers of Chip and Blaze, Tinkerbell, Cody and the other dogs as Mommy stepped right up to the edge with one leg in front of the other, the front slightly bent. Wrapping both hands into the inside of the warm outfit he was wearing to better grab his chest, and tucking her finger into his collar, she held him close and whispered, "don't worry baby, I've got ya," then before Zoby knew it, he was being thrust forward, her arms fully extended out in front of her at head level.

The Knob erupted in laughter and cheers.

"The Lion King, yes!" People yelled. "It's perfect!" Bewildered, Zoby looked around at hikers, dogs, and woodland animals alike all cheering and rolling in hysterics as Mommy kept the pose for more people to take their photo.

"Epic, dude. Epic!" He heard Cody yell.

"Going in the history books, this is so exciting!" Came Tinkerbell's exuberant agreement.

"Definitely a new one, kid. You're larger than life now!" Chip and Blaze chimed in.

As she kept the pose just a bit longer for still others to capture the moment, Mommy laughed and said to the other hikers, "I've walked over 700 miles for this photo!" Zoby took it all in. The Knob was abuzz with hilarity and continued cheers and shouts of approval.

Following their photo shoot, after they returned to the far ledge to continue watching the sun itself now actually rise over mountainous horizon, Zoby was all gleeful smiles with a joyful heart. All the other dogs on the ledge were around him now, and even many of the woodland friends Chip and Blaze had been able to gather were there, congratulating him for the hike and for foiling the Squirrel Mafia so many times, all rooting him on. Truly feeling proud of himself and his accomplishments, the sky ablaze with the fire of the rising sun which illuminated the white edges of his fur, he stuck his chest out, threw his head up and proclaimed what had become his mantra, "small dog, big adventures!"

Watching the scene below unfold, Ariana trembled with anger at the current spectacle, as well as haunting memories intruding from another incident at this location years ago. That oversized white rat of a domestic was quickly becoming the darling of the trail. Seething, she blasted them all in her head.

That southern shrew of a pony, Shelby, had made it her mission to utterly destroy Ariana's credibility with all woodland creatures anywhere near the trail after she brought the pack of coyotes into their midst, especially since Allie had been severely wounded. Any resources within 2-300 miles had utterly dried up after that.

Well, she could be patient. Virginia had plenty of miles left.

"You just celebrate now, Zoby," she hissed under her breath. "Because you won't be for long."

CHAPTER 11

The Blue Ridge Parkway, The Priest, and Starting Shenandoah

Mid-May brought with it the peak of spring's surreal beauty in the mountains. As Zoby, Mommy and Uncle Stan hiked north along the Appalachian Trail entwining itself with the Blue Ridge Parkway for about 125 miles, both the views and proliferation of wildflowers had them stopping in awe frequently. Rhododendrons created bright pink tunnels arcing across the trail, varieties of azalea spritzed the air with their fragrant perfume, and the dainty white-pink flowers of mountain laurel made the trail appear as though decorated for a wedding. Chip romped through a field of trillium playing hide and seek with Zoby, and Blaze's scarlet feathers began to blend in with the blossoming Eastern redbud trees – although Mommy caught a photo of his crimson body contrasting magnificently amongst white dogwood blooms. Uncle Stan and Mommy sang a silly song about building up buttercups every time they passed displays of the sunny yellow flowers, with Mommy making Zoby pose amongst them in a cheery photo shoot.

It also brought an early season heatwave. By the time they made their way across the James River Footbridge, past the 800-mile mark and were entering The Priest Wilderness, temperatures were in the high 90s, plus the southern humidity made the forest feel like a sauna. The thick, soupy air made it difficult to breathe on the climbs and overall left hikers and animals alike feeling exhausted and slightly dehydrated at the end of each day.

However, a highlight during this time came in the form of a visit on trail from Mommy's friend, Malisse and her golden lab, Luna! Just in the nick of time, Malisse brought Mommy her summer gear to switch out from her winter gear, and joined the group for a day and night backpacking and camping with them. Still a puppy, Luna had never been backpacking before, so Zoby plus his woodland friends got to show Luna the ropes of being a hiker dog, especially in the heat.

"Luna!" Zoby ran up to his new friend as she caught up to where he and Mommy were resting on a bald with spectacular mountain views. "You're doing great!" He encouraged her, "now we get to rest and take pictures with our Mommies before we hike on. Make sure to have your Mommy give you lots of water cuz it's so hot today."

"You ain't joking," Luna gasped, her tongue hanging out as she completed the climb in the direct heat of the open sunshine on the bald, "and you mean we're not done yet?!" Luna flopped down and rolled over on her back, not quite joking as she mocked immediate death by heatstroke.

Laughing as he pounced on her playfully, Zoby informed her, "no silly, we've only gone three miles! We still have six to go before camp!" Plus, he thought, he had done six additional miles that morning before meeting up with Luna, but kept his mouth shut on that point.

"Aaaaargh!" Rolling back over onto her feet and heading to where Malisse was pouring water into a cup, Luna looked back at Zoby, who had been joined by Chip and Blaze, and rolled her eyes at them. "Y'all are *crazy* to think this is fun."
Chuckling, Zoby responded, "the saying goes, 'embrace the suck,' right guys?" With Chip and Blaze nodding and laughing in agreement, Zoby ran toward the rocks where Mommy and Uncle Stan were sitting, "it's better than snow and ice, trust me!"

Mommy, Uncle Stan and Malisse walked out onto the pile of rocks and took turns snapping photos of each other, including the dogs in their captured memories as well. Just as the dogs were starting to walk across the rocks back to the grassy bald, Uncle Stan, a few feet ahead of them, yelled out and stumbled a few steps backward.

"Whoa! Stop! Grab the dogs!"

Curious, Zoby and Luna sprang forward instead of backward. That's when Zoby saw the brown-and-grey patterned snakes that had been soaking up the sun on the rocks lunging toward him around the side of Uncle Stan.

"No, Zoby, get back!" Blaze flew up the rock pile at him hollering, at the same time Mommy caught him and snatched him up, and Malisse grabbed onto Luna's collar, dragging her backwards.

"Sssso you're Zoby," the closest of the copperhead trio hissed at him, drawing out the "s" and "z" sounds, "ssssuch a pleasssure to meet you. Ariana sssspoke of you to usssss."

"What? Zoby, who is Ariana? What is going on here?!" Luna was panicked and pulling against the leash Malisse had clipped onto her.

In the meantime, Uncle Stan had been able to grab his trekking poles and was poking them at the copperheads in an attempt to move them off the top of the rocks down the cliff, to clear the way for the dogs and girls to return to the grassy bald and the trail.

Hissing at Uncle Stan, the snake who had spoken to Zoby lunged toward Uncle Stan's foot, taking a swipe at him around the trekking pole he had aimed at the snake.

"HEY!" Zoby yelled and pushed himself out of Mommy's arms.

"Zoby!" Mommy, Uncle Stan, Malisse and even Luna all screamed in unison.

The copperhead turned its triangular head toward Zoby, hissing as he focused his beady eyes on him. "Think you're ssso fearlessssss, do you?" As he started to strike toward Zoby, Luna let loose with a string of loud barks, distracting him just a fraction of a second long enough for Mommy to grab Zoby again, and for Uncle Stan to get a trekking pole under the snake's belly and fling him off the rock down the cliffside of the boulder pile with the other copperheads.

As the group scrambled off the rocks back onto the bald, the snake hollered and hissed, "thisssss isssn't the lassst you'll see of usss!" Adrenaline pumping, the group reconvened at their packs, everyone talking at once. As Mommy leashed him back up, she nuzzled her face in his and quietly admonished him, "baby boy, I know that nasty snake tried to get Uncle Stan, but you've *got* to stay in Mommy's arms. You really are the bravest dog I know, but you gotta be smart, too. That snake's venom could kill you if he bites."

Wait, what? Zoby looked over at Chip and Blaze as Mommy set him down. He didn't like snakes, sure, but he'd mostly seen garter and black rat snakes while hiking with her. Chip came over to him and threw his little arms around his Zoby's front paws. "Kid. That was a close one. Copperheads are nasty, and if they're consorting with Ariana, they're gonna be even nastier."

Blaze chimed in, "yeah, and I think they weren't expecting you here, they would have been more camouflaged and waiting in stealth. These guys strike without warning. Rattlesnakes at least give you warning. But now we know they're on Ariana's resource list, so we'll keep a close ear to Trail Talk again. He made a mistake telling you as much as he did."

"OK that's it," Luna's impatience had her tapping her paws and shaking her head, "you guys gonna tell me who Ariana is now, and what is going on?!"

As the group started off on the trail again, Zoby laughed and said, "sure, we've got six miles to tell you everything. Get ready for some crazy tales of adventure…" and he, Chip and Blaze regaled Luna with stories she could scarcely believe as they hiked on to camp.

The following morning, they bid farewell to Malisse and Luna, and continuing north, made their way up a mountain called The Priest, where they stopped at the shelter to read the hilarious "confessions" thru-hikers wrote into the log book. Following tradition by adding their own, Uncle Stan and Mommy decided Zoby needed to confess *his* "trail sins" to The Priest as well. Hysterics ensued, as Chip and Blaze rolled over with laughter while Mommy and Uncle Stan shared all his embarrassing trail moments in the log. Like when he puked on Uncle Stan's bed in a hotel. Or how he nipped at Mommy when she checked his paws everyday, (c'mon, don't touch his paws!) Or how he refused to eat dog food anymore and only wanted to yogi for human food. Or when he was snuck into a hotel stuffed inside Mommy's bag...

Mortified yet enjoying the merriment and high spirits of all after their visit to The Priest, that night they camped beside the Tye River – taking a refreshing dip at the end of another hot day – and the jovial atmosphere continued as one of the other groups of weekending hikers built a large bonfire with hot dogs and s'mores to share for all.

As they sat outside their tents with full bellies, Zoby contentedly half-dozed, half-listened to Mommy and Uncle Stan discuss plans for their upcoming days hiking through Shenandoah National Park. While Uncle Stan stroked his ears, he learned both his daughters, Courtney and Carissa, as well as his granddaughter Careis and the family beagle would be joining them the first three days through the Park. Mommy said they needed to make reservations at one of the Park's campgrounds, to establish a "base camp" where the entire group would camp each night, then the girls would slackpack Mommy and Uncle Stan along the AT each day.

"This heatwave is supposed to break about the time we hit the Shennies. It's supposed to cool down quite a bit, and rain every day that week," Mommy said, looking at her phone. "A lot of storms in the forecast."

At that, Zoby looked up in alarm. He hated storms even more after that night with the tornado and the Squirrel Mafia. He wasn't crazy about hiking and camping in the rain for a week, either. But ... that was all a few days away. Right now, his belly was full, there was a nice breeze on a warm summer night, and the soothing sound of the cascading river beside them lulled him into a deep, peaceful sleep.

Three days later, after a zero at the lovely mountain home of trail angels Mommy had met at Spy Rock named Lewis and Betty, they met up with Stan's family and began the 101 miles of the AT through Shenandoah.

Mommy and Uncle Stan were slackpacking while Zoby went with the girls and the female beagle named Bagel, (which he found amusing, but she didn't see the humor), to get their campsite set up. They would then be parking at the road intersection where Mommy and Uncle Stan were finishing for the day, and the girls had plans to hike down the trail to meet up and surprise them, which Zoby was excited about. He loved surprising Mommy!

As they set off down the trail, the wind was kicking up wildly with low rumbles of thunder in the distance. Trying not to shake and stay brave in front of Bagel the Beagle, Zoby controlled his fear until a clap of thunder boomed so loudly all three girls screamed, and even Bagel gave a hound dog "roo" in response. The skies opened up and sheets of rain cascaded down upon them as the wind lashed at the trees and the ground shook from thunder.

Zoby froze. Flashbacks of the storm and tornado in the tent flew through his mind.

"Come on Zoby, let's keep going," the girls urged him on. Coming over to Zoby, Bagel saw there was something more going on than just the storm. "You okay?"

Beside him, he felt a tug on his paw. Looking down, he saw Chip. "C'mon kid. You got this."

Taking a deep breath, he nodded at Chip, and looking at Bagel said, "I'm okay. Had a bad trail experience with a storm, I'll tell you about it later. Let's go."

Legs still shaking and heart still pounding, with the storm raging around them, Zoby mustered up all his courage and kept moving forward. With continued encouragement from Blaze above him, and Chip and Bagel on either side of him, he made it a bit further before Courtney decided to take mercy on him, and scooped him up in her arms.

"Now why am *I* not getting carried by Auntie Courtney?" Bagel pretended to be jealous.

Slowly, the storm let up to light sprinkles and the sun even tried to burst through the clouds. Just as Zoby was beginning to stop shaking, he heard …

"Look who's here, oh my gosh!" and, "ZOBY! Baby boy!!" Mommy and Uncle Stan were running up the trail toward them.

Setting him down, Courtney laughed and told him to go get his Mommy. Racing toward her, Zoby let out happy yip yips down the trail, making Chip and Blaze laugh in delight.

As Mommy swooped him upward and spun around in circles, smothering him in kisses and praising him for hiking in the storm, he didn't see the squirrel and the snake watching nearby.

From the hollow log she hid in just out of sight from the humans and domestics, Ariana cast a maliciously knowing look at the copperhead coiled beside her.

"Seems our poor domestic is just *traumatized* by his last storm experience," she said with a smugly cruel tone, "wouldn't it simply be *terrible* if he has another one, Venom?"

With a vile gleam in his eye, the snake hissed in reply, "sssstorms are forecasssst all week. Gather the ressssourccess, Ariana."

Glaring at the revolting reunion between the domestic and his human, she sent a nasty grin in the serpent's direction.

"Oh, I'm on it, Venom. This domestic is *not* getting out of Virginia."

That storm was the first of many, and brought with it a cold front, that when combined with constant rain made for miserable hiking and camping. Everything was cold, wet and muddy. Thankfully they had a base camp with the family and were slackpacking, so they didn't have to set up and tear down each day in the rain. They were even more fortunate to have Carissa and Courtney cooking breakfast and dinner for them, even if they did have to eat it in the car or their tents to get out of the rain!

And Zoby was the most fortunate, as Auntie Courtney didn't want to hike in the rain with Mommy and Uncle Stan every day, so she took Zoby with her to the Inn where she sat by the fire and read, with Zoby snuggled up beside her.

He did *not* mind missing the cold, wet, stormy hikes those days. Nope. Not at all.

He did, however, miss the actual hiking, and seeing Chip and Blaze during the days. The chipmunk and bird stayed at their camp each night and morning between the rain though, and the three of them kept Bagel entertained with trail stories of foiling the Squirrel Mafia. Which, Blaze cautioned Zoby, he had heard through Trail Talk Ariana was gathering resources in northern Virginia now, and to be extra careful.

****

Their last night with the family, the humans went out for dinner at the Lodge, leaving Zoby and Bagel behind at camp. Inside the tent, Zoby was content to steal Mommy's down quilt to curl up in and sleep, but Bagel wanted to chitchat through the tent while she was leashed outside.

"Zoby! Tell me more stories about how you've thwarted the Squirrel Mafia!"

Rolling his eyes, Zoby called out, "Bagel, we've told you all the stories! Lie down and rest until they get back. I bet they bring us leftovers!" At the thought, Zoby's stomach rumbled.

Bagel continued her chatter just outside his tent, but he merely mumbled in response as he got comfy and sleepy in Mommy's quilt, which felt like a toasty warm hug wrapped around him.

Suddenly, Bagel started her hound dog "roo" that signaled an alert. "Rooooooo! Rooo, rooo!" she howled, and Zoby could tell she was pulling at her leash.

"What? What is it?" Zoby yelled above her howls, "Squirrel Mafia attack? Chip, Blaze!"

"It's that mean German Shepherd a few sites over! He's attacking a poor baby deer!" Bagel cried. "Roooooooo!"

"Chip! Blaze! What can we do?! Get help!" Zoby yelled over Bagel's howls. That dog has a set of lungs on her, Zoby thought.

Chip popped his head up under the tent vestibule. "So don't tell anyone I know how to do this, kid, but we need you out here." Chip said as he unzipped the door to the tent.

Dumbfounded, Zoby stared in shock at the open tent. "Wha?... How?..." he stuttered.

"Don't ask, just help us out. Go stop the German Shepherd! I'm trying to get Bagel's leash undone, but it's a little too big for my paw fingers!"

Popping out of the tent and under the vestibule, Zoby took in the sight. The terrified fawn was caught in a triangle of blocked paths, the bath house creating a barrier on one side, a line of closely parked cars and the Park's golf carts on the second side, and the German Shepherd securing the third. Every time she tried to dart past the dog to freedom, he jumped up, clawing, and snapping his teeth at her. There was a cut on one of her legs already.

"HEY!" Zoby yelled. He and Mommy had a nasty altercation with this dog once already on trail when it came after Zoby as they passed a shelter. Zoby and other thru-hiker dogs knew him to be unfriendly and enjoyed scaring other animals – and even humans – just for the fun of it with his size and aggression. "Leave her alone you jerk, what is your *problem*?"

"Stay out of it, you little runt," the German Shepherd nastily tossed back to Zoby, "we're just having a little fun here."

Running halfway to where the scene was unfolding, Zoby angrily shouted, "are you crazy?! *She* is *not* having fun! You're just a bully, and a menace! What is *wrong* with you? Look how terrified she is, and she's bleeding!"

Turning in a rage of snarls, the cruel dog ran a few steps toward Zoby, "get out of here, runt."

Using his size to his advantage, Zoby made him think he was retreating in fear as he quickly darted under and between the row of parked cars to come up behind the petrified fawn. "Hey," he whispered from under a car, "you can clear the back end of this last golf cart right here beside me. I promise. You can make it."

The fawn's wild eyes looked at Zoby and she shook her head. "No, I can't jump that high!" she said in a strained, panicky voice, then backed up closer to the bath house as the German Shepherd was closing in on her to force her to run toward him in an attempt at safety and escape again.

"You can do it, I swear! Let me create a diversion so his focus is off you for a minute, then JUMP!"

Not waiting for her to agree, Zoby ran out in front of her, putting himself between the horrified fawn and viciously angry dog.

At that moment, Chip managed to get Bagel freed from her leash and the beagle bound over toward them as well, raising the alarm with her "roo-ing" of increasing volume.

"JUMP!" Zoby yelled. And the fawn jumped, easily clearing the golf cart as she leapt.

Cheering for a second, Zoby forgot to pay attention to the German Shepherd, who was now entirely focused on him. Sharp teeth gleamed at him and angry eyes told him without words he was about to be shredded. Games were over.

Freezing for a moment, he flashed back to another set of teeth. To the pain. To Mommy's tears.

"Zoby!!" Bagel yelled, "RUN!"

Just as he was about to be ripped into, Zoby snapped out of it and bolted back toward the cars. Reaching the safety of the low clearance of one, he lay between the bottom of the car and the ground while the German Shepherd paced and then turned his attention to Bagel.

Seeing what was about to happen, Zoby yelled, "noooo! Bagel, run!" but was interrupted by the pounding of hooves shaking the ground beneath him.

Seemingly out of nowhere, a half dozen doe and a large buck with an impressive rack appeared. One of the doe was accompanied by the formerly terrified fawn still sporting a wounded leg. With a fierce glare, the buck lowered its rack and aimed it at the German Shepherd.

"You have until the count of three to get out of here, or else the games will *really* begin. And I promise, *you* will not be the winner," he said. "One... two..."

Growling at the buck, then doe, then fawn then even at Zoby and Bagel, the dog angrily retreated, heading back to its campsite, where his owner in his tent was seemingly oblivious to the entire scene that had unfolded.

Letting out a breath he didn't realize he had been holding, Zoby crawled out from under the car and went over to Bagel to check on her.

"Zoby." The buck's baritone voice commanded authority.

Surprised, he looked up. "You know who I am?"

The buck laughed quietly as Chip scampered up to sit in his rack and Blaze fluttered over and landed on it. "Of course he does, kid!" Chip laughed. "The whole forest knows who you are by now! This is Knox, he's one of the good guys."

"I was already on Team Zoby," the buck said with a deep chuckle, then with a serious look Knox took a few steps closer to Zoby and continued, "but I am now in your debt, for you helped save my daughter tonight."

The doe and fawn stepped forward. "We won't forget it," the doe said.

Walking to Zoby, the fawn dropped her face nose-to-nose with him. "Thank you," she whispered shyly and quickly went back to her mother.

As the deer began to leave, Knox looked into Zoby's eyes. "You showed a lot of courage tonight, Zoby. I'm impressed. And as I stated, am in your debt. You have our gratitude."

Chip, Blaze and Bagel walked alongside Zoby back to their campsite. "Kid, you just won over any doubters with that. Knox will get the Trail Talk talkin' and nobody doubts his opinion."

Smiling proudly, Zoby shrugged and said, "well that's awesome … but what *won't* be awesome is if Mommy, Uncle Stan and the girls get back and I'm out of the tent and Bagel is off her leash!" Laughing, he continued as he raced toward their site, "Now work your chipmunk magic and get us back in where we belong!"

CHAPTER 12

Trail Angels Provide The Final "Steps" through Virginia

Ariana was seething.

Looking at the woodland creatures gathered around her, she channeled her mother's terrifying, barely controlled fury as a tool to control those she needed to use. Reigning in her temper, she coolly addressed those gathered with a voice coated in both fire and ice.

"This domestic has been enjoying the lap of luxury out of the storms which *frighten him so*," she said the last three words mockingly, "but more concerning, he has thus far managed to evade all attempts at getting him off trail. Mostly through sheer *luck*," her voice beginning to rise in intensity, "but moreso through the aid of our pathetically misguided fellow woodland creatures playing hero and coming to his rescue," she spit out scathingly.

Pausing to let that sink in, she continued, "therefore, the problem lies not only with this domestic, but with the turncoats among us."

Seeing the nods and hearing the low murmurs of assent, she grinned wickedly.

"Therefore, as we plan our next battle, remember who the *real* enemies are … get *them* out of the picture and the domestic will follow." As a small cheer started to rise up, she gave the careful, final push without making it a direct order, just as she had planned.

"May you choose to act accordingly."

Unfortunately, their time with Stan's family came to an end. The girls and Bagel could only stay the first three days of the time it would take them to hike through Shenandoah, so they still had three more days to complete the Park – with more rain and storms in the forecast each day.

Unbelievably the morning they had to say good-bye dawned sunny and clear. Reluctantly packing up the tents and their gear to begin full backpacking again, Mommy, Uncle Stan and Zoby lingered over breakfast, gave hugs and finally waved farewell as they started out on trail again. Enjoying the first warmth of sunshine in four days, they jovially made their way eight miles up trail before stopping for lunch at Big Meadows Lodge, where the trail passed it.

Coming out of the Lodge was like the sunshine had been a hallucination, as reality was once again full of damp gray mist, dripping trees and intermittent showers. By the time they were nearing the place Mommy had earmarked for camping, the skies had opened up and it was a full-on downpour.

"I am so sick of camping in the rain!" Mommy was saying to Uncle Stan, "it's going to be awful setting up in this, and we're camping right next to the Park's Inn. I wouldn't be opposed to seeing if they have an available room tonight, and get us out of the rain!"

Hopefully, Zoby looked at Uncle Stan, jumping up and wagging his tail. He wanted out of the awful rain too – even Chip and Blaze had taken cover from the torrential downpour, which with the distant rumbles of thunder, he knew was about to turn into storms.

Thankfully, Uncle Stan chuckled and agreed, "I like the way you think. How about I race on ahead and see what is available?"

Mommy and Zoby happily agreed. As Uncle Stan took off down the trail, Mommy looked down at Zoby, wet through his raingear but still smiling up at her, and simultaneously felt awful yet proud that he was hiking through the rain and a wet trail full of puddles and mud.

Picking him up, she cuddled him close to her, and giving kisses, said, "you really are the best dog ever, little man. Even a few months ago you wouldn't have hiked through this rain and mud, I'm so proud of how much you have grown and all the fears you are conquering out here."

Happily giving Mommy kisses in return, Zoby snuggled into her chest as she decided to carry him the last mile under her umbrella, which did keep him a little warmer and drier, as the distant thunder came closer. He shivered at that. Man, he really hated storms and hoped a room would be available for them at the Inn.

As luck would have it, a woman in the lobby overhearing Uncle Stan pleading with the front desk for some place to stay out of the rain, any room at all, rearranged her family's accommodations for the night to open up a one-bedroom cabin for them. Full of gratitude, Mommy cried and hugged her, then off they went to the cabin to get warm and dry for a good night's sleep.

****

As Ariana watched these events unfold, her anger boiled over.

Turning to Venom, her voice livid and shaking, she cursed the humans and their luck at getting the cabin available, raging over how it *yet again* spoiled their plans for the night.

Everything had aligned to perfection – the storm that terrifies the domestic, the planned campsite next to a river swollen with rainwater and raging along the rocks, plus the hostility that had been building in her recruits that was at a fever pitch – that domestic, his tramily and their turncoat friends should have faced their hike's end that night.

Venom however, was the juxtaposition of eerie calm in the reflection of her outrage. Hissing through his forked tongue as his yellow eyes gleamed in the gray mist, "Ssssettle down, dear. It'ssss merely a delay, an *opportunity*. We shall re-organizzze our planssss, and further ssstir the pot amongssst our resourcessss."

Narrowing her eyes, Ariana glared at the cabin the domestic and his humans were now occupying. "Watch out, little one. This is only a reprieve until the inevitable, for you *and* your turncoat friends."

What Ariana and Venom didn't see was the chipmunk camouflaged in the hollow base of the tree near them, where Chip had previously tucked himself in under covers of leaves and pine needles for the night, wide awake and overhearing everything.

The rain continued off and on – more on than off – for the last two days of their trek through Shenandoah. On their last day as they were about to exit the Park, a friend of Stan's named Kamper showed up with trail magic of hot coffee and cookies, and offered to watch Zoby while they hiked the rest of the miles through storms that day.

Chip had shared the information he had gleaned with Blaze, who had been largely absent from their group while he was out doing what Blaze does best with Trail Talk and his own recruits. When Chip overheard Kamper saying Zoby could stay in his truck while he does trail magic, Chip looked at Zoby and nodded emphatically.

"Hey kid, you need to stay back today," Chip comforted Zoby, whom he knew didn't care for staying with a stranger, no matter how nice, while he worried about Mommy on trail. "Look at me, kid." Zoby slowly raised his sad eyes to Chip's. "We don't know exactly when or where they have their next battle planned, but we know it's coming. If you can stay off trail for even part of the day, especially during a storm, then do it."

Heaving a large sigh, Zoby agreed. Then was relieved he had agreed, and that Chip had stayed near the truck, when Blaze returned to the road crossing where they were meeting Mommy and Uncle Stan at the end of the day with a report – and a slightly wounded wing.

"They had plans again for today. All I know is it was supposed to take place at a swollen river crossing where the beavers and squirrels chewed through an old footbridge that has been washed away now. There were several dozen Squirrel Mafia there today, and I caught sight of Venom nearby."

At this Chip threw his arms around Blaze and grabbed him by his bird-wing shoulders, "are you crazy? They saw you, and did something didn't they – that's what the cut is on your wing? They're out for *us* now too, you bird-brain!"

Flapping his wings to remove Chip's paws, Blaze snapped back, "of course I was careful! I had other eyes out there helping me see, you know! Yes, a squirrel went after me when he saw me, and got two more following me for a minute. One got a claw on me, but I'm fine. I've experienced worse." Looking at Zoby's wide eyes, he assured him, "There are more good guys than bad guys, and they know how to help camouflage me, have my back, or will go into an area and report back. They helped today, and will always have our backs, ok?" Zoby nodded.

"I know you're worried, but settle down!" Blaze admonished Chip. "We have a job to do and I'm *not* going to let Ariana or Jezebel scare me off from helping Zoby and his tramily get to Maine!"

Chip dropped his shoulders then looked at Blaze in apology. "I'm sorry, you're right. All this rain and drama has my brain waterlogged and overworked, I guess. And I haven't been to my therapist in two months now," Chip added woefully, while Blaze rolled his eyes at Zoby.

Blaze chuckled and uncharacteristically wrapped a wing around the chipmunk in a hug, "it's alright, Chip." Then he continued, looking at Zoby, "Ariana is raging at all the missed opportunities. First you were off trail with Stan's daughters, then had the night at the Inn, now today got off trail with Kamper. The Trail Talk grapevine coming from Maine says she has a short leash around her neck from her mom. She lost 100 miles of her Jezebel-imposed Virginia deadline this week."

At Zoby and Chip's looks of surprise and fear at that bit of information, he nodded and continued, "yes, apparently Jezebel has told her to get you off trail before Harper's Ferry. She now only has about 50 miles left. I *guarantee* she'll be doing everything she can in the next few days to ensure you don't make it there. The wrath she will face otherwise ... that short leash is becoming a noose," Blaze shuddered.

In what was becoming a providential streak of generosity from the trail community, Mommy had received an offer from an online trail angel friend named Nikki to stay at her place when they were north of Shenandoah in Front Royal. It was Memorial Weekend, but fortunately she was in town and more than willing to take them all in, and even slackpack them to within six miles of Harper's Ferry over the next three days. This would see them through a section appropriately named "The Rollercoaster" in northern Virginia, where the trail goes through 14 miles of steep climbs and descents. They would cross the 1,000-mile mark, as well as the VA/WV state line, setting them up to cross the Shenandoah River Bridge into Harper's Ferry.

Their first day slackpacking with Nikki was mercifully sunny and clear, a welcome change from the week of gray and rain in Shenandoah. Blaze was nursing the wound on his wing but followed along, just a bit slower than usual, while Chip scampered along near them on trail the entire way. Zoby kept a cautious lookout for anything that seemed at all out of the ordinary. Aside from seeing more unwelcome, nasty looks and insults from squirrels than normal, Zoby decided he could relax when they stopped for lunch at a picnic table near a trailhead with some other thru-hikers.

Steps, a southern gentleman from Alabama whom had connected with Mommy and Zoby on trail over their shared time living in Tampa Bay along with Steps' knowledge of the Rays and Zoby's namesake in Ben Zobrist, was one of the lunchtime hikers. Of course, Zoby was able to yogi some lunch from him. Steps had a soft spot for Zoby, as his own small dog at home was dearly missed.

"Y'all are slackpacking *again*?" Steps laughed, "didn't y'all slackpack the whole way through Shenandoah?"

"Not the *whole* way," Mommy laughed back, "only *four* of the six days!"

"I mean, if someone is going to offer to slackpack us," Uncle Stan chimed in with a chuckle, "we aren't stupid enough to say no to that!"

Belly full, Zoby curled up between Steps and Uncle Stan in the warm sunshine and half-listened to the conversation between his humans as he fell asleep. Waking to Mommy gently lifting him and saying it was time to get back on trail, he yawned and looked around for Chip or Blaze. Seeing neither, he was slightly alarmed, but one or the other usually fell in beside them as they returned to the trail after a break. And as a bonus, he learned Mommy had contacted Nikki about Steps joining them the next few days to slackpack while he healed from an ankle injury!

A few miles later, as they stopped at a stream to gather water, Zoby heard his name being called. Turning, he expected to see Chip or Blaze, but instead recognized the fawn he had helped that night in Shenandoah just downstream, slightly hidden among the brush and trees.

"Zoby!" she called again, "Come here!"

Walking over to her, he saw her mother with her, then heard the baritone voice belonging to her father, Knox. "Zoby." He said, that one word carrying authority.

"Knox, hey, how are you guys doing?" Zoby started out with a cheerful greeting, until he saw the look in the buck's eyes. "What's going on?"

"There's been an incident."

"Blaze. Chip. Nooo, what happened?!" Zoby just *knew*, instinctively, the incident involved his friends.

The fawn stepped forward and nuzzled Zoby nose-to-nose. "They're going to be ok," she said, then quickly retreated to her mother's side.

"What happened?!" He couldn't keep the fear and guilt from his voice. Here he had been falling asleep in sunshine with his humans petting and feeding him while his friends were in trouble, and because they were helping *him*.

Knox didn't sugarcoat it and dove right in. "It was a setup. There was an arranged meeting with a former informant to the Trail Angels whom unknowingly had been converted to the Squirrel Mafia side. This raccoon apparently had a negative experience with a domestic over the winter, which left him scarred – literally – but was still pretending to be a Trail Talk informant on the side of the Trail Angels."

Zoby felt the tears stinging his eyes as he imagined the betrayal his friends felt, on top of whatever else had happened. Blinking them back and squaring his shoulders, he looked Knox in the eye. "Tell me what happened."

"The raccoon, he went after Chip, personally. Thankfully Blaze had enough foresight to have a couple Trail Angel woodland creatures casually hanging around, just in case, because Ariana has been whipping the other side into a frenzy lately and things have been tense along the trail. It started an all-out battle amongst coons, squirrels, chipmunks, and birds gathered in the area. Chip and Blaze were the targets of the Squirrel Mafia, and as such, they have some wounds." At this, Zoby closed his eyes and shook his head, the tears barely restrained. "But they're ok," Knox continued. "Zoby, look at me."

Zoby opened his eyes and did as told.

"They are ok. They're spending the night in a safe place and are being taken care of. More important, this incident has emboldened the Trail Angels to fight the good fight, to take care of their own, and made us even more determined to help you. No one, and I mean *no one*, takes lightly the Mafia going after other woodland creatures. We may disagree on our stance regarding domestics, but we don't fight one another over it. What was meant for evil will be turned to a greater good."

"And..." Knox looked pointedly at Zoby, "I personally have seen you in action and seen your courage." Looking fondly at his daughter, he said in his deep voice, "I don't forget the debt I owe. While Blaze and Chip recover, I will personally be keeping watch over you on trail."

****

Zoby continued the hike that day with a heavy heart, and could tell Mommy was noticing he wasn't being himself. Forcing himself to be chipper, he amused them with pretending to chase after bunnies, and even pulling at his leash to "go after" Knox and his family when they were in eyesight along the edge of a meadow. It worked well enough to have Mommy, Uncle Stan and "Uncle Steps" as he was now being called, laughing as they finished their 20 miles that day and met up with Nikki at her car.

Fishing cold drinks out of a cooler, including cold water for Zoby, Nikki took them out for dinner and ice cream, a stop at an outfitter, and then to her home.

The next two days, the trio of humans and their dog hiked through The Rollercoaster, passed the 1,000-mile mark (Mommy cried), and finally reached the West Virginia state line where they sang a song about mountain mamas and country roads taking them home.

And all the while, Zoby checked in with Knox – who seemed to have the woodland authority to prevent any misfortune in his presence – and fought back the guilt and worry in the pit of his stomach over his friends being hurt. But most of all, he wondered what Ariana had planned for *him* on trail next, for he knew it was coming.

Two days later, as they were dropped off for the final time by Nikki and said their good-byes to her, with only six miles to go before walking into Harper's Ferry, he found out.

CHAPTER 13

The Showdown at Harper's Ferry

After enjoying three days of sunshine following the six days of rain in Shenandoah, the rains were forecast to return that morning with early thunderstorms but clearing in the afternoon. Then actually it was supposed to get quite hot the following days, as the calendar would be flipping the pages yet again into June.

But as they hit the trail that morning, the gray mist that so frequently shrouded these mountains was once again covering the trees and hills in a fog so thick the hiker tramily could barely see one another as they moved along the trail.

Thunder rumbled overhead.

Zoby knew it was not just a warning for the impending rainstorm, but that a storm of another type was brewing on the trail as well.

Knox had kept Zoby updated on Blaze and Chip's conditions – both were healing nicely and planned to return to the trail and Zoby's side today as they crossed into Harper's Ferry. Everyone knew Ariana would do whatever she could to keep Zoby from walking across the Shenandoah River Bridge that day, and the entire woodland chain of animals on both sides were on alert.

They hiked the first nearly five miles through scattered sprinkles, dense fog and muffled thunder around them. As they neared the Shenandoah River, Zoby foolishly began to hope maybe Ariana had simply admitted defeat and returned to Maine to face her mother.

With a streak of lightning flashing across the treetops above them, the wind rushing through their leaves, and as a crashing boom echoed through the mountains, the heavens opened and rain fell in sheets upon them.

Zoby froze. He couldn't see Uncles Stan and Steps ahead of him anymore, and even tethered to Mommy via his leash, he could barely make her out through the rain and fog.

And he knew his thoughts of just moments ago had indeed been foolish, for it was then he saw the coyote off trail to his right. Fangs gleaming, he emitted a low growl for only a second before he lunged.

Mommy had seen it too, and screaming his name, yanked on the leash pulling Zoby both back and up toward her where she dropped her trekking poles and snatched him into her arms. Unfortunately, the quick movement on wet rocks sent her off balance, and she fell – still holding Zoby in her arms – down the embankment to her left, a steep slope which ended in the rocky cascades of the Shenandoah River below.

The coyote lept after them, snarling and aiming for Zoby as Mommy tumbled and slid, kicking at the coyote and screaming for help to Uncles Stan and Steps.

The coyote's teeth caught on the leash tethering Zoby to Mommy, snapping it, and as Mommy took another rolling tumble toward the river, Zoby found himself tossed from her arms and landing on his side painfully against a pile of rocks.

"ZOBY!!" He could hear Mommy scream in panic but could no longer see her.

Uncle Stan was coming down the embankment through the pouring rain as carefully as he could without falling himself, while Uncle Steps was racing ahead on the trail to come back up the hill toward them from a different angle. Suddenly, Stan yelled, "copperhead!" as his forward motion down the hill came to a sudden halt.

But all Zoby could see were the teeth and claws in front of him as the coyote grinned and moved in. "So, we meet again," he said as he slowly took a step closer and lightning zipped through the sky, illuminating his golden eyes.

Fighting the flashbacks of another set of teeth and the pain, Zoby instead focused on how he had gathered every bit of strength and courage he had that day to be smart, stay alive, and help Mommy get through the trauma too. He had to do the same thing now.

Through the mist, he saw Uncle Stan nearby going after the large copperhead - which had been joined by another - with his trekking poles and throwing rocks at them. He couldn't see Mommy through the gray fog, but could hear Uncle Steps had reached her, and she was hysterically screaming about the coyote and Zoby.

In the fraction of a second before the coyote lunged at him, Zoby used his small size to his advantage and shrank back into a crevice in the rocks he had landed on. And in the following second as he considered what to do next, he heard through the storm the woodland animal chain come to life around him. Suddenly squirrels, chipmunks and birds went head-to-head in unseen battles within the dense fog and deluge of rain.

Leading the charge, Knox and two doe went after the copperhead Uncle Stan was battling. Startled by the large buck and his rack a little too close for comfort, Uncle Stan shimmied away from the scene and let the pounding hooves of the deer take over, crushing the snakes beneath them.

Looking for Zoby, not seeing him, but seeing the coyote, Uncle Stan heaved a large rock at the coyote that distracted the animal enough to turn and look at him with a menacing growl.

With the coyote's head turned, Zoby slipped out the back of the crevice with the intention of running to find Mommy, when he came face-to-face with none other than Ariana herself.

In that moment, Zoby had enough.

His friends had been hurt. Innocent creatures were wounded or dead. His humans were even being threatened. Anger pulsed through him, fueling his courage and providing clarity through the mist.

"This. Ends. Now." Zoby growled at Ariana, then not waiting, lunged at her with his final word.

Meanwhile, Knox had charged the coyote, wounding him with his impressive rack, sending the beast scrambling down the embankment and disappearing into the mist.

Angry squirrels who had gathered to watch the scene or take up battle with Trail Angel squirrels suddenly focused their attention on Zoby and Ariana, in shock at both the courage and then the aggression shown by the little dog.

A large fox squirrel, Ariana herself wasn't much smaller than Zoby. Caught by surprise, he had the advantage over her for a moment, but she quickly and adeptly turned herself around in his grip and sent them both rolling further down the hill toward the river.

Over the sound of the thunder and the own booming in his ears of his boiling blood rushing through them, he heard Mommy screaming for him in panic. No way, *no way,* was he allowing her to be caught up in this woodland fight and fall into a panic attack where she would be more susceptible to getting hurt.

Throwing his paws against some rocks to catch him and Ariana from skidding and rolling any further, he had to release Ariana at the same time. In doing so, the force had her flinging to the side and hitting a tree stump, momentarily stunning her.

Two smaller squirrels seized the opportunity and angrily jumped on

Zoby, spinning him to also face the traitor of a raccoon, that with only one smirk told Zoby what he needed to know. This animal had hurt his friends.

Screaming out in frustration, Zoby rolled onto his back and shook the squirrels off, and while doing so, had Trail Angel squirrels launch a counterattack on the raccoon, who took off like the coward he was. Zoby looked around then, only to see Ariana watching it all, then rapidly retreat toward the river.

"Oh no you don't!" Zoby yelled as he sprinted after her, forgetting about Mommy in his haze of fury to get Ariana and end this battle.

"There he is, y'all he's over here!" Zoby heard Uncle Steps yell from only a few feet behind him. Suddenly he remembered Mommy, but for the first time in his life, his need to right the wrongs by going after Ariana pulled stronger at him than letting Mommy know he was ok. Looking back briefly at Steps, he also saw Knox nearby. "Take care of Mommy and the Uncles," he yelled at Knox, then ran faster than he had ever run before after Jezebel's daughter.

Pushing his way through obstacles, and shaking off other squirrels trying to stop him, he put on one last burst of speed and jumped toward her, just before she reached the rocky base of the Shenandoah River near the steps of the AT leading up to the Bridge.

Landing on her and rolling yet again, Zoby pinned her down, with a forceful paw on her neck and windpipe, preventing her from speaking. Growling into her stunned face, he said, "I could end you right here, right now. You've hurt my friends, and boy do I want to hurt *you* in return. But I'm not going to. Why? Because I believe your bigger fear is failure and facing your mother's fury." Seeing her eyes widen, then narrow, he knew he was right. "So here is what is going to happen. I'm going to throw you into that river." Her eyes widened again at that. "Oh yes, I am. If you make it out alive, you can decide if you return to Maine or not. I on the other hand, am going to march into Harper's Ferry with my Mommy and Uncles today, and *you* will have failed. And after this, you know what I'm going to do then ..." Zoby lowered his face even closer to hers and growled out the words. "I. Am. Going. To. *MAINE*. Tell Jezebel I'll see her there."

With that, Zoby grabbed Ariana in his mouth and tossed her into the roaring cascades of the Shenandoah River.

Regaining his composure and taking a deep breath, Zoby turned around to head back down the trail to find Mommy, and realized dozens of stunned eyes were focused on him. It was then he also realized the storm had stopped and the sun was breaking through the clouds. Formerly angry squirrels intent on attacking him slowly backed away in stupefied bewilderment, or ran off in newfound fear. Cheers and applause broke out amongst the Trail Angel woodland creatures gathered, and Knox offered a regal nod in Zoby's direction before gracefully bounding off, just as Zoby saw Blaze and Chip emerge from under the steps on the Bridge.

"Chip! Blaze!" Zoby yelled and ran over to them, his exuberant hugs making his friends slightly wince from their healing wounds, but all were laughing with happy chatter filling the air. "You're here, you're ok!" Zoby was beyond relieved and excited to see his friends.

"Kid, I gotta say… what a show! Wow, that was something else!" Chip had climbed on Zoby's paws and grabbed his face, pulling him forward to smack him with a kiss on the nose.

"Zoby, wow," Blaze began, "*you* did that. Do you realize *you* won this battle almost completely on your own? We are *so* proud of you." Blaze flung his wings around Chip and Zoby in another group hug.

Mommy and Uncles Stan and Steps came racing around the bend in the trail calling for Zoby.

"Zoby!!" Mommy ran over to him, tears streaming from her eyes. "Oh my God, baby, you're ok, you're ok!" Cradling him in her arms, she smothered him in kisses, which Zoby eagerly returned, removing her tears with his love. Uncle Stan came over and rubbed his ears and kissed the top of his head, and then Uncle Steps joined in on the happy reunion.

"Y'all, I don't know what on earth that was all about, but we certainly deserve a nice break in Harper's Ferry tonight and tomorrow after *that*." Steps stated in a perplexed southern drawl.

Stan agreed with a bit of incomprehension still baffling him, "I don't think anyone would even *believe* us if we tried to explain what just happened. Copperheads. Bucks. Coyotes. Squirrels." He shook his head as if trying to figure out the puzzle of it all.

"What *did* just happen?!" Mommy laughed. "All I know is, now that is behind us, the sun is out, the skies are blue, and we are about to make this iconic walk across the Bridge into Harper's Ferry and get our photos in the thru-hiker yearbooks at the ATC! Let's goooo!"

****

Although approximately 100 miles shy of the actual halfway point, Harper's Ferry has long been considered the "emotional" halfway point for a thru-hiker on the Appalachian Trail. Residing at the point where the Shenandoah and Potomac Rivers meet, surrounded by the mountains rising from the two rivers, Harper's Ferry is a historical landmark as well, particularly during the Civil War. For thru-hikers, the Appalachian Trail Conservancy is headquartered there, making it a poignant "must-stop" to have their polaroid photo taken beside the ATC sign to be added forever into their hiker yearbooks.

As Zoby triumphantly accompanied Mommy across the Shenandoah River Bridge, into Harper's Ferry and to the ATC headquarters, Chip, Blaze, Knox and other Trail Angels cheered them the whole way. Puffing his chest out and throwing his head back in his now-recognized stance and proclamation, he along with the woodland creatures enjoyed yelling, "small dog, big adventures!"

Mommy got choked up and cried happy tears, which made Zoby's heart swell with pride for her. For them. They had done it. Made it to Harper's Ferry.

Against all odds.

About a mile downstream from the Bridge, Ariana managed to pull herself out of the sweeping current and onto the rocks along the edge. Bruised and possibly sporting a broken bone in her arm, nothing hurt more than her pride. *How* had that domestic managed to get out of yet another of her traps, surrounded by a coyote, copperheads, squirrels, a raccoon, a raging river and even a storm and fog working in her favor?! She had even managed to separate and distract the humans with all the chaos, yet that overgrown rat of a dog still somehow came out on top. Literally, she remembered as she rubbed her raw throat he had pressed on. Angrily, she held her aching side and arm as she stumbled across the rocks, soaked, cold and humiliated.

She could *not* return to Maine. No way.

Not only would her mother's outrageous fury be unmatched, she likely would throw Ariana out of the den, no matter that she is her daughter. Actually, the fact that Ariana *is* her daughter would be all the more reason to shun her, the utter mortification that the one failing in the cause and bringing disgrace upon her being her own flesh and blood. Any family or friends caught associating with her would then also be shunned, but Ariana knew none would take the chance of being shamed themselves, or of facing Jezebel's wrath.

No, she would not be making the return trip north.

Maybe it would be best to let Trail Talk believe she had perished in the river. Yes, she decided, that would be best.

For now.

CHAPTER 14

Understanding the Past, Understanding Today

Late that afternoon in Harper's Ferry, while Mommy and the men went out to dinner, Zoby huddled with Blaze and Chip on the deck outside the private suite Mommy booked for their tramily. They told him of the deceitful raccoon, their former informant and friend, and the trap he laid for them to be attacked.

"Kid, the crazy thing is," Chip continued the story, "most woodland creatures on either side of the domestic debate draw the line at someone authorizing a coordinated attack on a specific animal from the other side. Kind of an unspoken rule within the world of the Squirrel Mafia and Trail Angels. So Ariana only hurt herself by giving the command to go after me and Blaze; she actually lost some followers by having us intentionally injured in a private attack with you not present. And Ryder, that traitor, has enemies now on both sides."

Fortunately, the woodland Trail Angels Blaze had instinctively gathered came to their rescue before things got too rough, so their wounds were only superficial, and as Zoby looked them both over, any signs of injury were healed or nearly healed already.

Zoby himself was sporting a few small cuts, and even more bruises. He knew he would be sore and hurting the next day, so he was glad they had a nero out of town planned rather than a long, full day of hiking. Mommy had cleaned and treated his cuts, and she had done the same for herself. But it was minimal damage to both of them, he knew, compared to what might have been.

"Today, between the fog and rain and all the chaos, I didn't get a good look at him, but that copperhead – he was the same as the one I saw on those boulders with Luna, right?"

Blaze cast a sorrowful gaze downward, then looked at Zoby directly, "that was Venom. *Was* being the operative word. He has always had a mean streak, but it's been worse with Ariana around these past couple years. He has bitten three domestics – that we know of – and even more humans. He enjoyed it, and he was a threat to all on the trail because of that. We Trail Angels make it a point to not do more than is necessary to end a battle or confrontation … and today unfortunately what Knox and his family did was necessary. Venom was out of control, and he absolutely would have bitten you and your tramily had he gotten any closer."

Shuddering, Zoby thought about what could have happened to Uncle Stan when fighting Venom and his buddy off, if Mommy had rolled onto them when she fell, or how the venomous bite of a copperhead would likely be lethal for a small dog like him.

"And the coyote, I recognized him from the alpaca farm. He's the one that hurt Allie." At their nods, Zoby began pacing and went on, "Ariana had a few new recruits, but she had some faithful ones that followed her hundreds of miles up this trail. They had various plans for over a week, over 150 miles, that kept getting foiled by our human trail angels assisting us, or by changing plans like going to the Inn instead of camping. That's a lot of time and energy they're devoting to getting me off trail." He stopped and looked pointedly at Blaze and Chip. "*Why* do they hate domestics so much – and it's time you tell me – why do they hate *me* so much? Why small, white dogs?"

Passing an understanding look between the two of them, Chip and Blaze settled in around Zoby to share the history of the Squirrel Mafia. Climbing up on Zoby's back, Chip told him to lie down and get comfortable, as the chipmunk took his own advice and stretched out in a bed of Zoby's soft hair, propping his chin in his arms on top of Zoby's head as the two friends gazed upon the cardinal as he began his tale.

"It hasn't always been this way on the trail, you know. Domestics visited our forest homes with their humans and, outside of hunting season, woodland creatures largely didn't fear either human or canine in their midst. Oh, there may have been an occasional scuffle between a domestic and animal, but the incidents were few and far between."

Looking right at Zoby, Blaze stated, "as a dog, I'm sure you are aware of the long-running animosity between squirrels and canines." Zoby nodded, thinking to the very first toy Mommy ever brought home and taught him to play with – a small, stuffed squirrel. Matter of fact, every toy he had over the years, no matter what it was, they affectionately called it a "squirrel" after that initial introduction to playing "fetch and kill" with his stuffed squirrel.

"But there's a big difference between *playing* with squeaky, cotton-stuffed fabric, and *actually* going after a real squirrel," Zoby stated to his friends.

"Unfortunately kid, a lot of domestics translate what they learn at home to *our* home. Trust me," Chip stated as he dropped his head upside-down to be eye level with Zoby. "It's why so many squirrels and chipmunks –"

"– and birds," Blaze interjected.

"... and birds, we move to the forest, away from parks and city streets where most humans walk and run their domestics. It's safer." Chip finished.

Looking upward through the tips of his eyes, Zoby blinked and nodded at Chip. "OK, I can see that. So when did things change, and how did Jezebel and Ariana get so powerful?"

Blaze laughed. "Hold on, we're getting there." And with that, Blaze began to recount how the Appalachian Trail was the first long-distance trail of its kind, the dream of a man named Benton MacKaye in the mid-1920s, taking nearly 30 years to construct, and was considered officially completed in the early 1950s. Humans enjoyed day hiking and light backpacking, occasionally bringing their dogs, but actually walking the entire trail in one year – or thru-hiking as it is now known – was not its intention, even to its founders. The first man to thru-hike was a World War II Veteran named Earl Shaffer, who set out to "walk off the war," and he was followed by Emma "Grandma Gatewood," who became the first woman to walk the entire trail alone.

"By the mid-1970s," Blaze continued, "thru-hiking was becoming popular and common enough the ATC began rewarding hikers with patches and certificates of completion. But it was in the '90s and early 2000s, when internal frame backpacks became common and lighter weight, that the trail started to become more crowded with humans."

"And their dogs." Chip added.

With a nod, Blaze resumed his story, "With the introduction of even lighter weight packs and gear, the ultralight backpacking craze began, so thru-hiking the AT became less of a dream and more of a reality to more and more humans. And yes, to their *dogs* as well. As you well know Zoby, there is backpacking gear made now specifically for dogs – packs, booties, clothing, sleeping bags ..." Zoby nodded, as he had many of these items himself for their thru-hike.

"And here's where the Squirrel Mafia enters the picture," Chip tossed out, encouraging Blaze to continue.

"That's right. See, due to these advances in gear, somewhere in the last 10-15 years, dogs began accompanying their humans more and more on long-distance section hikes, or complete thru-hikes of the trail. Most of these dogs, their humans kept off-leash while hiking, therefore behavior from the parks and city streets began to occur with more regularity on the trail."

Blaze paused, and looking at Zoby, he took a deep breath and flung his wings out in frustration.

"Even though I believe with all my heart the trail should be a sanctuary to wildlife, humans and even domestics, there's still a part of me that understands why the Squirrel Mafia formed. Squirrels in particular were constantly being terrorized in what should be the safety of their home. Off-leash dogs chased, even wounded – and occasionally killed – squirrels up and down the trail. What was once an *un*common occurrence became common. The surviving squirrels from the attacks, and loved ones of those who didn't survive, they banded together, up and down the trail … and the Squirrel Mafia was born."

"But it got worse!" Jumping down from Zoby, Chip animatedly joined Blaze's narrative. "Domestic off-leash dogs on trails didn't stop at squirrels and chipmunks and birds, there began to be more reports of them going after larger wildlife too – coons, foxes, coyotes, fawns, and even elk and bears! That's what really did it, Zoby, the bears!"

See," Blaze sidestepped Chip and leaned in to Zoby, "black bears aren't naturally aggressive toward humans. But you get a dog, especially one off-leash thinking it can take on a bear, well, the bear winds up fighting the dog and humans get involved. Bears were getting relocated away from their homes and families, or worse, they were put down. Now there's some truth to that being a result of domestic interference, but more often a bear is relocated or euthanized due to its behavior around human campgrounds and their food sources. BUT … The Squirrel Mafia made it their mission through Trail Talk to get the woodland creatures believing this was happening due to domestics ruining the safety and sanctity of our own lands and home."

"And it worked," Chip chimed in again. "The Squirrel Mafia grew in its size up and down the trail, recruiting new members and constantly reminding the woodland chain of the danger of domestics on trail. Each year as the thru-hiker bubble also got larger, and more domestics joined their humans on trail, there would be more stories – some true, some exaggerated, some completely made up. And then, there was Jezebel."

"*Now* we're getting somewhere," Zoby said, which resulted in Blaze indignantly scowling at him. Laughing, he soothed Blaze's ruffled feathers, "I wanted to know the full story, really. I actually do empathize with why the Squirrel Mafia feels the way they do. Not that I agree with the tactics they employ as a result of their beliefs – it's never ok to hurt someone because you fear them or disagree with them. But, you know … I wanna hear how Jezebel came into power and what the story is with little white dogs like me."

"First, you also need to understand a bit about the hierarchy of the Squirrel Mafia," Blaze smiled at Zoby, "but I promise to get there quickly for you."

Zoby chuckled, and Chip resumed his lounging position between Zoby's ears.

"The squirrel population along the trail is large, but especially in Maine," Blaze began again. "They outnumber humans 20 to 1 up there." At Zoby's wide eyes, Chip tipped his head down again and said, "Seriously! And they're crazy up there!"

Chuckling, Blaze agreed with Chip. "You'll see when you get up there, Zoby. You noticed Ariana's size, right?" Zoby nodded. "Maine squirrels are larger, thick in population, and extremely aggressive. They scream with their chatter echoing through the forests, and even literally throw nuts at domestics *and* humans on the trail. They are *extremely* territorial, and well, a bit irrational. Which overall, makes them intimidating. They have used that to their advantage in establishing the Squirrel Mafia, even convincing their own natural predators to side with them over their unified cause to get domestics off trail."

Excited, Chip jumped down again. "There's no real 'leader' to the Mafia, as in there's not a royal family or democratic vote for President, to borrow human politics and terms. It's more the use of intimidation and influence. And *that*, kid," Chip went eyeball-to-eyeball with Zoby, "*that* is where Jezebel excels."

Blaze agreed, "Our furry little friend here is correct. About six years ago, the previous leader took ill. Trail Talk turned to constant chatter about that leader's young and very beautiful daughter, Jezebel. Aside from her exceptional beauty, she is clever, creative, and initially charming ... until you see the other side of her, which to be blunt, is pure evil. Most know that now, but back then, there were many fooled by her charms. Including another powerful leader, the one widely viewed as being her father's second-in-command and likely successor upon his death, Ahab. Cunning and shrewd, Jezebel managed to steal Ahab's heart, married him and in essence became the true ruler of the Squirrel Mafia, for Ahab bowed to her every request and demand, even – as rumor has it – killing for her."

"Men are idiots," Zoby proclaimed. Then laughed as he realized his statement in the presence of three males, himself included.

"Yeah well..." Chip blushed and confessed, "I've been taken a fool for a woman once or twice."

Blaze rolled his eyes, then at Chip's glare sheepishly also admitted, "there *is* a certain female back in Georgia I do become a bird-brain around."

"I'm just a fool for Mommy. But she's a female, so she counts," Zoby laughed. "Go on with the story, Blaze."

"Well, here is where truth becomes blurred with manipulated half-truths, and/or outright lies. But I'll tell you the widely accepted version of the story at the time," Blaze settled back in to his storyteller mode. "Jezebel and Ahab spent about three years frequently traveling the trail, maintaining the Mafia and gathering more recruits, as well as planning "incidents" to get domestics off trail."

"Been there, done that," Zoby chimed in.

"Exactly my point," Blaze turned and looked Zoby in the eye. "Three years ago there was a small white dog thru-hiking with his humans. A Poodle or Bischon with Maltese mix, small but still larger than you. They were on a mission to get this dog off trail, with a planned encounter in Virginia, the Triple Crown area."

"Jezebel had given birth to Ariana, who was nearing a year old, and all who knew them well at the time relate how she hated traveling to begin with, especially with a child in tow. She wanted to rule from their home in Maine, and send others to do the Squirrel Mafia's dirty work on trail, but Ahab enjoyed the social life and travel. Despite his shortcomings, Ahab was quite beloved by many."

Zoby caught the "was" in Blaze's last sentence, confirming his gut instinct on this story.

"Devious and underhanded, Jezebel set up a second attack Ahab was supposedly unaware of, for she wanted to *ensure* this domestic was off-trail so they could return home, where undoubtedly she would use her wiles to convince Ahab of their need to stop traveling the trail and instead rule by intimidation, threats and violence, as was starting to become the norm. She enlisted a hawk to be near the planned scene at MacAfee Knob with the job of grabbing the domestic and 'dropping it' off the ledge, if their original plan failed."

"Oh my gosh!" Zoby exclaimed. "That is crazy! What was the original plan?"

"Actually, no one really knows. All who were involved in planning it mysteriously disappeared or refuse to talk, following what happened there," Blaze answered.

Eyes wide, Zoby slowly asked, "sooo what happened there?"

At that, Chip scampered down again to join Blaze. "I was there."

Zoby sat upright. "You *were*?! As part of the Trail Angels, like you've been there for me?"

"That's right kid, I was there," Chip started but frowned, "but I wasn't a

Trail Angel at the time. It wasn't as organized as it is now, or set up for being in place for counterattacks against the Squirrel Mafia. It was actually *this* incident that changed all that." Chip paused, then went on.

"For me, it was simply a coincidence that I was there. I was born in Catawba, Virginia, that's my home. I now make Springer Mountain my base as a Trail Angel, but spend most of thru-hiker season traveling the trail. With domestics, like you."

"Because of what I saw that day," Chip added.

Blaze picked up the story again, "No one seems to know exactly what happened that April day. It was evening, chilly, and a little early for the thru-hiker bubble, but a few were passing through the area already. The only eyewitness from start to finish of the incident is Ariana."

"If you believe *her*," Chip said with a snarl.

"Well, people did. And do." Blaze responded, then shrugged. "She was a child, she saw what she thinks she saw."

"What did she see?!" Zoby asked impatiently.

"*Something* got the domestic's attention onto Jezebel, Ahab and Ariana," Blaze continued. "Now mind you, this is over 700 miles into the trail, and there had been no reports of the dog being a threat to any woodland creature, never chasing or endangering anyone. Yet that morning, something caused him to not only leave his owner's side, but lunge at ... supposedly, Ariana. *Their* version states he went after Ariana, but Jezebel – being the protective and loving mother, of course – jumped in front of her daughter, therefore the domestic latched onto her."

"She *was* wounded, pretty badly, on her back leg. She tries to hide it, but still walks with a slight limp today. Of course, she got her wish by using her injury as an excuse to not travel any longer, once she returned to Maine," Chip interjected into Blaze's story.

Blaze gave a pointed look at Chip to let him continue, "so the domestic has Jezebel by her back leg. Ahab comes running over, the dog drops Jezebel and grabs Ahab instead. Just as this is occurring, the hawk Jezebel had employed swoops in, and instead of snatching the dog in his talons and likely freeing Ahab by doing so, he grabs Jezebel and Ariana. The hawk, being an accomplice to Jezebel, drops her and Ariana to safety on a tree nearby, where Ariana states Jezebel commanded the hawk to return for Ahab. From the tree, they then watch the hawk return to the scene." Blaze paused and looked at Chip.

"And this is the only part I saw," Chip said sadly. "It all happened so fast, and I didn't see the initial attack on Jezebel or Ahab, only the hawk flying away and then returning. Now remember, all that I'm about to tell you happened in a matter of seconds. The dog's humans, a young couple, as well as two other hikers on the Knob had run over to the dog. The female owner was grabbing for him, commanding the dog to drop the squirrel. Just as the hawk started to swoop down again and was beaten back by the trekking poles of the other hikers, the dog looked over at it coming in from the direction of the ledge, and tossed Ahab from his mouth – in that direction. Ahab went flying toward the edge, landing near it, then rolled from the inertia of the toss ... and went over the edge to his death."

Zoby closed his eyes, imagining the scene. "What did the domestic say? Why did he go after them? Did he actually toss Ahab over the edge on purpose?"

Chip and Blaze looked at each other. "We don't know," Blaze replied.

Baffled, Zoby looked back at them. "What do you mean? No one ever talked to him to get his side of the story? He was just assumed guilty and now *all* of us small white dogs are like *him*?"

"No kid, of course not. You know we would have," Chip said softly to Zoby. "But his humans ... they turned around and hiked back down to the MacAfee parking lot after the incident and got off trail. Turns out the husband had been nursing an injury, and the hawk thing freaked the wife out so badly they decided to end their hike. We never saw the domestic again."

"What really got me," Chip went on, "was how Jezebel somehow managed to have no eyewitnesses other than herself and Ariana, my own poor account of not seeing the whole thing, and the hawk who of course backs up anything Jezebel says."

"So..." Zoby saw the next chapter clearly, "Jezebel used Ahab as a martyr to rally the Squirrel Mafia and recruit more resources. Ingenious. She cleverly manipulated her daughter into a domestic-hating machine to do the same up and down the trail over the years, calculatingly using her to do her dirty work while she controls the entire operation from Maine." Seeing his friends nodding, he added, "And now *I'm* out here, a small white dog who may have just repeated history, by potentially killing her daughter by tossing her into the river." Zoby closed his eyes and put his head in his paws. "I played right into her game."

"Hey kid, don't give her that much credit," Chip wrapped his little arms around Zoby's neck. "You're right, but you're also wrong."

Blaze stepped over and wrapped a wing around them. "Chip's right, Zoby. You're astute but remember there's another side of the fallout from that day. Many woodland creatures had already seen Jezebel for the manipulative shrew she is. There are many theories floating around as to what may have 'actually' happened that evening on MacAfee Knob." Blaze paused, making sure Zoby was listening before he continued.

"As such, the Trail Angels united like never before and became a strong opposing force to the Squirrel Mafia. As the attacks on domestics increased in frequency and violence, more and more have detracted from the Mafia and joined the Angels. The attack on me and Chip – that did more harm. I wouldn't worry too much about what happened today with Ariana. You're right, Jezebel will spin it precisely the way you stated, but the only ones who will buy into her craftiness are the ones who are already wrapped around her evil little paws anyway."

Feeding off the comfort of his friends around him, Zoby felt his anxiety slip away. Instead, it was replaced by exhaustion. The dramatic events of the morning combined with the emotional upheaval of the evening made him rapidly feel like he would drop dead asleep in an instant. Saying as much to his friends, he bid them good-night and headed into the room and bed, where Mommy would be returning from dinner shortly to join him in much-needed slumber.

That night, the nightmares haunted him again. Shadowy silhouettes and shifting outlines of figures around misty bends in the trail, obscured by fog and rain. Then the shadows would have teeth, or claws, and come tearing at him from the side or swooping down from the sky … and then … was it him? Did he have a shadowy figure in his own gleaming teeth? Obscure thoughts and vague memories entwined in his mind, confusing him … or was that real voices he heard? Was Mommy hurt, was she calling for him? He couldn't tell. Then out of the darkness, diabolical laughter with evil eyes and those gleaming teeth slashing into his side as the pain he knew so well burst forth once again …

"Zoby!! ZOBY! Wake up, baby, wake up. Little man, it's mommy, you're ok. You're ok." Opening his eyes in the dark, he made out Mommy's face and felt himself cradled in her arms. "You're here, baby, you're here with me now." Mommy covered him in kisses. "That was a bad one. Understandable, little man. I had a bad dream too." Zoby gave Mommy kisses in return, hating hearing she had a bad dream and that his had woken her. "It's ok baby. Let's go back to sleep."

Snuggling in against Mommy's chest, as the images from both real life and his dreams converged, he vowed to get to the bottom of what happened three years ago on MacAfee Knob and set things right for future dogs, and their humans, on the Appalachian Trail.

CHAPTER 15

Norovirus, Birthdays and The Half Gallon Challenge

The parade of human trail angels lining up to help the tramily kept right on flowing through Maryland and into Pennsylvania. With the extreme heatwave hitting the area, the offers to slackpack and bring food and beverages to the hikers on trail were a true Godsend. First, two thru-hiker alumni from Maryland reached out to Uncle Stan and Mommy, wanting to help.

David came first, with his teenagers along for the day, and slackpacked the group across the Potomac River out of Harper's Ferry further north into Maryland, greeting them on trail with cold drinks, then again under a pavilion near the end of their hike with more drinks and dinner from town. The following day, "Wizard" slackpacked them 21 more miles through Maryland, setting them up to cross the Mason-Dixon line into their seventh state, Pennsylvania, the next day. Wizard also met them on trail with lunch and cold drinks, then again at a road crossing near the end of their hike with dinner and even a quick trip down the road to get ice cream.

Unfortunately, at the end of this particular day, the queasiness Mommy had been fighting all day finally turned into full-on nausea following the ice cream expedition. As they returned to the trailhead in Wizard's car with less than a half mile to hike in to their campsite, she became overwhelmed with a sudden all-consuming weakness, shaky legs and feeling like she needed to throw up. Walking over to the edge of the parking lot, she laid down, her face white and hands clammy, while Zoby tried to give doggie kisses to help her feel better.

Looking helplessly at Chip and Blaze in a nearby tree, he said, "guys, I don't know what to do for her. I can help her out of panic attacks, but she hardly ever gets sick like this."

Sympathetic, Blaze fluttered down, landing in a bush near them to get a closer look at Mommy without getting her attention. Looking at Zoby he said, "she hasn't thrown up yet, but I bet she will. I've seen this in humans up and down the trail. After watching her symptoms all day and how she looks now … my guess is norovirus. And Zoby," Blaze waited until the dog looked at him, "that's a form of flu that dogs can catch from their humans. You may be sick now, too."

Well, Zoby thought, that explains his own queasiness, which he had been attributing to worry over Mommy. "Great. Just great," is all he said in response to Blaze though.

After a bit of discussion, with Mommy insisting to the men it was just something she ate and she'd be fine to get through the night and continue on to Pennsylvania the next day, Wizard carried her pack in to their campsite and everyone helped her get set up.

Not a moment too soon, for shortly after changing and lying down, she began getting sick.

And Zoby joined her.

From there, for 17 hours through the night and next day, Mommy was miserably ill, her body relentlessly and repeatedly trying to purge itself of everything in her. Zoby had been sick a few times through the night also, but was feeling better by morning … only he was worried about Mommy and tired from a night of no sleep. He knew Uncles Stan and Steps had come near their site in the morning and talked to Mommy through the tent about altering their plans. The men were hiking 10 miles to Pen-Mar State Park, just before the Pennsylvania border, where Uncle Stan's sister, Sue, would pick them up. They had planned to stay with Sue later in the week, but Mommy and Zoby being sick changed things.

Suddenly, Mommy sat up in the tent and grabbed her phone. Looking at the date on it – June 3 – she moaned and reached over to pull Zoby close. "Baby boy. It's your birthday," she said with tears in her eyes, "I'm so sorry we got sick for your birthday. This is *not* how we were supposed to celebrate it."

Every year Mommy made a big deal out of his birthday, actually *their* birthdays, as hers was only four days later. He always enjoyed the first week of June because of the way she made him feel so special, and then he got to do the same for her. Curling up beside her in the tent, he put his paws on the crook of her arm then laid his head on top of his paws, in a way he knew she enjoyed cuddling with him. She lay her head near his, and finally – mercifully – they fell asleep for a few hours.

Zoby woke up to the warmth in the tent with the shade having shifted and afternoon sun hitting them directly. Carefully moving away from Mommy so as not to wake her up, he walked to edge of the tent and whispered as loud as he dared for Chip and Blaze, to see if his friends were near.

Popping up under the vestibule, Chip cheerfully yelled, "hey kid, happy birthday! You're feeling better?"

"Shhhh!" Zoby shushed him, glancing at Mommy who stirred but stayed asleep. "It's warm in here, but yes, I think we're both starting to feel better. What a birthday," he added with an eyeroll.

With a grin and placing his finger over his mouth in the universal "quiet" signal, Chip slowly and quietly unzipped the tent door and motioned for Zoby to come out.

Doing so, Zoby was greeted by a lineup of his woodland friends whispering not so quietly as they sang "happy birthday" to him. Chip, Blaze, Knox and his whole family, and several of the Trail Angel birds, chipmunks, squirrels, bunnies, coons and more had gathered to wish him health and happiness on his birthday. Then Chip produced an actual birthday card on white birch bark, signed with prints from Shelby, Allie, Eli, Tinkerbell and Luna, even Peyton, the bear who had intervened with the wild boar in Georgia, among many others Zoby had met on his journey so far. Truly touched, Zoby hugged and thanked his trail friends, before Chip motioned him to get back into the tent because Mommy was waking up.

****

Late that afternoon, after Mommy hadn't been sick for several hours, Uncles Stan and Steps came for them. Helping pack up, then carrying her gear out for her, they hiked the half mile back to the road crossing from the night before, then Uncle Stan drove them to his sister's home in Pennsylvania. Mommy cried from relief and gratitude for Sue and her husband Mark, that she didn't have to stay another miserable night in the tent, but instead actually had a real bed and a shower, and laundry to disinfect her clothes and gear. They set Mommy and Zoby up in the "basement suite" and even made soup and bread for her empty stomach.

Then Mommy cried again when Sue produced a little bag of specialty dog biscuits with a bow on it, saying, "I hear it's someone's birthday," with a big smile, as she gave it to Zoby. Marietta, Stan's mom, cuddled with Zoby while she and Uncle Stan snuck him table scraps along with his treats, endearing Stan's sister and mom to him forever.

Zoby snuggled in next to Mommy a little while later thinking what a nice birthday it had been after all, and exhausted, they both fell into a deep sleep.

Their days at Sue and Mark's flew by. Enjoying their time with Stan's family and friends, they took an extra zero, which also gave Mommy more time to recover from being sick. As Mommy regained her strength, the men slackpacked her the 10-mile gap they had hiked that morning, then the whole group rejoined forces and finally officially crossed the border into Pennsylvania together on the AT.

Chip and Blaze high-fived and did a little dance with Zoby for entering the northern half of the trail and nearing the official halfway point. His friends had set up their temporary homes in a tree just outside the basement door of his and Mommy's "suite" at Mark and Sue's, so he was able to catch up with them and the Trail Talk frequently. As of yet, no signs of Ariana after Zoby tossed her into the river several days ago. Blaze said the official stance from Trail Talk was they were giving it a little more time before declaring she must not have made it out. Interestingly enough, also no word on Jezebel's reaction to the showdown in Harper's Ferry, or any concerns of her daughter's whereabouts and well-being.

They zero'd again on Mommy's birthday to fulfill her own birthday wish of giving back to the trail community that had given so much to her by providing a day of Trail Magic. Setting up under a pavilion on the AT at Caledonia State Park, the tramily and all of Uncle Stan's family came out to help them cook breakfast, lunch and dinner for their thru-hiker friends, as well as provide fruit, snacks, drinks, and even power banks to recharge their devices. Carissa and Careis drove into town, bringing Bagel, as well as party hats and decorations. All the hikers signed an AT card and sang for Mommy while Zoby got some extra love and treats for *his* birthday that day too. His heart was full, happy to see Mommy so happy and getting love from so many of her special hiker friends and tramily for her birthday. Then Stan's family had ice cream cake and more cards and treats for her *and* Zoby back at Mark and Sue's house.

And to continue the celebration, the next day, they officially hit the halfway point!

Approaching the sign, Mommy and even Uncle Stan got choked up. They had walked 1,097 miles from Georgia. Crossing that point meant with every step forward there were now more miles behind them, and less miles before them to reach Maine and Katahdin. Zoby had to admit, that was pretty cool to think about.

As they moved on from the halfway point to the 1,100-mile marker and took another round of photos and video, Chip and Blaze were teasing Zoby about the Half Gallon Challenge.

"So you gonna do it?" Chip bantered with him, "do you have what it takes?"

Zoby scowled. He loved ice cream and all, but consuming an entire half gallon of it? There was no way, he'd be sick. Who comes up with these crazy challenges anyway?

Thru-hikers gathered around the outdoor seating at Pine Grove General

Store, right on trail, where they sold half gallon cartons of ice cream to celebrate the halfway point with their infamous Half Gallon Challenge. If one consumes an entire half gallon in an hour or less, they win the challenge,rewarded with a little wooden spoon inscribed with "Half Gallon Challenge." Silly yes, but as they arrived toward the end of the day, a couple dozen hikers they knew had already been there and done that, plus Sue was there eagerly anticipating watching her brother eat himself sick with ice cream ... and so *both* Uncles Stan and Steps decided to give it a go.

"Maybe Zoby here should go for the Half *PINT* Challenge," Uncle Steps laughed, as Mommy was buying a pint for herself.

"OH, now I bet he could do *that*!" Mommy replied, giggling. Looking at Zoby she said, "what do you say buddy? Shall we split this pint and make it our own Half *Pint* Challenge?"

"Yes, do it!" Chip and Blaze cheered in support and laughter.

"Well, alrighty then, let's do this!" Zoby said as he dove headfirst into the pint as soon as Mommy opened it, making everyone around the general store bust out laughing.

"Oh my goodness, am *I* going to get any?!" Mommy was hysterical watching him go to town on the pint of ice cream, while Sue snapped photos of all the hikers, including Zoby.

Uncles Stan and Steps were nearing the end of their half gallons, and both were shivering with frozen tongues and lips from consuming such a large quantity of the frozen dessert so quickly. Uncle Stan was laughing about getting brain freeze, wondering if Zoby was getting one too.

Suddenly, it hit him. "Yup," Zoby said, taking a breather from the pint and looking up with frozen eyes at Chip and Blaze sitting nearby. The only support he got from them was more laughter, and as he started shivering, snickering also from his human tramily.

Whatever, he thought, and dove back into the pint.

While Mommy celebrated Uncle Stan finishing his half gallon, closely followed by Uncle Steps, and took their celebratory photos ... Zoby finished not just *half* the pint, but the *full* pint.

Realizing this, Mommy, Sue and the Uncles laughed and cheered, along with other thru-hikers gathered around nearby. "I guess that means if he finished the full *pint*, he'll finish the full *trail*!" another hiker called out.

"You *bet* he will!" Mommy cheerfully tossed back in return.

Utterly freezing, belly aching, and shivering but triumphant, Zoby stuck his chest out, tossed his head back in his favorite and now characteristic pose, then stuttered out through chattering teeth, "ssss-ss-small d-ddog, bb-bb-big ad-vventures!"

Chip and Blaze fell over laughing.

In stark contrast to the jovial atmosphere in Pennsylvania, at the same time hushed and trembling voices whispered bad news through the dark tunnels under boulders in Maine. *No one* wanted the unenviable task of reporting the update coming through Trail Talk to Jezebel.

Staring straight ahead into her mirror as she precisely went through her nightly ritual, Jezebel sneered at the reflection of the servants in her bedchambers. "Do you think I am a *fool*?" she snarled into the looking glass, while continuing in a haughty manner, "that I am somehow not aware of the chatter concerning my *own* daughter, in my *own* den?"

Giving sidelong glances to one another, the maidservant squirrels chose to remain quiet rather than answer.

"Becca," she snapped, as Becca flinched like she had been slapped. "Get me the informant."

Breathing a sigh of relief it wouldn't fall on her shoulders to officially inform Jezebel her daughter was still missing and the domestic was still on trail, then feeling guilty because it would be his, she scurried out to retrieve Marcus from the room next door.

Wringing his hands at being summoned, he attempted to control his shaking and the darn stuttering of which he had rid himself, that magically seemed to reappear around Jezebel.

Seeing him enter in the mirror's reflection, Jezebel slowly turned with an eerie calm which those who knew her best meant she was anything *but* calm underneath the façade.

Before Marcus could begin his pitiful stuttering, Jezebel merely held up one paw to stop him. "Tell me," she began, with a cool voice but fire in her eyes, "precisely how many days has it been since I was last informed of my daughter's pathetic performance in Harper's Ferry?"

"Um, n-nine, M-miss Jeze-b-bel."

"Nine days." Jezebel said slowly, as she lifted her chin and kept her gaze in a manner she knew was intimidating just above the informant's eyes, (what *was* that pitiable creature's name again?) "Nine days," she repeated, "and *no one* has the courage to tell me that which I already know?" She cocked her head to one side in a mocking manner, as if she actually expected an answer to her rhetorical question.

Marcus dared to slide a glance to Becca and the other maidservants. How did he respond to *that*? "Um, M-miss Ariana, we thought she would be back in M-maine b-by now –" he started.

"You *thought*?" Jezebel cut him off with a disdainful laugh. Smirking, she lowered her gaze to stare right into his eyes. "You thought, did you? Oh *do* enlighten me. Just what did you … *think*?" she taunted.

Noting Becca and the other servants imperceptibly moving backward, Marcus knew this was not good. Attempting a different tactic, he took a deep breath and managed to stop wringing his hands as he took what he hoped would be perceived as a compassionate step forward. With his palms up and a sorrowful look on his face, he stammered out, "M-miss Jezebel, as a m-mother, this m-must be a t-terrible time for you –"

Cut off by the simple widening and deepening fire of Jezebel's eyes, and the barely audible gasp coming from Becca beside him, he knew he had gone the wrong direction with that tactic. Cringing, he closed his eyes and waited for the inevitable blow to come.

Pushing herself up from her plush vanity stool, Jezebel straightened to her full height, and lifting her head while keeping her gaze on Marcus who still wouldn't look directly at her, she slowly walked over to him. Stopping nearly nose to nose with him, she simply waited until he raised his eyes to look into hers.

"Do you *think*," she began derisively, "that I am full of – what? *Pride?* – for that worthless daughter of mine? That she hasn't *humiliated* me with her repeated failures, absurd excuses and pathetic performances?" She spit out the words in contempt. "She's *useless*. I'm heartbroken over what a weak and lamentable *joke* she turned out to be." With a sorrowful laugh and shake of her head, she scornfully added, "my own bloodline, a sad excuse of what should have been a powerful creature. Too much like her father, they received the same fate."

"Anyway," she said, turning her attention solely back on Marcus. "This whispering, this murmuring and chatter through the tunnels," she made talking gestures opening and closing the fingers of her paws in Marcus' face, "these discussions and rumors, while *no one I employ* has the courage to speak to me … *this* is what I find unacceptable."

She paused a moment to let that sink in. Cocking her head and leaning in, she broke into a wicked grin as she grabbed Marcus by his lapel, lifting him off the ground to meet her taller eye level. "Don't *you*?"

"Y-yes, yes, of course, M-miss Jeze-bb-bel. Unacceptable." Marcus managed to get out.

"Good." Jezebel tossed him against the wall. "Then you understand why you no longer have a job or a home. Get your things and get out. Tonight." At Marcus' stupefied look and Becca's tortured gasp, she included the maidservant in her cruel gaze as she continued declaring her punishment on him, "You are shunned from the den, and anyone who supports or heaven forbid, goes with you, shall be as well."

She turned her back and slowly strolled back to her chair. Looking at the scene behind her in the mirror, she roared, "GET OUT! Now!"

As there was a mad scramble toward the door, she called out, "Becca."

Immediately forcing the tears forming in her eyes to retreat, straightening her back and taking a deep breath, she turned toward Jezebel. "Yes, Miss Jezebel?"

"Come here, dear."

Becca hesitated only a moment, but Jezebel caught it. Her barely controlled fury snapped. Marching to Becca, she grabbed the younger squirrel by her chin and pulled her face upward. Eyes blazing, her voice was low with intense heat. "I don't believe my instincts are off here. You think I was cruel to do that to him, don't you?" Pausing, she continued, "Don't answer. I already know. And I also know you, how shall we put it, *care* for that imbecile, don't you?" There, the answer was clear in Becca's eyes.

"Well, my dear. As you know, siding with a shunned former den member results in the same punishment yourself. But…" she grinned maliciously, "that would put you *together*, out *there*, wouldn't it? I believe the *true* penance for you, my dear … is to stay right *here*. By my side. Never. Seeing. Him. Again." Becca couldn't stop the tears from welling up in her eyes, which caused Jezebel to scornfully pull Becca's chin higher as she angrily glowered her final warning, "Trust me, I'm watching you. You wouldn't want anything even *worse* befalling him, now would you? Don't try anything you will regret." She released the girl and walked back to her vanity.

"Now," she said to her, "let's address the real problem underneath all this nonsense wasting my time and energy. The domestic. We need to enlist Brady's expertise." She smiled as she saw in the mirror Becca's damp eyes widen in fear at that. "Yes indeed," Jezebel stated to her reflection, "it is time for Brady."

CHAPTER 16

Rocksylvania, Angry Porcupines and New Jersey Bears

Before they knew it, the hiker tramily was hugging farewell to Stan's family and making their way onward into the northern half of Pennsylvania, or "Rocksylvania" as it is nicknamed by the AT community. And aptly so, as the trail is comprised of rocks of all sizes, many areas nothing but boulder fields in all directions. For over 150 miles, hikers walk across more rock and stone than dirt underfoot, traversing helter-skelter jumbled-up piles of boulders, and the worst – the ones Mommy called "shark's teeth rocks" – smaller rocks littering the trail in such a way they can't be avoided, with pointy angles extruding from the ground like teeth. They say Pennsylvania is where shoes go to die, but it's also where any hikers with pre-existing foot injuries such as plantar fasciitis really do want to die.

That last description included Mommy.

Mommy daily struggled with foot pain after hiking with a full pack across 15-20 miles of rocks each day. Some days were worse than others, and on the worst days, Zoby tried his best to make her smile and laugh through her pain and tears. He was thankful the Squirrel Mafia had been largely quiet and inactive since Harper's Ferry so Mommy could focus on getting through the rocks of Pennsylvania. Adding to the exhaustion was being on constant lookout for snakes among the rocks, although it helped greatly to have Uncles Stan and Steps "sweeping" the trail in front of them.

Yet Pennsylvania still abounded with blessings in the form of Trail Angels – of both human and woodland creature variety. In Boiling Springs, a thru-hiker alumni friend of Stan's named "Radagast" met them and slackpacked them for part of the day while he did trail magic for other hikers. In Duncannon, a trail angel family - Chrissie, Doug and Kate - met them in town and brought treats for all, including Zoby! They also had birthday cards for Mommy and Zoby, then treated the entire tramily to lunch and ice cream before they hiked their way out of town. As they reached Highway 501, Stan's close friends, John and Christine McBride, met them on trail and took them to their home for the night, drove them into town to resupply, and provided hot meals, showers, laundry and a bed for a night. And finally, in Palmerton, Courtney, Carissa and Careis drove to the trail to meet them for Father's Day, taking them all out to brunch and then dinner, and the tramily was treated to a night at a home belonging to a friend of Uncle Steps.

All this helped make Rocksylvania tolerable for Mommy, but what she was unaware of was the help the woodland Trail Angels were providing as well. Following Harper's Ferry, there was a large shift occurring, as many former Squirrel Mafia were detracting and moving over to the Trail Angel side. Chip and Blaze were actively keeping an ear on Trail Talk, but no one had seen or heard from Ariana, and most were presuming she didn't make it out of the river. Chip and Blaze however, weren't convinced of that, therefore were keeping an even tighter net around Zoby and his tramily, enlisting the help of local woodland trail angels each day to follow them along the trail to ensure their safety.
Two weeks after Harper's Ferry, the day they were waiting to be picked up by the McBrides, Chip and Blaze had pulled Zoby to the side of the parking lot with a Squirrel Mafia update.

"Hey kid, we've got confirmed word from Maine," Chip had climbed up on Zoby's back the way he seemed to whenever he was letting Blaze take over the conversation.

And indeed, Blaze was full of new information he had confirmed via multiple trusted sources between their location and Maine. "There was a bit of a scene a few nights ago in Jezebel's chambers. As several of us suspected, that coldblooded she-devil could care less about her daughter's safety, said horrible things about her, and is *much* more concerned about appearances – how Ariana's an embarrassment to Jezebel, calling her pathetic and a joke. Apparently, in private she is totally *fine* with her daughter succumbing to the same fate as her father, even seems happy to be rid of her – although in public she is turning on the waterworks and convincing the Squirrel Mafia in the northern states you are the devil himself, returning to finish what the other small, white domestic started three years ago."

"Wait," Zoby interrupted, "how do you know what is being said in *private*, in her own den, as opposed to the show she is putting on in public? Up until now, you've told me her public commands, combined with Trail Talk theories as to the truth. Do you *really* have someone on the inside, that close to Jezebel, double-crossing her?"

Chip hung his head upside down over Zoby's face and grinned. "We do now."

Blaze sighed and continued, "well, I was getting there, guys, if you'd let me finish."

Zoby smiled, it was becoming a running joke that Blaze took the long route in his stories while Zoby cut to the core. "Sorry, go ahead," he said and settled back in for the tale from Maine.

"Ok, I'll cut out the details," Blaze laughed, "so there is this maidservant to Jezebel, Becca, who was secretly engaged to one of her informants. Secretly, because Jezebel has to give her blessing to those closest to her getting involved romantically – which rarely happens. So what really ticked Jezebel off wasn't Ariana missing, but that everyone was talking about it behind her back, and no one was courageous enough to directly give her updates. Therefore, she called this informant – Marcus – into her chambers, gave him a regal tongue-lashing and also apparently slapped him around a bit, then fired and shunned him from the den."

Despite himself, Zoby felt began to feel a bit of compassion for Ariana and animals such as this Marcus, who had to live with such manipulative evil on a daily basis.

"It gets worse, or better – for us," Chip chimed in.

"Right," Blaze continued, "For Jezebel then forbade the maidservant from leaving to go with him, giving her a virtual death sentence of having to remain by her side and never see him again. She threatened Becca that something worse would happen if she tried to leave."
"Would Jezebel actually ... *kill* ... her if she left to be with him?" Zoby just couldn't wrap his mind around such sinister realities from someone like Jezebel.

"Well, yeesss...," Blaze drew it out thoughtfully, "but you have to think like a maniacal psychopath. If Becca loves Marcus enough to give up her home, job, family, friends and even safety ... what would be worse than losing *her* life? Losing *him*. Jezebel would kill Marcus, to hurt Becca. So to protect *him*, she has to stay where she is, and lose him forever."

Zoby's mouth fell open and he just stared at Blaze, not knowing what to say.

"So," Blaze bleakly went on, "with his shunning, Marcus has crossed over to the Trail Angels wholeheartedly now, and we're working to keep him safe and hidden from Jezebel's resources, and Becca is the insider 'double-crossing' Jezebel, as you put it."

Understanding fell over Zoby, and he genuinely felt bad for two squirrels he didn't know up in Maine. "So, to keep tabs on Marcus, and get back the only way she can at Jezebel, Becca is basically an undercover Trail Angel now."

"You got it," Chip jumped down and pulled Zoby's face toward his. "So their heartbreak works in our favor, gotta look at the silver lining here, kid. We've got ourselves a direct-to-the-shrew-herself inside informant."

Taking a deep breath, Zoby said, "Ok, ok, you're right. So, what is Jezebel doing about *me* now? There's no way she's letting me just hike my way on up to Maine."

Blaze and Chip looked at each other. "You're right," Blaze said, then flung his wings out in frustration. "But all we know is she has something truly fearsome in the works. Becca is too afraid to give more details at this point because apparently she and one other are the only who know besides Jezebel, so it is too risky to her safety to tell more. All we know for sure is it's not in Pennsylvania, so we're getting you out of this state and then tightening the Trail Angel net even more."

That had been six days ago. With each day passing and they got closer to the New Jersey border, Zoby grew more cautious and anxiety settled in. It was now their final night camping in Pennsylvania, with a long 20 miles planned the following day to end on the border at a hotel in Delaware Water Gap. Mommy's feet were hurting from the plantar fasciitis, but she was insistent to Uncles Stan and Steps that she was going to make it the next day if it killed her.

"I want *out* of this state," she laughed but meant it, then changed the subject. "Hey guys, so I'm reading in FarOut these comments about a large, angry porcupine living at this campsite," she giggled and went on, "apparently it keeps campers up all night with its loud noises, obviously unhappy with hikers in its home. I want to know what an angry porcupine sounds like!"

Uncles Stan and Steps laughed and got out their phones to read the comments in the app as well. "Seems like we might be in for an interesting night, y'all," Uncle Steps chuckled as he settled into his hammock.

While his human tramily found it amusing, this exchange had Zoby alarmed. Calling out to Chip and Blaze, he asked them about this "angry porcupine."

Blaze chuckled. "We're on it. Her name is Maude, yes seriously," he added at Zoby's grin, "and she's just an elderly and cantankerous resident who doesn't like people in her space. She's harmless, not part of the Squirrel Mafia, nor a Trail Angel. Just a grumpy nuisance, and a bit of a joke along the trail, if I'm being honest. She knows the Angels are near your site in force, and she's none too happy about that, either. We've warned her to leave you and yours alone."

Feeling better, Zoby chuckled over the cranky porcupine and said good-night to his friends.

****

"What in the dickens is *that*?" Mommy and Zoby sat straight up in their tent in the dark, on high alert as Uncle Steps yelled out in alarm.

Coming from his area of the site, they heard it, a high-pitched whine, almost like a toddler on helium trying to scream. "Oh my gosh, it that the angry porcupine?!" Mommy and Uncle Stan yelled back in unison.

Bewildered, Zoby barked and called out for Chip and Blaze. Shushing him as the porcupine continued her screeching, Mommy yelled over to Uncle Steps asking if he was ok. He said he was, but the porcupine was right under his hammock and was afraid its quills would wind up in his backside if he moved.

"We've got to get it away from you," Uncle Stan responded, "without getting hurt ourselves."

"Chip, Blaze!" Zoby yelled for them. "Where are the Trail Angels? Get Maude out of here before she hurts my tramily!"

"We're on it!" Blaze called back. "We've got someone who will be here in a few. Just try to keep your tramily away from her." As he ended his sentence, Maude's screams filled the night air again, and around them, she hollered back at Blaze and Zoby.

"What is wrong with you, Blaze? Siding with a domestic and humans? Out here in *our* space? I don't care for the Mafia, but I don't understand helping those who invade our homes, either! I want you, them, and everyone – OUT of MY space!" Maude's screams went up a decibel.

"Oh my word!" Mommy exclaimed, trying not to laugh, "I wanted to hear an angry porcupine, I guess I got my wish," she said as she finished putting her shoes on, grabbing her headlamp and unzipping the tent. Alarmed, Zoby started barking and jumped out of the tent ahead of Mommy, to block her from going out. Instead, Mommy panicked that Zoby was out of the tent with an angry porcupine at their site and tried to grab him in her arms, just as Zoby turned around from facing the tent and instead came almost face-to-face with Maude, hanging out beside them just under Uncle Steps' hammock.

"Zoby, get back!" Uncle Stan yelled, as he attempted to get around Zoby to divert Maude away from them with his trekking poles.

Maude huffed bad-temperedly at Zoby as she continued her screeching, "so you're the little rat dog that has the forest in a tizzy." Hissing at Uncle Stan as one of his trekking poles made contact, she took a step closer to Zoby, right as Mommy wedged herself between her dog and the porcupine, her own trekking poles in hand. Grabbing Zoby and forcefully shoving him back in the tent as he howled his disapproval, she and Stan poked and shoved Maude away from Uncle Steps, much to her shrieking displeasure, freeing Uncle Steps to now get out of his hammock and help.

"Blaze!" Zoby yelled. With the vestibule open, he could watch what was happening. "Where is this help of yours?"

And then he saw it. At first, he thought it was a weasel, which he had only seen in a zoo from his carrier with Mommy. Then it emitted a sound that was a cross between a bark and a scream, and Uncle Stan yelled, "that's a fisher cat!"

"What's a fisher cat?!" Mommy yelled back. "It looks like an overgrown weasel!"

"Blaze, you rotten skank, you," Maude hollered crossly at the cardinal. "You sic'd *Clinton* on me? That's low, even for you." Calling to Zoby in the tent, she yelled, "I hope they *do* sic Brady on you now!" Glaring at the fisher cat, she sent out one last screech before zooming off into the forest, with only a split second before Clinton took off after her.

Headlamps glowing, trekking poles hoisted and mouths hanging open, the human trio gaped at one another, then burst out laughing. "We have certainly had our share of unbelievable animal encounters lately," Uncle Stan said.

"I'll take the blame for this one," Mommy laughed, "sorry, Steps, I *did* say I wanted to know what an angry porcupine sounds like!"

As the humans talked and retreated back to their shelters, Zoby looked through the mesh of his tent right at Blaze and Chip. "What did she mean by that – who's Brady?"

Looking at one another, they said, "We'll talk in Delaware Water Gap." And Blaze added, "oh, and Clinton won't actually hurt Maude, just chase her. They have quarreled with one another in this area for years. Well ... Unless she quills him," he laughed. "But she knows better."

Two days later, on a zero in Delaware Water Gap, Chip and Blaze lounged under a tree with Zoby, who had a gloriously full belly of food from a BBQ restaurant and treats from the bakery next door, where his humans were currently sitting outside with other thru-hikers stuffing themselves silly with the sugary concoctions.

"Alright guys, cranky Maude's parting words to me – who is Brady?" Zoby was so deliriously stuffed at the moment, he actually almost didn't care.

"Brady is, to put it simply, a serious threat." Blaze said, then waited as Zoby finally opened one eye to look at him. "In the form of an extremely large, extremely aggressive, black bear."

That got Zoby's attention.

"We have been preparing for this possibility, Zoby," Chip came over to him and put his paws on either side of Zoby's face. "We knew Brady was a weapon Ariana or Jezebel would use if you got this far. And to be honest, Brady also just goes out on his own, without directives from the Squirrel Mafia, because he doesn't care for either domestics *or* humans."

At that, Zoby's eyes grew even wider. "Wait, are you saying this bear could go after not only me, but Mommy and the Uncles too? Or any other of our hiker friends?!"

Blaze fluttered down and landed beside Chip. "He's a problem, Zoby, even without being a resource to the Squirrel Mafia. The Rangers have relocated him twice. His home is New England, in Massachusetts, but he's been moved to various parts of New Jersey and New York. He always makes his way back to the AT, and well, he could be anywhere from the New Jersey border to the Vermont border."

Zoby had studied the trail enough with Mommy to know that encompassed several states and hundreds of miles. Saying as much to his friends, they nodded, "Four states and about 350 miles," Blaze confirmed, "and we think Jezebel has reached out to him. Yes, we do and we're trying to confirm it," Blaze added as he caught Zoby's low gasp and fearful eyes, "and we have reached out to get our own resources ready. If she has, and he's in the area, it could be soon, because she doesn't have much patience for you getting further up this trail."

Zoby shuddered. Angry porcupines aside, he knew it had been too quiet the past few weeks.

They hiked out of Delaware Water Gap in yet another downpour, crossing the state line into New Jersey on the bridge over the Delaware River under umbrellas, with Zoby in his carrier and sprays from passing trucks soaking them. Only a few miles ahead, they hit the 1,300-mile mark and celebrated not only the milestone, but also that the rain had stopped.

Hiking around Sunfish Pond, they made a stop at Mohican Outdoor Center for dinner, where Mommy had a package to pick up containing new shoes and insoles, which she hoped would help her feet, still aching from Rocksylvania. Uncles Stan and Steps hiked on ahead to claim their campsite on a ridgeline for that night, while Mommy worked on getting her insoles and shoes ready to go, plus also needed to stop for water, while the men had already done so.

As Mommy and Zoby hiked the last mile to the campsite, Chip and Blaze followed alongside the two of them closely. More closely than normal, Zoby felt, and attributed it to the fact they were now in New Jersey, apparently Brady's territory. They reached the ridgeline and the trail meandered along open rock faces with stunning views out over the rolling layers of mountains, with the sun turning everything golden as it was just beginning its descent.

Reaching the Uncles already set up, Mommy exclaimed over what a beautiful campsite it was, the views from the ridgeline there, and oh look – blueberry bushes covering the field on the hill beside their site. Getting the tent set up and Zoby settled inside, she and Uncle Stan grabbed their cameras and some plastic bags to watch the sunset and pick blueberries.

Forgetting his anxiety and relaxing over the soothing sounds of Uncle Steps softly talking to his wife on the phone, Mommy and Uncle Stan chatting with two other hikers who had joined them while filling up on blueberries and watching the sunset, he felt himself being lulled to sleep inside the tent.

That is, until he heard Mommy's slightly panicked, yet excited, voice.

"Oh my God. Oh my God. Stan. STAN!" he heard her yelling under her breath. Going to the tent doorway, he could see Mommy still facing the ridge, blueberry bushes and sunset, while Uncle Stan and the two other hikers were at the edge of it looking back toward the campsite, but Zoby couldn't see past them. Mommy was flailing an arm backwards toward Uncle Stan to get his attention, while gesturing with her other hand toward the hillside. "Look!" she hissed, getting him to turn around. Then, they both said it, "*bear*!"

Zoby froze. Without seeing the bear, he *knew* it was Brady.

And that meant trouble.

CHAPTER 17

New Jersey Bears, Part 2

Shaking inside, but aware enough to make as little noise as possible, Zoby hissed under his breath, "Chip! Blaze! I can't see him, is it Brady?"

Chip raced over to the tent and hid in the back vestibule. "Get back from the screen, Zoby," he whispered, "we don't know if he knows this is you and your humans. He's usually stealthy and discreet when he's going to attack, and it's typically at night or early morning. He doesn't just walk out into an open field when it's still light out like this. I think he came for the berries. If he doesn't see you, or me and Blaze, he might just leave everyone alone."

Doing as told, Zoby disappeared from the screen toward the back side of the tent where Chip was, but angled his neck in a way he could still see out as much as possible. "Chip," he said, I can*not* let anything happen to Mommy or the Uncles."

"Zoby," Chip admonished, "while we love your bravery … you can*not* take on a bear."

Zoby had been watching the humans as Steps had hung up and bounded over to the group with a couple sets of trekking poles. Now they all were slowly backing up, keeping their eye on the bear. Mommy kept glancing toward the tent – checking on him, Zoby knew.

"Blaze went for help," Chip said, "it's nearly impossible finding anyone willing to take on a bear for the sake of a domestic, especially one as mean as Brady. But we have someone, who is on his way, but he wasn't quite in the area last we heard. Blaze is hoping he can find him and get here in time for whatever may happen."

"That's supposed to make me feel better?!" Zoby yelped loudly, then covered his mouth with his paws.

Eyes wide, he realized Mommy had heard him. "Zoby, quiet!" she yelled the command he had been trained to follow quietly, but still loud enough to carry across the hillside field. Zoby looked at Chip, whose eyes had also widened.

Mommy had just inadvertently told Brady whose campsite he was at, if he wasn't already aware.

Moving back to the door, he saw the humans had backed all the way under the trees in the campsite, still facing and watching the bear. Brady had moved far enough up the hill into the field Zoby could now see him, sitting amidst the blueberry bushes with the sunset streaking colors behind him. If he hadn't been so terrified, Zoby would have thought it actually made a pretty scene.

Already alerted by Mommy's call to him, the bear then caught sight of Zoby through the tent, and with a nasty glint in his eye, a grin spread across his face. "Zoby," was all he said.

He guffawed and bluffed, causing the humans to retreat even further and start banging their trekking poles together, yelling at the bear.

Maniacal laughter came from Brady as he reared up, saying, "I'll never understand why humans think their trekking poles and shouts are actually going to scare me off." Letting out a roar, he said, "no, it actually *ticks me off.*"

"Mommy!!" Zoby screamed for her, "Chip, you've got to unzip this thing for me! *MOMMY!*" Zoby was going crazy, pawing at the tent door, fear making his chest tight as he watched the bear roaring, up on its hind legs, only about 50 yards from the woman who was his whole world. The woman who had saved his life … he had to save hers.

"Chip, let me OUT! She saved my life! I've got save hers! *Chip!* Let me *OUT!*" he screamed.

Watching the bear rear up, the humans all seemed frozen for a few moments. The two other hikers who had joined them broke the silence, yelling, "RUN!" and took off toward the trail behind the campsite.

"NO!" Mommy yelled, grabbing for them but they shook her off, continuing through the site, "you're not supposed to run!" They paused for a moment, and seeing the bear staring right at them, froze.

They were standing right beside Mommy's tent, with Zoby inside.

Brady looked at the two hikers, and the yellow tent he knew contained the domestic. He wasn't sure which human had yelled the dog's name earlier, but decided it didn't matter if he actually got the domestic's owner too or not. With the hikers in the position they were, he could do it all at once – destroy those humans *and* the domestic. Maybe for fun go after the other three then too. And then collect the nice reward Jezebel had promised him for ridding the trail of the domestic. The humans were just extra. And goodness, he loved the look of terror on their faces.

Mommy watched the scene unfolding. Looking at the bear still up on its hind legs bellowing, and then over at the two section hikers in the wrong place at the wrong time, she realized they had stopped right beside her tent. Where Zoby was.

Not thinking, she jumped into action, screaming, "Zoby!!" and raced to the tent. Out of the corner of her eye she saw the bear drop back down and begin to charge. She heard Stan and Steps screaming behind her, but all she could focus on was getting to Zoby.

Chip unzipped the tent.
Brady was 40 yards….

Zoby flew out and ran into Mommy's arms.
She didn't even question how.
30 yards…

Everyone was running.
20 yards…

Mommy tripped over a rock, dropping Zoby and landing face-first on the ground.
10 yards…

With Brady's teeth and claws glistening in the last of the golden sunset, Zoby growled and started toward him. Ignoring Mommy's screams that tore at his heart, he charged. He would die trying anyway, before that bear got to Mommy.

And in a blur of grayish-brown and white, something else with fangs and claws jumped onto Brady before dog and bear reached one another.

"Oh my God!" Mommy yelled, just as Uncles Stan and Steps had reached them after turning around when they realized Mommy fell. Uncle Stan grabbed Zoby and Uncle Steps helped a bleeding Mommy up.

"Go, run *now*, while the bear is distracted!" Uncle Stan yelled.

"What is that, a wolf?!" Mommy yelled back, dumbfounded. "Wolves don't live here!"

"It's a coywolf," Blaze told Zoby, flying over them, "Name's Dex, he's here to help. *Go!* Get to safety, *now*!"

The bear and coywolf –a hybrid between a wolf and coyote indigenous to the Northeastern U.S. – were tearing into one another, a frightful scene that had the trio of hikers and Zoby somewhat frozen in awe even as they dodged behind trees and rocks on the trail. And, it looked like Brady might have been winning the battle, as the bear currently had the coywolf under him, paws on its neck, ready to take him out.

Then Mommy screamed.

A second bear came charging up the path toward them, flew past and dove onto Brady.

"*Peyton*?!" Zoby heard Chip and Blaze yell in disbelief.

"Y'all, get over here!" Steps gestured to a large boulder pile just below the rock outcropping along the trail's ridgeline that hid them from view. Barely able to peel their eyes away from the scene with two bears and a coywolf, they all followed and huddled behind the boulders.

"Oh my God, I've never been so scared," Mommy said, shaking and holding Zoby.

"Shhh," Uncles Stan and Steps shushed her. "Just stay quiet and pray they take this out on one another and leave the campsite. Or we may be sleeping here on these rocks tonight."

Zoby tried to see around the edge of the boulder, but couldn't. Where were Chip and Blaze?

Meanwhile, Peyton had gotten Brady off the coywolf and both had teamed up to go after Brady. The bears rose up on hind legs, claws and teeth bared and clashing, while Dex snarled and lunged at Brady's sides and hind legs, trying to injure and take him down that way.

Zoby heard the sounds of the fight, and also heard the animals shrieking and bellowing at one another, dropping names and past transgressions he didn't understand, but recognized it had nothing to do with him and Jezebel, but had a feeling Chip and Blaze would know and would fill him in. That is, if they made it through this.

Mommy was still shaking, and unable to help with the fight between the animals, he focused on trying to calm her down. Completely hidden below the ridgeline ledge in the boulders, no one had a direct line of sight, but all listened with wide eyes and held breath.

Suddenly, about 150 yards away from where they were hidden, a roaring bundle of black fur went rolling over the edge of the ridge, a freefall of at least 100 feet to another ledge and steep embankment far below them.

Mommy shrieked while everyone gasped, watching. Uncle Steps shot up and told them to stay there while he raced over to a large tree closer to the scene. Zoby squirmed and pushed at Mommy's grip on him, and finally got free. Hating to ignore Mommy's yells again, he ran over beside Uncle Steps, who reached down and grabbed him, to Mommy's relief.

Zoby watched as Peyton looked over at them by the tree, then walked over to where Dex was lying, wounded but alive. "What in tarnation…" he heard Steps whisper in bewilderment under his breath as the bear lowered his head and shoulders to the ground then hoisted the injured coywolf onto his back. Looking back at Zoby, Peyton called out, "I told you to make me a fan. Tossing her into the river? You made me one."

And then he disappeared into the forest in the direction away from their campsite.

Mommy and Uncle Stan had left the boulders and climbed back over the ridgeline, walking toward Steps and Zoby. In shock, and as darkness was falling around them, the trio stood there staring at the now-empty field on the other side of their campsite and the forest on the other side into where the bear and coywolf had disappeared.

"I don't even know what to say," Mommy let out the breath she'd been holding, allowed herself to shake uncontrollably, and taking Zoby back from Uncle Steps, just buried her head in Zoby's and started crying.

Blaze and Chip called out to Zoby from the tree they were in. Looking up, Zoby saw his friends and shook his head, "not now," he said, comforting Mommy. "Zoby," Blaze said patiently to him, "we just want you to know it's safe here tonight now. We're going to go talk to Peyton, we had no idea he was here, but he saved everyone tonight, including Dex, who was our only resource on hand against Brady. He won't let anything happen to you tonight, not that I think Brady even survived their combined attack and then that fall."

Zoby nodded, and tried to figure out how to let his humans know that.

As if on cue, Uncles Stan and Steps began discussing if it was safe to stay there or if they should break camp and set up elsewhere in the dark.

"It doesn't matter," Mommy said. "I'm going to have nightmares about a bear charging me and going after Zoby no matter what. I'm too tired to think right now, let alone tear down camp, hike elsewhere and then set up camp again anyway."

"Hey! Did you guys see a bear up here tonight?" Startled, they all turned around at the new voice in the dark, just turning on his headlamp as he approached, wearing a Ranger uniform.

"Oh my gosh, yes!" Mommy said, then asked how he knew, why was he asking?

"I'm Mike, a ridgerunner here, and there's been reports of an aggressive bear in this area. About 20 minutes ago, two section hikers came flying down the trail toward me and said a bear was attacking a campsite on the ridgeline."

Mommy and the Uncles filled him in on the events. He informed them the "wolf" was likely a coywolf, and it's not uncommon for them to attack bears, then said he would put together a team to search for the bear that fell off the ridge in the morning. He told them he believed the second bear would leave them alone; he had a chance to attack them, but went after the other bear instead. Zoby didn't think Mike believed them that the second bear took the wounded coywolf with him, though. But he won Zoby's heart when he looked at Mommy still trembling and made an offer.

"Tell you what, he said, "if it makes you feel more comfortable, I'll set up camp here with you guys tonight, too. I'll stay awake, and I have bear spray. Just in case anything happens again."

Looking at each other and nodding, the humans all agreed and started back toward their campsite. Zoby thanked God for sending Mike, and between him and what his woodland friends had assured him, he knew they would be safe that night now.

"Hey," Mommy said looking at Zoby as they reached the tent with the door still unzipped, "how on earth did you get out of the tent, anyway?"

That night, Zoby and Mommy both dreamed of another attack, in another time and place, when nothing intervened at the last moment, and Zoby nearly died as a result.

May 2018

Lying on the stainless steel table with his mind muddled from the painkillers they had given him, and body uncooperative to his commands, Zoby still had fully functional eyes and ears. The animal doctors were lamenting a tragedy – *his* tragedy. How it was such a shame, they were saying, that the surgery would be so expensive, and it probably wouldn't save him anyway.

"I know it's hard, but she's doing the right thing," one said to the other.

Looking at Zoby, the second one agreed, "putting him down is the selfless thing."

What?!

Wide awake and alert as he could be, Zoby struggled against the medicine making his body feel so heavy, and the searing pain that ripped through him when he moved. There was *no way* the doctors were correct! Mommy would *never* not give him a chance to live! He *had* to get through the doctors to tell Mommy he was going to be ok, that he would live!

The animal doctors had their backs turned to him, and then three more nurses and technicians came through the triage door, followed by a sobbing Mommy and his Nana, his Mommy's mommy, who was also crying.

His heart broke. He *had* to make Mommy feel better and stop crying. He was going to be ok!

She walked past all the medical staff toward Zoby, making eye contact with him while unending tears rolled down her already tear-streaked and wet face.

He *had* to get up. He *HAD* to.

Gathering every ounce of strength, pushing through the blinding pain and the weight of the medicine, he lifted his head and began to push himself up on his front paws, the whole while not taking his eyes off Mommy.

The entire room gasped collectively.

Doctors and techs rushed over to try and re-situate him, but Mommy reached him first, crying harder than ever. Burying her face in his, Zoby kissed her tears and despite the pain, put his paws on her chest, in the way he knew calmed her down. She pulled back and looked him in the eye, and he begged her, just begged her with his eyes and whimpered … "don't do this, Mommy. Let me fight."

With a cry, she looked at the medical staff and at her mom. "I can't do it! I can't, I'm sorry, I won't do this. Look at him! He's trying to tell me to let him fight, to give him a chance. He's made it so far, against all odds."

She looked at the surgeon who had accompanied her in, "you said he wouldn't even be able to open his eyes to look at me while I said good-bye, and *look* at him! He's a fighter. He shouldn't even be *alive* right now! I've *got* to do the surgery, he *has* to have a chance to live, and to be my Zoby again afterward!" Sobbing, she buried her face in his.

The medical staff all had tears in their eyes, or rolling down their faces. Zoby looked at all of them, and again pulled himself up put his paws on Mommy's chest and kiss her. She was right.

And that's exactly what the surgeon said. "You're right. But the cost..." she trailed off.

"I don't care! I'll max everything, I'll borrow, I'll hold a fundraiser, I'll figure it out." She looked at her mom, who nodded. "We'll figure it out. Somehow. Just please, please .... Let him live."

Throwing herself around Zoby, holding him as tightly as she dared with his injuries, she wept with him in her arms. Looking down into his eyes, she said, "baby boy, you've got to fight like you've never fought before. You've come this far, you need to come through this surgery. Hold on with all you have. Come back to me. OK? Come back afterward to Mommy. And little man, I promise, if you get through this, I will work my butt off to give you every experience, every adventure, to give you the best dog life you've ever imagined. You're my best friend and biggest inspiration. I love you so much."

Zoby kissed her in return, promising to fight, to come back to her.

"I love you so much, my baby boy," she kept repeating as the staff escorted her out of triage so they could prep Zoby for surgery.

"Did you see that?" The tech said wiping her eyes, while rubbing Zoby's ears. "He talked to her. He really did. What a little miracle he is. I can't believe he managed to move his body like that, he's so wounded and drugged up."

"There's nothing in this world like a dog's love," the other responded, while setting Zoby's anesthesia line, "and this one is a real fighter. He makes it through this, he's my hero."

And then Zoby's world went dark one last time, before he came back to his Mommy.

CHAPTER 18

The Dog Days of Summer

The morning following the bear attacks, Mommy and the Uncles lingered over breakfast and packing up while talking to the ridgerunner, who was coordinating efforts to locate Brady.

"If the bear is still alive, he won't have gotten far, and we'll find him. If it's the bear I'm thinking of, he's already been relocated twice, and with the aggression he is showing around here, it's likely he will be put down. Again, if he is even still alive."

Zoby's heart hurt a little at that. Although Brady would have injured or killed him and his tramily, and he knew that, he still hated to hear that either way, the bear didn't really make it past last night's confrontation.

While the humans talked, Blaze and Chip pulled Zoby aside to fill him in on Peyton and Dex. The coywolf had mostly minor injuries, unfortunately a lot of them, so it would take a while to heal. A New York resident, he had traveled to New Jersey specifically to follow Zoby and his tramily through the mid-Atlantic states and New England, in case Brady showed up. He had nearly reached them when Blaze found Dex to tell him the bear obviously, had indeed shown up.

Peyton was a complete surprise.

He told Blaze and Chip that Eli, the elk from the Smokies, was like a brother to him. So after hearing of their adventures there, he kept an ear to Trail Talk and was consistently impressed with the little dog foiling that heinous Ariana. He *really* disliked her. So when he heard Zoby had tossed her into the river, he became not only a fan, but extremely concerned Jezebel was going to pull out the big guns to get Zoby off trail – he just *knew* she would employ Brady. If there was someone Peyton disliked more than Ariana, it was Brady.

"Why?" Zoby asked, "I heard some of their yelling during the fight, but none of it made sense."

"Because Brady killed Peyton's father." Chip stated bluntly.

Jaw dropped, Zoby looked at Blaze, who nodded. "It's one of those things no one can prove, but everyone knows. There's been a long-standing rivalry between Peyton and Brady. It's why Peyton lives in western North Carolina now, around the Smokies region. He is originally from New England, like Brady, but after the mysterious death of his father, Peyton relocated himself. First it was Virginia, then the Smokies. He's a bit of a loner, except he is very close to Eli, and overall he is a good guy."

"Most of all, he has zero tolerance for violence on the trail for no reason, and detests the Squirrel Mafia," Chip added, "so he makes a *great* Trail Angel!"

"But," Zoby cocked his head and looked at them quizzically, "you didn't ask him to come all the way up here. You were surprised to see him last night."

"Correct," Blaze answered. "He followed his gut about Jezebel and Brady, and knew the deranged pyscho that he is, Brady would seriously wound or kill you and your tramily, and enjoy it. He wasn't going to let another tragedy happen to someone whom he had grown fond of – and that's a direct quote from him. Apparently, he's been quietly following us through northern Pennsylvania – and no one knew." Zoby was shocked to hear that. "Anyway, he is visiting family now that he's up here, and who knows, with Brady gone, maybe he'll decide to move back home."

"Wow." Zoby felt overwhelmed, in many ways. "I think I need some time to process all of this."

Chip scampered over to Zoby and hugged him. "Just one more thing, kid. You are brave for sure, but also a fool for your Mommy. I mean, you charged a *bear*." Chip laughed but quickly sobered up and looked at Zoby, "you said she saved your life. There's a story there, and you can tell it when you're ready. But don't lose *yours* trying to save *hers*, that won't do her any good, you know." Chip leaned into Zoby with his paws on his face, "gotta stay smart, kid."

"Yeah," Zoby nodded, then shook his head in an attempt to clear it, "this has been a lot guys. I need some time to process it all, and I think Mommy does too. She said we're staying with a trail angel for a few nights, so maybe that will help, with a lot of things."

"Dawn!" Chip exclaimed. "Yes, Dawn is one of our favorite human trail angels. You guys are in for a treat staying with her and Ned. Just what the trail doctor ordered!"

Yes, Trail Angels Dawn and Ned were definitely what was needed for both Mommy and Zoby at that point on the trail. With a beautiful home near several of the trail road crossings, they took in thru-hikers they had a special bond with each year, and loved providing trail magic. For Mommy, it was a welcome relief to slackpack a few more days after Rocksylvania, getting the extra weight off her feet, then being able to soak, ice and massage them at night. And for all, it allowed them to decompress from, and process, the drama on trail in a safe environment. Zoby loved curling up on couches and chairs with Uncles Stan and Steps when Mommy was working on her feet, and one morning they all snuggled up under the front porch on the outdoor furniture while they waited out a rain shower to get back on trail.

Chip and Blaze once again set up their home-away-from-trail in a tree near Dawn and Ned's front door, and kept Zoby updated on Trail Talk while they slackpacked each day through New Jersey. Brady had been found by the Rangers, and as suspected, hadn't survived both the attack and the fall. The death of the aggressive bear terrorizing the trail even made local human headlines. But it really got Trail Talk going with the additional information Peyton had traveled nearly 1,000 miles back to his home to protect Zoby and his tramily, and enact his final revenge over his long-standing feud with Brady. So far, he was staying in the area, but Blaze suspected he would return to the Smokies and the few close friends like Eli he had there. Dex was healing, and would make a full recovery. He still intended to stay close to the Tramily as they moved through the area, just in case Jezebel had another trick up her wicked sleeve.

And, along those lines, Becca had only reported that Jezebel was, of course, furious about Brady, but had no further details. Chip and Blaze were reluctant to push harder and alienate their new source, so with the Tramily safely ensconced in Dawn's home for a few days, they were patiently awaiting any updated word from Maine.

Their last night in New Jersey and first night back on trail after staying with Dawn and Ned, they camped at a drive-in movie theatre. Mommy had been excited about it all day, as the Warwick Drive-In was another "must-stop" experience along the trail for thru-hikers. With a large grassy hill at the back end of their lot, the hiker-friendly theatre owners allow them to camp for free. For only $5 hikers could rent a radio to watch and listen to the movies, and of course they typically also bought concessions just like normally going to a movie.

However, it was here that Mommy noticed a puffy blister on her ankle, one she recognized as being one of her worst nightmares – poison ivy. That night she got calamine lotion and wrapped it, but knew it was likely going to become a problem.

Despite that, it was a fun experience for all, especially since they were surprised by Stan's good friend and hiker, "TryTry" that night! She then picked them up the next morning at the drive-in and slackpacked them into Uncle Stan's home state, crossing the New York border. She met the group at Bellvale Farm Creamery, where she treated all, including Zoby, to their delicious ice cream, then the Tramily headed out backpacking north on the trail again.

Summer's heat scorched the trail as they made their way through New York the end of June and into July. The humidity and bugs were torture to deal with, water sources were drying up due to a drought in the area, and as suspected, Mommy's itchy poison ivy spread with large, angry blisters on her leg.

Mommy and Uncle Stan decided to have her poison ivy treated at an Urgent Care. The Tramily had made plans to get off trail for the 4th of July holiday, going into New York City (where Zoby and Mommy had never been), so with her poison ivy needing time for the medicine to take effect, they went into the City earlier than planned. Mommy and Uncle Stan stayed with his daughter Courtney and her fiancé, Dave, while Uncle Steps hiked on a bit further north, then met his wife and stayed with his niece in the City. They had fun playing tourist, then met up with Steps for fireworks. All were sad to say good-bye to him, who unfortunately, they would not see on the AT again. Shortly after returning to the trail, Uncle Steps had to get off permanently due to a heart condition that required surgery and recovery time. The tramily was back to Mommy, Zoby and Uncle Stan as they left the City and returned to the AT in New York.

Meanwhile, while they were in the City, Dex fully recovered, and Chip and Blaze finally got an update from Maine.

Two days following Brady's death, a furious Jezebel snatched a large acorn and hurled it into her mirror in a fit of rage, shattering the glass. Snatching a large shard of it, she whirled around and marched up to Becca and her burly bodyguard – now her informant to replace Marcus.

"Tell me," she said to them, brandishing the shard of glass in front of her, slowly moving its tip from the chest of one to the other, "how the only three people in the forest who knew about my deal with Brady are standing in *this room*, and *yet*," she stopped to suck in her fury before it exploded again, "and yet," she continued more slowly and controlled, "both Dex *and* Peyton magically appeared on site with a counterattack? And at a site that *wasn't even planned?!*" As her voice rose on the final words, she gripped the broken shard so tightly dots of red appeared on the edge of her palm around the glass.

Calmly, the bulky bodyguard reached out and opened her palm to reveal the cut, and removed the glass from her hand, while saying, "Miss

Jezebel. This is not a result of anything but Brady being a hothead, a volatile tool in our shed. He was unpredictable and therefore, unreliable, as he proved by acting on his own will that night before our planned encounter further up the trail. As much as it is a shame to lose him as a resource, the fact is ..." he looked at Jezebel with unfeeling eyes, "enlisting him may have been a slight oversight – not *mistake*," he stopped Jezebel's angry defiance he could see in her face at that, "but we need to remember the irrational thinking of the Trail Angels. They perceive Brady as violent and aggressive, a threat to the trail in general, therefore they equate the same to the Squirrel Mafia for using him as a resource."

An eerie comprehension flowed into Jezebel's eyes and demeanor, resulting in a spine-chilling calm as she looked at Becca. Taking the handkerchief from her maidservants' pocket, Jezebel coolly wrapped her bleeding palm, never taking her eyes off the girl. "And Becca, do you agree with this assessment?"

Taking a deep breath, she started, "Miss Jezebel. You want open communication and honesty from your informants and the Squirrel Mafia. So I bring you that." Looking straight back at Jezebel, knowing she may be greatly punished for what she was about to say, she continued, "yes, I agree. There is a detraction occurring along the trail you need to not only be aware of, but take into consideration with future plans. Brady has indeed terrorized the trail and we have lost support through the mid-Atlantic and New England states as a result of the confrontation the other night. To answer your earlier question, no one outside of this room knew about your deal with Brady."

That she could state honestly, for she hadn't told the Trail Angels those details. "But the Trail Angels are ... wily and resourceful," she finally landed on being able to say without lying or upsetting Jezebel, "and they suspected Brady would be used, as the domestic entered his territory. Peyton himself has widely stated to Trail Talk he assumed this, and combined with his own history with Brady, he made the trek north to counterattack."

She stopped and held her breath for Jezebel's reaction.

Thoughtfully, Jezebel twined the end of the bandana through her fingers. Walking back toward the mess around her vanity, with her back toward them she said over her shoulder, "so *you* think we need to be more ... subtle?"

Becca cast a look at the bodyguard, not sure from whom Jezebel was expecting an answer. She cleared her throat and said, "it may be the perceptive and wise move for now, Miss Jezebel."

Turning, she glared at Becca. "Are you insinuating I have *not* been perceptive and wise?"

As Becca opened her mouth and started to stumble around an answer, the bodyguard/informant cut in. "Of *course* you are always the perceptive one with not only good judgment but impeccable acumen, Miss Jezebel. I do believe flying under the radar until the domestic – *if* the domestic," he corrected himself, "makes it to the northern states where we have a stronghold over the Trail Angels would indeed be in the best interest for both yourself and the Squirrel Mafia."

Eyes slowly moving back and forth between the two, Jezebel finally snapped out, "fine. We lay low. But, we do so by undetectably going after the humans." Becca's eyes widened, causing Jezebel to narrow hers and walk slowly back toward the maidservant. "Get the *humans* off the trail, get the *domestic* off the trail." Waiting until Becca nodded, she continued, "summer is hot, miserable hiking weather. Poison ivy, bugs, stinging insects, snakes, contaminated water sources, heatstroke, multiple possibilities for injuries – we use *all* of it. Get in their heads. This is a mental game now. If they make it through … " Jezebel's eyes gleamed with anticipation, "we'll be waiting in the north."

"So you're telling me it's probably not a coincidence Mommy has poison ivy?" Zoby looked at Chip and Blaze incredulously.

"Sorry kid. Probably not," Chip looked at him sorrowfully. "The squirrels could have easily rubbed it up against her without her knowing. And yes, the Squirrel Mafia does have more control over the mosquitos, gnats, biting flies, bees, yellow jackets – basically the insect world – than we do. I mean, they *thrive* on biting and stinging humans, after all."

Heaving out a large sigh, Zoby shook his head. "So what can I and the Trail Angels do?"

Looking at Chip, Blaze sighed as well. "Not a whole lot, Zoby. We'll do what we can, but you just have to stay positive and give her a lot of love. Sorry for the pun, but the dog days of summer are brutal and mentally difficult for most thru-hikers to get through anyway, and it's about to become even worse for your Mommy."

****

And so they hiked on through the miserable July heat and humidity, wearing bug nets over their heads which barely deterred the mosquitos and gnats, dodging snakes (both venomous and non-venomous), stinging insects and their nests, and filtering then boiling highly questionable water. Thru-hiker friends of theirs contacted giardia, everyone was swollen from bug bites, and many hikers were getting off trail to treat poison ivy.

Yet they made progress, and mercifully had the assistance of human trail angels along the way. Crossing New York off the list and entering Connecticut, they journeyed along the Housatonic River, met Stan's friends Nicki and Ryan, who brought trail magic to them, hiked through trail towns and stopped at Great Falls one afternoon where a human trail angel named Diane had met them and was bringing trail magic pizza to the Falls. While they waited, Mommy literally watched her poison ivy spread across her leg, so off they went for a second round of shots and medicine at an Urgent Care, with an unplanned stay in Salisbury, Connecticut.

There, another trail angel whom had reached out to Mommy online met up with them. Lyndsay brought her adorable toddler-aged boys who loved hiking even at that young age, and they also loved Zoby, who enjoyed being spoiled by them. Chip and Blaze got a kick out of the kids hiking with their mother while the tramily slackpacked across the 1,500-mile mark and the border of Massachusetts, celebrating Zoby hitting state number eleven on the trail.

In a scary moment just after crossing into Massachusetts, Mommy had picked Zoby up because the heat from the sun on the hot rocks was hurting his pads on as they crossed over Mount Race, and on the very steep, rocky descent, "something" near her feet caught her off guard, and she took a nasty tumble down the sharp boulders, still holding Zoby. Uncle Stan saw her fall, and convinced she had broken bones, commanded her to stay still while he got help.

Amazingly, Mommy was ok, save for a lot of deep cuts and even more bruises, but at first, they weren't sure Zoby had survived the fall without broken bones. Even Chip and Blaze were calling out to him, concerned the fall may have ended his hike, but Zoby was initially just dazed and in a little bit of shock. His ribs hurt and one paw was banged up, but he could walk and would be fine. He was more concerned about Mommy when he saw her ripped pants and the blood all over her, but she insisted she was fine, and they hiked on to where Lyndsay was meeting them.

That day, they decided it was time to have the ongoing pain in Uncle Stan's stomach / groin area looked at by a doctor, so Lyndsay took them to the hospital before saying her farewells. Between Mommy's fall and what turned out to be Uncle Stan's double hernia (but not requiring an emergency surgery), they took an extra zero in Great Barrington, Massachusetts. In the hotel, Mommy and Uncle Stan looked at their wounds, poison ivy, bug bites, recent doctor bills and prescription bottles, and laughingly called themselves "the walking wounded."

But Zoby could tell Mommy was struggling. It was all getting to her, just like he had been warned it would.

And yet, they hiked on. From Great Barrington to the Vermont border was a long, 4-day stretch of 17-20 mile days in the scorching heat. Zoby knew Mommy was hurting from the fall, and the bugs always ate Mommy alive, but she was marching on despite all that as well as having dried-up water sources on trail in the drought.

Thankfully, they were once again blessed by a former thru-hiker trail angel, "PTL" and his wife, who met them on trail in the morning providing trail magic of hot breakfast and cold drinks, and again in the afternoon for a lunch of hot dogs and burgers – and they gave Zoby his own meals, too!

Massachusetts was full of trail towns and interesting stops, which Zoby loved – like the ice cream stand in Cheshire, relaxing in a hammock at The Cookie Lady's home on the trail, getting breakfast at Mt. Greylock's Bascom Lodge, and staying at the free, volunteer-run shelter on the trail – Upper Goose Pond Cabin – where they had bunks and made blueberry pancakes for hikers. Being able to get hot meals or ice cream, and refill their water in dry spells really helped to ease the heat, bugs, and monotony of the trail during this stretch.

Taking his inspiration from Mommy's grit to continue on, Zoby marched on as well, daily telling Chip and Blaze to report up to that witch in Maine that they were still coming for her. They loved his positive, upbeat attitude, as did the other woodland trail angels that came out to meet the "famous" domestic named Zoby who was still on the trail despite all the plotting against him. It was becoming a daily occurrence to have other animals mimic his chest-out, head-up pose, calling out, "small dog, big adventures!" as he passed by. Zoby was humbled and amazed by the support, and always told them so.

The drought finally came to an end as they crossed the 1,600-mile mark and the Vermont state line, and they slept in a shelter that night in a downpour. Unfortunately, the rain did not bring with it a cooldown in temperatures, but instead made the trail feel like a swampy sauna, and if Mommy thought the bugs were bad before, it was nothing compared to the constant swarming attacks they experienced in southern Vermont. Even Uncle Stan was being bitten, by both mosquitos and biting flies now, and both humans were beyond miserable. The rain lasted off and on for days, shrouding the trail in a gray mist once again, enveloping them in a grayish-green tunnel with no views, muggy and full of bugs and mud. Both Mommy and Uncle Stan were mentally struggling to get through each day.

Finally after a week in Vermont, Mommy broke down. Saying the constant buzzing and attacks by the bugs were like an AT-form of Chinese water torture, and she couldn't take the heat and constant itching, with her back, legs, arms and even face swollen with bug bites and the remnants of her finally-fading poison ivy, the cuts from her fall scabbing over and painful bruises just beginning to fade, she laid in the tent and cried. Her head was aching in the tell-tale sign of a migraine. Zoby tried everything he could to console her, covering her in kisses and loving on her. She finally fell asleep with him curled up in her arms, and Zoby lay there fuming. The Squirrel Mafia had attacked her body and mind, and maybe had finally broken her spirit.

CHAPTER 19

No Rain, No Pain, No Maine

"Chip? Blaze?" Zoby softly called out from the edge of the tent after Mommy had left at dawn, heading to the shelter to talk with Uncle Stan.

The night had been rough. Mommy had a migraine and Zoby couldn't make her feel better. They both had barely slept, and the continued thunderstorms through the night hadn't helped.

Chip appeared under the vestibule in response to Zoby's call with a cheerful, "good morning!" then frowned when he saw the look on Zoby's face. "What's up, kid?"

Zoby looked at Chip sorrowfully, "She's really struggling, Chip. I mean, have you seen her body? She's covered head to toe in itchy bug bites, the poison ivy, cuts and bruises … and last night she got a migraine. We've got to do something to help her. What can we do? We can't let the Mafia win this way … I'm afraid Mommy is about to break."

Their cardinal friend popped up under the vestibule beside Chip. "I just heard your Mommy and Uncle Stan talking in the shelter. Another round of storms is coming," Blaze gave Zoby a pointed look, knowing despite his accomplishments in them, he still hated storms, "and hopefully those couple hours will help her migraine get under control so they can hike a few miles to the next road crossing. She's trying to contact a shuttle to take them into Rutland a day early."

"OK, that's good. I think she needs to get off trail and heal her body a bit more. But guys, there's got to be something the Trail Angels can do. Do you have human trail angels in the area, or can the woodland chain come up with a way to counteract what has been done to her?"

Chip opened the tent door to wrap his little arms around Zoby in a big hug. "We are a little low on trail angels, both woodland and human, the closer we get to Maine, kid. Jezebel's power and influence is strong in the north." At Zoby's crestfallen look, Chip tried to remove the sadness from his eyes. "But we still have our resources, many are willing to travel for you and go up against the Mafia stronghold … and you know we have an inside source now. We're going to get you not only to Maine, but all the way to Katahdin. Trust us, kid," he said, pulling Zoby's face to his own and giving him a smooch between the eyes.

As Chip zipped the tent back up and returned to Blaze's side, the red bird also tried to comfort Zoby. "We'll see what today brings with how your Mommy is feeling and if they can get off trail so she can rest and recover. We *promise* to put the woodland trail angels to action to do what we can to get her spirit recovered as well."

They heard Mommy returning from the shelter and scurried off, while Zoby put on his happy face and danced around for her, with happy yip yips like he knew she loved. It worked, as she smiled through her pain, kissed and snuggled up with him, and said, "we get to sleep in today, baby boy. Let's try to get a few hours in while it rains, and then we're gonna get off trail a day early for a zero, ok? You good with that, little man?" she said, petting him between the ears and smiling into his face as he happily rolled his head into her hand and looked up at her with pure adoration. He really did have a way of making her feel better, she thought.

After slowly hiking the few miles to the next road crossing that day, the Tramily got a shuttle into Rutland, Vermont, where Mommy spent the rest of the day, and a zero the next, sleeping off the remnants of the migraine, as well as simply resting her body to recover. They had decided to hire an early shuttle back to where they got off trail, then do a long slackpack to make up the miles they were supposed to have gotten in the last two days, so it would actually all even out. A local bus ran by the trailhead where they planned to end their slackpack that would return them to Rutland. Their route that day would take them over Killington, a 4,000-ft peak and the highest point on the AT in Vermont, as well as past the 1,700-mile marker.

Shivering a bit as they got into the shuttle before dawn, Mommy said, "it's cooler out this morning than it has been. Maybe the bugs won't be so bad," then laughed with an eyeroll, "oh I'm just dreaming on that one, aren't I."

Starting off, they had a rock scramble climb out of a gorge, where Zoby saw Chip and Blaze join them. Calling out a greeting to his friends, he saw Chip give a huge smile in return. "Hey kid! We've got some surprises in store for your Mommy!"

Blaze spread his wings and laughed in an uncharacteristic moment of glee. "The weather is even working in our favor, it's cooler out! Plus we gained control over the mosquitos through the rest of Vermont!" Blaze could barely contain his excitement. "We managed to get *both* our frog and bat trail angel leaders in the next 65 miles to the New Hampshire border to make a deal with the mosquito and fly clans. If they leave your Mommy and Uncle Stan alone as they pass through, they won't feed on them. This is a *first*, Zoby, it's amazing! You are *truly* pulling together the woodland chain to stand up to the Squirrel Mafia and fight for you!"

Zoby couldn't believe it. Looking back at Mommy making her way up the rock scramble while laughing with Uncle Stan, he breathed a huge sigh of relief. "That *is* amazing, guys. And will be a *huge* help. I know she's feeling better physically, it's all about getting her back into this mentally. And *that* will be a huge relief for her, both physically and mentally."

"Oh, and we have some other surprises, too!" Chip cheerfully added. "Speaking of, I need to get them set. See you up the trail!" Zoby laughed as his friends disappeared, wondering what was in store for them that day.

****

Mommy noticed the lack of bugs, a stark contrast to the incessant swarming of their previous couple hundred miles, right away. "I'm afraid to jinx it, she laughed, but 4 miles in, no need to wear the bug net, and no bug bites so far must be a new record," she laughed with Uncle Stan. "And the cooler weather is also a welcome relief," he agreed.

In high spirits, they continued several miles along converging streams with small cascades and pretty mountain views, which had them stopping frequently for photos. Then they came to a widening of a stream with a wooden bridge, surrounded by wildflowers and milkweed.

And hundreds of monarch butterflies.

"Ooooh my gosh!! Monarchs!" Mommy gasped, her eyes wide with utter delight. "It's a sign! For *me* ... monarchs, it's my trail name!" Frozen with joy, she could hardly believe what she saw.

Huge smiles on their faces, Chip and Blaze grinned like fools at Zoby.

"You guys did this?" Zoby shook his head in disbelief. "Monarchs? It's so perfect. But how?" He laid down in a patch of sunshine within a bed of wildflowers as Mommy took him off leash so she and Uncle Stan could wander, taking photo after photo of the butterflies, flowers and river.

"A little way up the AT is an official Monarch Waystation, you'll pass it in a couple days. It's basically a safe haven for monarch butterflies and caterpillars, with their host and feeder plants. Several of those same plants grow here. We just convinced a migrating group of monarchs to feed here instead of there today, it was pretty simple, but an experience we knew would mean a lot to your Mommy, with her trail name and all," Blaze explained.

Truly touched, Zoby hugged his friends. They all turned as Mommy laughed in delight while a monarch landed on her shoulder and another fluttered around her head. Laughing, Chip returned the hug, then with a wink pranced away, calling out, "but wait, there's more!"

It was hard to move away from the babbling brook with the enchanting field of dancing butterflies and colorful wildflowers, but they still had over ten miles to hike that day.

Several miles later, they reached a split from the AT on a blue blaze to ascend the actual peak of Killington, which was a very steep bouldering rock climb. Upon reaching the top, Mommy turned around and gasped. It was their first higher-elevation view in months, with layers of mountains spread out around them and their first glimpse of the Whites along the horizon, their not-so-distant future New Hampshire hikes awaiting. Zoby could tell finally getting views like this once more was adding to Mommy's enjoyment of the day, and the thru-hike, again.

Zoby spotted Chip and Blaze gesturing him over to a grassy area below the rock ledge they were on, next to some older, moss-covered logs. Zoby went over to them, as Mommy followed him and called out to Uncle Stan, "there's a grassy area out of the wind over here, it's a good lunch spot!"

Taking their packs off and leaning up against the rocks in the soft grass, they pulled out snacks and their packed lunches from a deli in town. Zoby of course, with Uncle Stan wrapped around his paw, got beef jerky and nearly half the deli meat out of his sandwich. Giggling at their interaction, Mommy suddenly gasped in pleasure as she caught movement out of the corner of her eye under the mossy logs near them.

"Look, a bunny rabbit!"

Catching the eye of Blaze up in a tree nearby, Zoby grinned. This was another of their surprises. "His name is Jack," Blaze laughed, "despite not being a jackrabbit. He's a snowshoe hare. And willing to come out during the day to see your Mommy."

"I'll do anything to go up against the Squirrel Mafia," Jack said, "and I don't normally get a chance to do much. I'm happy to put a smile on your Mommy's face today." Going up to Mommy and Uncle Stan, he accepted their offerings of lettuce and spinach from their deli sandwiches. Mommy even had some baby carrots she had packed out since they were slackpacking and she didn't care about the weight.

Saying as much, she giggled over the hare eating from her hand. "When I was little, I had a wild bunny for about a year. His mommy had abandoned him, so we took him in, nursed it to health and raised him before returning him to the wild. I named him Bun-Bun."

Uncle Stan chuckled at that, "of course you did." Jack nearly choked on the carrot he was eating, "and I thought Jack was bad," he laughed.

Unfortunately, just then a loud group of day hikers ascended the peak just behind them on the rocks, making Jack nervous. "Sorry guys, I'm out," he said as he bounded back under the log to his den below.

Grinning from ear to ear, Mommy looked at Uncle Stan and picked up Zoby. "That was *so* cool, wasn't it? And he didn't even seem to care that Zoby was with us! What a great day. It's cooler, still no bugs, the monarchs and flowers, great views, and now a rabbit! I'm *loving* today!"

Zoby beamed at Blaze up in the tree. "More to come," Blaze promised, then flew off.

Descending from Killington, they decided to detour over to the ski lodge and lift area, both closed, but gave them even more views to appreciate. On their way back to the AT, they went down a long series of grated steps. As Zoby took the steps with no fear or problems, Mommy exclaimed over how proud she was of him, for that was something he never would have done on his own before. He honestly didn't even realize what he was doing, which made him understand he had indeed overcome silly fears and obstacles in his life. And even better, it came on a day that continued to add to Mommy's brighter disposition.

And a few miles later, coming around a bend in the trail was a sign reading: "500 Miles to Katahdin." Perched on a branch right next to the sign, in all their crimson glory, was Blaze along a with another male cardinal friend.

Stan and Mommy gasped and exclaimed over seeing them right next to that sign. "Cardinals are a symbol of good luck!" Uncle Stan declared.

Mommy was choked up. "It's also a symbol of a blessing from a loved one who has passed on. I'm claiming it as a message from both our dads," she said, wiping a tear.

Choked up as well, Stan agreed. "Luck and love from above."

Teary-eyed himself, Zoby mouthed, "thank you," to Blaze as he and his friend obligingly posed for pictures before flying away.

And one last treat for the day, a couple miles later, they hit the 1,700-mile mark, posing for pictures with the numbers made out of fern leaves on the ground, with a certain silly chipmunk dancing around them, making them laugh at his antics as he "stole" nuts from Uncle Stan.

Finishing the hike and waiting for the bus, Zoby doing his roly-poly on his back in the grass, Mommy sat beside Uncle Stan in the late-afternoon sunshine and said, "I needed this. What a great day. All these beautiful reminders – from the cascading rivers and mountain views, to the special moments with monarchs, bunnies, cardinals and chipmunks … I needed today," she repeated with a nod. "And not a single bug bite," she added with a laugh. "Three days to New Hampshire, then only two states re-Maine! Let's do this!"

****

Three days later, after truly enjoying northern Vermont with stops at The Lookout – a shelter with a rooftop deck offering 360-views of sunset (where they were treated to a spectacular one!), seeing more monarchs in the official Wayside on trail, stopping at a farm stand for amazing food and watching more butterflies dance amongst the owner's radiantly colorful gardens, cheering on their friends Parkour and JetPack as they bridge-jumped into the White River, and finally, stopping for enormous ice cream cones just before the border … they walked onto the bridge over the Connecticut River where the New Hampshire border resides.

Tears in her eyes, ecstatic and full of joy, Mommy felt refreshed and ready to tackle the final two states. She had long been looking forward to these final miles, seeing the splendor of the challenging White Mountains, and taking those steps into Maine and its beauty as well.

"Zoby! ZOBY!" she yelled in elation, "We're in New Hampshire, buddy! We're almost there!"

Zoby had the biggest grin on his face for those state line photos, and just down the bridge, a chipmunk and cardinal high-fived one another as they watched.

CHAPTER 20

The Great Whites, Part 1

"They're in New Hampshire."

Jezebel pursed her lips and cast a quick shifting glance toward Becca in her new mirror. "Yes, I am aware," she said with a cold smile, "and they shall be welcomed appropriately."

With that, Jezebel sent a last gaze into the mirror checking any imperfections in her made-up face or coiffed hair, smoothed her dress, stood up and turned to Becca. "It is time." With a vile gleam of excitement in her eye betraying her calm demeanor, she directed, "Gather the residents in the assembly hall. We have a mob to … shall we say, *appropriately inform* … that the domestic responsible for my *beloved* daughter's death is now amongst us in the north." Warming to her story, she chuckled, "It's *my pleasure* to rally them to the cause."

With an imperceptible shudder, Becca left and did as told. From the back of the gathering, she watched as Jezebel, flanked on either side by her brawny bodyguards, recounted the tragic story of the loss of her husband. Full of emotion even Becca almost believed, she transitioned from the grieving widow to the grieving mother. With Broadway-perfect timing and storytelling, one could hear a pin drop as she openly wept, then seemingly gathered her courage, and bravely faced the crowd with a terrifying warning.

"This could be *your* family! *Your* husband, *your* child. Allow *me* to bear the burden of this grief for *all* of us. It is our duty, our *right*, to never allow another woodland creature to perish in the clutches of a domestic!" To the roaring cheers, she stepped forward, embracing the power she held in that moment to manipulate the masses. She paused, waiting for quiet to settle in.

"Especially *this* domestic. He has already proven to be a killer. We will *not* let him strike down another among us." As the cheers rose again, Becca felt a chill as she watched the diabolical pleasure spread across Jezebel's face. In that moment, Becca understood she was face-to-face with evil. She would send the entire gathering to their deaths and enjoy it, witnessing animals misguidedly acting in blind hatred while believing they were fighting for a righteous cause, because Jezebel – callously detached from her own daughter's *unconfirmed* death she was boldly waving as the red flag – was purely motivated by her own power over others.

Feeling ill at the scene, and violently missing Marcus at that moment, Becca vowed to take down Jezebel with the Trail Angels, even if it cost her life.

New Hampshire was stunning.

Not even officially in the Whites yet, where Mommy knew the beauty of locations along the trail such as Franconia Ridge awaited them, she was already relishing in the more northern, alpine-feeling views from the coniferous forests, so different from the rest of the trail. After her challenges of the last month, as they rolled into August and the final two states, she basked in her reward of the natural splendor surrounding them.

Ecstatic at Mommy's renewed joy, as they departed Hanover and made their way north toward the Whites hiking over Moose, Smarts and Cube Mountains for a few days, Zoby also stayed on high alert. Their first day hiking in New Hampshire, Uncle Stan had seen a coyote on trail but had scared it off before Mommy and Zoby reached him. Blaze and Chip weren't sure if it was Squirrel Mafia recon, or a coincidence. That first night camping in New Hampshire, Blaze had flown off to the north to meet with a Trail Angel leader flying down from Maine, and the next afternoon he had reported back to them of Jezebel's impassioned rally to stir the masses, uniting them in action against Zoby specifically, as well as all domestics.

And so, despite Mommy and Uncle Stan's delight in their surroundings, Zoby was uneasy as he knew they were actually hiking through enemy territory.

And at any moment, it would become a war zone.

****

That moment came on Mt. Moosilauke.

The day had dawned with sapphire skies and warm sunshine. Excited to officially enter the Whites and hike their first New Hampshire 4,000 footer (there are 48 in the state many peak-bagging hikers enjoy checking off the list, and the AT crosses over or near the peaks of about half of them), Mommy, Zoby and Uncle Stan started off with several thru-hikers they liked to call their extended tramily.

A beautiful Saturday, with the intersecting nobo and sobo thru-hiker bubbles and Moosilauke being a popular day hike, the trail was full of both humans and their domestics. With all the extra people and dogs, Zoby found himself lulled into what turned out to be a false sense of security.

For the first five miles, talking and laughing with their extended tramily, they enjoyed the climb up the mountain, even if it was steep. The only thing to bother Zoby were all the day hikers who didn't believe he had hiked to New Hampshire from Georgia, and kept telling Mommy he wouldn't be able to handle the rock scrambles of the White Mountains. Mommy and Uncle Stan would always reply, "he hikes better than *we* do!" and let it go, but Zoby just couldn't understand why humans were so condescending about his hiking abilities just because he was small. He had watched bigger dogs around him, even that very day on Moosilauke, struggle with what he found relatively easy over the rocks. Saying as much to Chip and Blaze, they agreed he needed to just used the pessimism from ignorant humans as fuel to his fire to make it to Katahdin and prove them all wrong.

Despite those interactions, he joyfully celebrated the 1,800-mile mark with Mommy and Uncle Stan. Spirits were high as they ascended above treeline to sweeping views of staggering beauty in all directions. Cheers rose amongst their friends as they reached the summit, photos were taken, and then many of their friends began the descent, as they were hiking further and backpacking that night in the Kinsman range ahead. Mommy and Uncle Stan were going to a hostel, to slackpack the Kinsmans the next day, so they had extra time to enjoy the summit and views before making the treacherous trek down an extremely steep and typically wet pile of boulders jammed up beside a series of waterfalls down the north side of Mt. Moosilauke.

The afternoon sun warming them and bellies full from lunch, Mommy and Uncle Stan both dozed a bit, lounging across the rocks on the wide, flat summit, as the crowds thinned out. Many day hikers had chosen the out-n-back route that avoids the steep waterfall descent, returning the way they came from the south side of the trail, and their thru-hiker friends had all departed ahead of them by the time they were ready to get going again in the mid-afternoon.

Still a bit groggy from his own nap, as they hiked back below treeline then started the ridgeline descent before the steep mile of waterfall rock scrambles would begin, it took Zoby a bit to realize Chip and Blaze weren't around. Odd, he thought, and for the first time that day, felt a pit in his stomach. Which grew larger as he saw more and more angry squirrels glaring and chattering at him from trees as they passed through.

"Is it just me, or are the squirrels up here bigger and ... well, *crazy*?!" Mommy laughed as yet another sent a shrieking loud chatter through the forest. "What is *with* them?!"

Zoby's eyes darted from side to side across the trail as he saw more and more eyes glaring at him and heard more chatter echoing off the spruce and firs around them.

"What the?..." Mommy yelped in surprise, "I swear, a squirrel is throwing *nuts* at me!"

Ahead of them on the trail, Uncle Stan laughed and tossed back a casual, "I guess they don't like us in their home." Then he continued, "Hey, I think we're starting the descent, I can hear the waterfalls just ahead, and these boulders are getting steep. There's some rebar and wooden stepping blocks built into the rocks up here. You may want to take Zoby off the leash as we work our way through this."

Catching up to where Uncle Stan had stopped, Mommy rubbed her arm and repeated, "I am not kidding, that squirrel was hurling nuts at me, and actually got me! I think it's going to leave a mark," she giggled, shaking her head and laughing it off, "anyway, yeah, you're right. This is pretty steep, and the rocks are wet." Turning to Zoby, she knelt down and unclipped the leash. "Baby boy, you need to stay close to Mommy or Uncle Stan, ok? I know you can do this better than we can," she laughed, "but wait for Mommy and be a good boy."

Carefully picking their way through the boulders and sliding down slippery wet rocks, they reached the start of the waterfalls that ran immediately adjacent to the trail, with no more than about six to ten feet max, oftentimes less, separating the pile of rocks that made up the trail from the swiftly cascading water beside it.

Seeing a larger pull-out that offered a good view of the first set of falls, Mommy and Uncle Stan exclaimed over the beautiful sight and headed over to it for photos.

And that's when it all broke loose.

Taunting Zoby, two enormous fox squirrels burst onto the trail ahead of him, further down the steep descent, showing him what was in their arms. Each burly one was manhandling his friends – now he knew what had happened to Chip and Blaze.

Something snapped inside him. "Noooo!" he yelled as he bounded down the rocks toward them. With their backs turned to the trail and the sound of the waterfall filling their ears, Mommy nor Uncle Stan saw him fly past or realized what was happening.

"No Zoby, it's a trap!" Blaze managed to get out before the oversize squirrel shut him up.

But as Zoby hit the next gear speeding after them anyway, the trees lining the steep trail and waterfall erupted as the woodland Trail Angels hiding in the wings made their presence known. Squirrels, chipmunks, birds and more animals were going one-on-one in their effort to either block or clear the way for Zoby and other Trail Angels to rescue Chip and Blaze.

Nearing what he thought was the edge of another rock pile with more like it below, just before reaching the squirrels holding Chip and Blaze, he made a split-second decision to jump from the edge down to the rocks below that would have him closing in on them fast, rather than take the time to rock scramble down the pile, and let them get further ahead.

Mistake. There were no rocks below.

Instead, the trail took a deceptive sharp turn to the right over tree roots one couldn't see until at that edge, and what was below the edge was open air to the slick, sharp rocks and crashing water of the next series of waterfalls beginning below.

Yelping as he realized his mistake, flying through the air past Chip screaming his name, Zoby frantically twisted his body to find something, anything, to grab onto. And indeed, he saw a large tree root jutting out of a dirt shelf, the last thing he would pass before falling to the water and rocks below. Closing his eyes, he grabbed for it with paws and mouth … somehow managing to get it between his teeth.

Frantically grabbing it with his paws and attempting to pull up, he was slipping on the wet surface of it without a solid grip, and feared it was only a temporary stop in his inevitable fall.
Then two large squirrels literally appeared out of nowhere on the other side of the root and one shoved his face and paws over it toward Zoby. "Give me your paw! Hurry, before they get over here!" Indecisiveness over whether to trust them evaporated as soon as he heard, "Zoby, my name is Marcus. We're here to help. Hurry! They're coming," Marcus said, as he and his friend grabbed at Zoby's paws. Zoby grabbed the root with his mouth again and gave them his paws, and amazingly the two squirrels pulled him up over the branch.

Where he came face-to-face with a great-horned owl easily as big or larger than Zoby himself.

"She's on our team!" Marcus yelled, as he pointed at squirrels coming at them in the other direction, "but they're *not!*"

All of them precariously balancing on the small dirt ledge holding the large root, Zoby suddenly found himself lightly grasped through his hiking outfit in the talons of the owl, quickly flying a short distance over the waterfall to land safely just a bit further down the trail.

Terrified on the few-second flight but looking back, he saw Marcus and his friend battling the other squirrels on the ledge and root. "Help them!" he begged the owl, then added, "and thank you!" The owl nodded and returned to ledge, grabbing the two Mafia squirrels in her talons and depositing them over the ledge.

Looking around, he tried to see where Chip and Blaze were, then heard Marcus calling him, "Zoby, over here!" and finally caught sight of the red feathers of his friend back up the trail above him, behind a pile of rocks that thankfully were on the other side of the waterfall.

Zoby raced to meet Marcus and his friend, and as an angry dog, squirrels and owl simultaneously converged on the two bulky fox squirrels holding his friends captive, the Mafia squirrels saw the outcome clearly. Bravado gone, they cowered at the sight of the owl's talons swooping toward them, the furious dog growling and charging at them, and releasing Chip and Blaze, disappeared through the rock crevices and off into the forest.

"Zoby, look out!" Chip yelled, pointing behind him.

Whirling around, Zoby barely had time to comprehend what was coming toward him. Not Clinton, was the thought flashing through his mind as the fisher cat leaped on him, causing both animals to roll down the rocks. Coming to a stop with the fisher cat on top, Zoby snarled and fought, then froze as he saw the glint of teeth coming at him.

Another set of teeth. Another time. The pain ripping through him.

A pair of talons brushed Zoby's head as they latched on to the face holding the glinting teeth, pulling the fisher cat off him and deeply wounding its face. Screaming in fury and pain, blood filling his vision, the fisher retaliated with claws and teeth toward the owl while Zoby righted himself and shook off the déjà vu of another time and place to take in the current scene.

"Run, Zoby, I've got this," the great-horned owl shouted to him.

"Zoby, over here!" he heard his friends calling him, toward a large recess in the rocks he had just tumbled down.

With the fisher cat letting out blood-curdling screams and temporarily blinded, Zoby nodded at the owl now perched in a low tree branch, and running off, hollered over his shoulder, "You saved my life. Twice. I can't even thank you!"

Reaching his friends, he tucked himself into the cave-like recess, then heard Mommy in a panic yelling for him. "Oh no, you guys, she's hearing the fisher cat and thinks he's got me!" Without waiting for them to respond, he leapt up onto the rocks, racing back up the trail and jumped into Mommy's arms as soon as he reached her.

"Zoby!! Oh my God, oh my God, baby boy. You scared me to death. What *is* that, screaming, is it on the trail?! Oh, I thought it got you, whatever it is. I thought I lost you." Burying her head in his, she kissed him, then pulled back suddenly, looking closely at him and seeing some blood on his white fur around a few cuts in his hiking outfit. "Oh nooooo, no, you *are* hurt! What *happened* to you?"

Uncle Stan reappeared from going down the trail to see what the screaming was. "I think it was a fisher cat," he said, "but it ran off when it heard me. I couldn't get a good look at it."

Looking at Zoby, he pet his ears and also saw the holes in his outfit. Quizzically, he wondered, "what did you *do* without us for a few minutes to get these, buddy?"

"I don't know, but I'm thankful he's here now, and is ok." Setting Zoby down, she told him, "we have less than a mile to go. You're staying on the leash or *right next* to Mommy, ok?!"

That was more than fine with Zoby.

That night at The Notch Hostel, after Mommy had tended to Zoby's cuts and decided they weren't bad enough to require a visit to the vet, and the humans were inside having dinner with their hiker friends, Zoby sat on the porch to their private cabin and formally met Marcus, and the great-horned owl, Sage.

"I am so sorry for everything that has happened because of me," Zoby started, but Marcus cut him off.

"It's not you. It's *not*," he insisted. "It's all Jezebel.

Sage nodded in agreement. "Zoby," she said in her smooth, comforting voice, "Many, *many* are starting to see through Jezebel, but too many still fall to her deceptive charms. And of those who don't, most aren't willing to stand up to her. Not up here in the north. The Trail Angels are gaining numbers here, but it's still a Squirrel Mafia-dominated area."

Zoby looked over at Chip and Blaze, relieved they were not harmed beyond some aches and pains from the ordeal. They had told him how the two powerfully built squirrels had abducted them while they also were dozing during Zoby's summit nap. Thankfully, Chip and Blaze had the entire woodland chain of Trail Angels on high alert, and all were following Zoby's daily progress, ready to assist at any moment. The Mafia bodyguards holding Chip and Blaze knew Zoby would try to rescue his friends, and set the trap with the hopes Zoby would fall over that ledge.

However, no one knew Marcus was in New Hampshire, or that he had been living under the protection of his should-be predator but Trail Angel leader, Sage. To do so, Marcus had also turned largely nocturnal to not only accommodate his guardian's lifestyle, but to stay off the radar of the Mafia, and be able to transmit messages through Trail Talk. Knowing Zoby had crossed the state line, the two had been making their way down the trail in New Hampshire to be ready to fight … and reversed their nocturnal lifestyle the last few days to do so.

Looking back at Sage, Zoby gratefully stated, "You saved my life. Others have along this trail too, but today … when that fisher cat had me and I saw its teeth gleaming, coming at me …" Zoby trailed off, lost in his mind again.

Wisdom being her gift, Sage reassuringly said, "what doesn't kill us really does make us stronger, Zoby. Whatever happened in your past prepared you for today. You are stronger. You are braver. You are an inspiration. Why do you think we fight for you?" Seeing Zoby looking at her in surprise, she smiled and continued, "sure, we are opposing Jezebel and the violence she incites for her own pleasure. But we also are inspired by *you*. Specifically *you*, Zoby." She paused and grinned widely as she added, "small dog, big adventures, right?"

Shaking his head but beaming, Zoby looked at the gathering of his friends. "I think it's time I told you about the time I was attacked …" he began to share his story.

And as he revealed the details of the large neighborhood dog that ripped him open for no reason other than he didn't like small dogs, how he nearly bled to death, how they nearly had Mommy put him down, how he barely survived the surgery, but then went on to heal and become even stronger and more adventurous than before …

… as he shared all this …

He became even braver, stronger, and more important to his friends. This was the dog they'd been waiting for, the one to overturn the Squirrel Mafia for good.

CHAPTER 21

The Great Whites, Part 2

"Incompetent as usual." Fuming, Jezebel kept her back to Becca and her bodyguard. "Do you mind telling me just how, *exactly*, that domestic *and his little friends*, escaped ..." eyes flashing, she whirled to them, "yet *again*? "

The informant stepped forward and simply stated, "they had help. A great-horned owl."

Jezebel narrowed her eyes. "Sage," she hissed out the syllable under her breath.

"Unconfirmed reports are saying that, yes. If indeed her, she was with, we believe, your former informant, Miss Jezebel. Marcus."

Hearing his name, Becca fought flinching at the jolt that ran through her in response, but Jezebel caught the look her in eye just the same.

Taking a step toward the maidservant with her eyes locked on Becca's, she sneered. "Marcus? The imbecile," she spat out, still keeping her eyes on Becca's and inching closer with each word, "he isn't clever or *perceptive* enough to have foreseen the attack, in that location, at that time, with precisely what resources at hand. Wouldn't you agree, Becca?"

Gathering her strength, she held Jezebel's stare. "Of course he's not, Miss Jezebel." After a moment's staring contest, Becca intentionally cast suspicion elsewhere. "The bodyguard team sent from Maine certainly did a lousy job. What *else* did they do?"

Eyes flickering with both appreciation and surprise at Becca's challenge, Jezebel shifted her gaze to her bodyguard. "Yeees," she slowly drew out, "that *is* true. And as they came from your team," she flicked the bodyguard's chest in annoyance, "to say I am disappointed is an understatement."

Taking a step back and holding both in her gaze, she stated, "I am just about out of patience with inept attempts at removing this domestic from the trail. You've been warned."

About the time Becca was being threatened in Maine, Marcus was enjoying his new role joining Chip and Blaze protecting Zoby as they made their way up to Franconia Ridge. All were excitedly chatting with Zoby about how much they loved this section of the trail, and Zoby knew Mommy had long-awaited this hike, eagerly looking forward to this day out of the entire AT.

Unfortunately, the day hadn't started off well for Mommy, though. The rocky terrain of New Hampshire was once again bringing out the foot pain of her plantar fasciitis, and that particular morning had been sheer torture with every step. The flowing tears and anguish on her face as she was passed by every other hiker on trail, some commenting she should take a zero, made Zoby's heart ache, as it also did for his woodland friends. Mommy told Uncle Stan to go on ahead because she didn't know how far she'd make it that day, their planned campsite would be full quickly, and she would catch him that night or in the morning. Zoby knew it was all made worse by the fact their hike this day was one she had been greatly anticipating.

But Zoby was incredibly proud of Mommy for pushing through the agony for several miles over rock scrambles to reach the ice-cold stream that originated right there from the mountain spring just before turning on the approach to the ridgeline. Stopping both to collect water and recover from the stinging, throbbing pain, she soaked her feet. The icy water and round of ibuprofen helped reduce the inflammation as well as numb the pain, so after an extended break, she felt much more capable of continuing on, and enjoying the day.

With a renewed smile on Mommy's face, they were now approaching the exposed, alpine zone summit of Little Haystack Mountain, where they would then traverse the high, serrated edge of Franconia Ridge for nearly two miles across Mounts Lincoln and Lafayette.

Crossing over to the north side of Little Haystack, the trail then cut a clear path across the rocky ridgeline, beautiful in its own right, surrounded by lush green alpine grass and mosses, low bushes and other vegetation. The rising peaks of green stood in sharp contrast around the sand-colored backbone of the trail and its gray-brown rocks lining either side. The sight of the tan-hued AT marking the spine of the emerald ridgeline set against azure skies as the sun sparkled across the stunning scene made Mommy gasp.

Even Zoby had to admit it looked like a National Geographic magazine spread.

"Oh. Oh, it is just *so* beautiful. Everyone was right, it's unbelievable,"

Mommy murmured as she slowly moved forward, just taking it all in. Then laughing in sheer delight, she picked Zoby up and spun in circles, "we made it up here, buddy! Thank you, Jesus for providing healing, and good weather! We can do all things!"

Staying discreetly off trail, Chip, Blaze and Marcus looked at each other and grinned. Seeing Mommy so ecstatically cheerful and giving praise after such a difficult morning made them want to help her and Zoby even more. It was turning out to be a pretty good day after all.

****

After spending an obscene amount of time to go two miles, for Mommy couldn't stop taking photos and videos, they finally were descending Mt. Lafayette off Franconia Ridge. They were supposed to summit one more 4,000 foot mountain in a few miles, Garfield, then meet Uncle Stan at a campsite on the descent from that peak.

But Mommy was exhausted. Physically and emotionally, the day had taken its toll on her. Stopping a mile short, before ascending Garfield, she managed to get enough cell reception to text Uncle Stan her coordinates and make plans to meet up in the morning. Making do with her location by setting up camp on a bit of a muddy slope next to a rather swampy pond, Zoby became anxious. They were completely alone at this site, something they hadn't experienced in over 1,300 miles since hiking with Uncles Stan and Steps, and many times being around other thru-hikers at camp as well.

Voicing this to his friends, they agreed. It wasn't sitting well with them, either, to be completely alone in the midst of Squirrel Mafia territory. Blaze flew ahead to the campsite they were supposed to stop at to return with Sage, whom had agreed to keep a nocturnal watch on them while on trail. This brought Zoby a degree of comfort, but his unease wouldn't subside.

Mommy made dinner for both of them, contacted Uncle Stan one last time, then turned in as the sun was setting, or "hiker midnight" as it was called along the trail. Exhausted, she fell asleep immediately. But in the twilight of the post-sunset glow, Zoby sat up, alert to the sounds around their tent.

"Sage?" Zoby whispered, not sure if his other friends had also turned in.

Chip popped up under the vestibule at the same time the owl responded with her silky, "hoooo ... I'm here Zoby." Chip smiled, quietly unzipped the tent enough to squeeze his little body through and climbed up on Zoby. "It's ok, kid. We're all up, and we've called in reinforcements. Nothing is going to happen tonight, I promise. Get some sleep." Chip popped back over to the tent door and comically blew Zoby a kiss good-night as he zipped it shut.

Right, Zoby thought, like he could sleep. He could *feel* the tension around the tent. Something was amiss, he just knew it.

Several hours later, in the middle of the night, a drowsy Zoby nodding off snapped to attention. He *definitely* heard something walking nearby. Checking on Mommy and seeing she was still sound asleep, he whispered to Sage.

"Keep quiet, Zoby," came her hushed answer, "he's hunting, and not for you. He doesn't see the tent yet."

"What?! Who is *he*?" Zoby replied in a strangled whisper.

Chip popped back under the vestibule with a finger to his lips. "Shhh, Zoby, seriously. Bobcat. Excellent hearing."

As if on cue, Zoby heard the low the growl and chuckle coming from near the pond, too near them, in his opinion. "Zoby? Well, well, well. Seems I have stumbled onto the domestic that has the Trail Talk tongues wagging." The voice outside the tent inched closer as Zoby looked at Chip with wide eyes at the next words from the feline. "I do believe this meeting may be kismet, as Miss Jezebel herself has personally reached out to me."

Sage sent out a series of "hoos" and warned the bobcat, "don't come too near. Just continue on your hunting, or become the hunted."

"Wow, the infamous Sage. I *am* in celebrity midst here tonight," the bobcat mocked. "You know, earlier this evening I couldn't decide whether to listen to – or *eat* – those overgrown squirrels on steroids doing Jezebel's bidding. Perhaps I should have gone with eat, for now I'm hungry. I'm sure there's a certain chipmunk and bird around here now, too."

Alarmed, Zoby stood up and gestured for Chip to leave the vestibule and enter the tent.

But the bobcat continued, pacing wide circles around their tent as he spoke, "But I wouldn't want to upset the Trail Angels, now would I?" Sarcastic chuckles followed. "No, can't have that. I personally don't care about the whole domestic drama, or the Mafia and Angels. I care about the domestics *hunters* bring with them, not *hikers*. To me, hiking dogs are harmless, not trained to hunt, so if it doesn't apply to *me*, I just ignore the Trail Talk. But … well … Jezebel has made an *interesting* offer," he paused right next to the tent and whispered inside it, "and I wouldn't want to ruin the surprise she has planned for you, Zoby."

Walking away, he called out, "see you up the trail."

As the bobcat stealthily slinked off into the night, everyone let out a collective breath. Zoby checked Mommy, still fast asleep. "Guys," he said, "who was that?"

Sage calmly responded, "he knew us. We don't know him. He's a loner cat, most likely. Even as a nocturnal creature myself, I've never seen him before, but don't worry Zoby, we'll find out."

Marcus agreed, popping under the vestibule beside Chip. "I know I'm new to this, but I can offer views from an insider perspective. If Jezebel is making offers, and coming this far into New Hampshire for new resources, that means she either doesn't have her normal recruits in Maine … or … she's lining up multiple resources for a big showdown."

Zoby stared at Marcus. "Is that supposed to make me feel better? Cuz it's not working, if so."

Apologetically looking at Chip who was rolling his eyes, then back at Zoby, he tried a different tactic. "Becca. She will inform us. Sage has an Angel Becca is directly reporting to, who in turn directly reports to Sage. It's almost like being in Jezebel's chamber. We will find out."

Sage hooted again, "we will Zoby. Trust us. Now, get some sleep everybody. I'll keep watch."

Meeting up with Uncle Stan after climbing Garfield just after dawn the next morning, Mommy feeling refreshed after a good night's sleep – which caused Zoby and friends to chuckle when she said it – the tramily hiked on. At lunch, after Sage had napped in the morning, Blaze informed Zoby they were flying north to Maine to learn what they could about the bobcat and any other intel. Chip and Marcus continued along the trail, and enjoyed that night's campsite as much as Zoby, Mommy and Uncle Stan did. One of the best views from a cliffside campsite on the entire trail, they were treated to a spectacular sunrise at Zeacliffs. Later that day they passed two waterfalls – one, Thoreau Falls, becoming Mommy's favorite on trail up to that point – and ended the day catching a ride with a day hiker heading into the town where they were planning to stay that night.

The Presidentials loomed as their next section. From notch to notch, it covers 26 miles, with most of it fully exposed above treeline crossing the highest peaks in New Hampshire, including Mt. Washington, the first peak over 6,000 feet since the Roan Highlands. Boasting wildly unpredictable weather at all times of year, extreme elevation gain and loss, and challenging, rocky terrain, it is one of the most difficult traverses on the entire AT.

Due to so many miles of it being above treeline where there is no camping, most thru-hikers make the rather pricey reservations – or try to do work-for-stay – at one of the Appalachian Mountain Club's huts scattered across the traverse. Essentially large bunkhouses with a kitchen and dining room but no heat or air conditioning, they do not allow dogs. This was something that had been bothering Mommy as to how to handle, because with Zoby being her therapy dog, that made him a service animal. However, she had tried to reach out to the huts multiple times to confirm they would accept a therapy dog as a service animal so she wouldn't have to fight them upon arrival if given a hard time, and had received no response. Their only other option on trail was to blue blaze a couple miles back below treeline to camp, adding several miles roundtrip to already long days of hiking.

That night in the hotel, Mommy and Uncle Stan sat discussing this, as well as the weather forecast for the mountain range. The observatory atop Mt. Washington was calling for thunderstorms and hurricane-force winds the next day, when they were supposed to be hiking it. Between that and the hut situation, they decided to zero out the weather first, then made arrangements with a shuttle driver to slackpack them, two long days, across the traverse by driving up the Auto Road to Mt. Washington, pick them up in the evening, then drop them back off the next morning. Slackpacking also got extra weight off Mommy's feet over this rocky terrain, and off Uncle Stan's double hernia that was beginning to bother him more and more.

Listening to them make plans on their zero while the storms raged outside their hotel, Zoby thought it was all a good idea. He certainly didn't want to be hiking in exposed terrain above treeline in this, *plus* worrying about bobcats, crazy squirrels and who knew what else!

When Mommy took him outside for a break between storms, he talked to Chip and Marcus about it. Blaze and Sage were due to return soon, but Blaze had sent a warning through Trail Talk to be prepared in the Presidentials *that* day – the day Mommy and Uncle Stan had decided to zero out due to the weather.

"So they were going to use the storms to their advantage," Zoby stated, as Chip and Marcus agreed. "Kid, it's a good thing you zero'd – it's dangerous enough up there in bad weather without Squirrel Mafia attacks on top of it," Chip said.

Marcus affirmed Chip's statement, "yes, and whatever they had planned, if I know them, it won't work as well without storms, wind and fog. If the weather clears up like they're calling for, then they'll cancel this attack and to prepare something else further up the trail."

"Zoby, another thing," Chip said, climbing up on the dog's back and hanging upside down over his face, "we're almost to Maine." At that, Zoby broke into a huge smile, but it faded when he saw Chip wasn't congratulating him. "Jezebel's entire community, ground zero for Squirrel Mafia if you will, is right on the trail, shortly after the Maine state line. Trust me, she has *no* plans of letting you get past her home."

"Personally, I think with canceling the Presidentials attack like I believe they will," Marcus confirmed, "they just might sit back and *let* you get to Maine, to be on their home turf … but with *no* intention of letting you get any further."

****

The weather indeed cleared, a little misty and foggy their first day across the Presidentials, but amazingly they had blue skies and no wind at the summit of Mt. Washington for their pictures at the sign, then mostly sunny, clear weather their second day. Mommy detested the grueling, six-mile long, rocky descent off Mt. Madison nearly all the way down to Pinkham Notch, which going slowly and carefully meant they ended the second day after dark. Zoby was just relieved to have gotten through the Presidential Traverse with nary a sign of the Squirrel Mafia.

Returning to trail with full backpacks to attack the Wildcats, the final section of the Whites in New Hampshire, Blaze and Sage rejoined them. Armed with intel from multiple sources in Maine, including Becca (who sent her love to Marcus), they detailed their findings to Zoby and the others at camp that night.

"Mahoosuc Notch. Just as we expected," Sage began, "it's Jezebel's home and the hub for the Squirrel Mafia. All squirrels and other animals living in or near the Notch will be there. Plus their resources – that is, if they are physically able to get into the Notch."

"Physically able to get into the Notch?" Zoby questioned, "what do you mean?"

Solemn, Sage looked at Zoby, "The Notch is a jumbled-up pile of boulders the size of buildings. Literally pieces of the mountains on either side of this gap that broke off and fell into the Notch on top of one another. Additionally, tree roots as large as you can imagine only existing in fairy tales wrap around and through them, creating a cave-like maze, an intricate system of tunnels and dens beneath the boulders and roots. It's extremely difficult for humans – or animals larger than humans such as a bear or moose – to navigate the Notch."

Chip, being Chip, having climbed up on Zoby's back and nestled in, exclaimed, "Hikers like to call it 'the most fun mile, or the most difficult mile' on the entire AT!"

Marcus returned to the story, "having lived there all my life ... well, until recently ... I can affirm it is full of large gaps between and under rocks – big enough to bury a moose alive – and that underneath the surface level of rocks and trail lies a very well-organized community, where Jezebel rules, and very few oppose her."

Blaze chimed in, "Zoby, we've got several days before we'll get there. Becca confirmed that with the Presidentials attack called off, Jezebel agreed to focus on organizing the Notch attack. My opinion is, we focus on our own recruits and counterattack. And in the meantime," Blaze smiled at Zoby, "you just enjoy the time on trail with no Mafia worries. This is one of the most challenging, but beautiful sections. You'll love it if you can relax and enjoy it – and you can. That's a gift, take it. We'll focus on the rest."

Zoby didn't see how, but he promised he would at least try to relax and enjoy their last days in New Hampshire and crossing the Maine state line. Actually, when he thought about it, he could barely believe they were really about to do so ... that he and Mommy had almost hiked from Georgia to Maine!

CHAPTER 22

The Most Fun Mile Or Most Difficult Mile

"Yeah buddy, that's how it's done! Show me and Uncle Stan up," Mommy cheered and giggled as Zoby yet again raced up rocks like a mountain goat. Didn't matter if it was a steeply angled granite slab, a sheer wall with tiny crevices to place your hands and feet, or a nearly vertical pile of jagged boulders – Zoby was zooming up and down all of them with ease. He was loving that it delighted Mommy and Uncle Stan to see him do so, so he played it up for them, even climbing up a vertical wooden ladder secured into a rock façade, completely on his own. Mommy and Uncle Stan were so proud, he couldn't hide his delighted grin as he peered back over the ladder down to Mommy recording him below.

As they worked their way through the final days of New Hampshire toward the Maine state line, the challenging terrain full of rocks and roots made it slow-going, but the dramatic views were magnificent. As a bonus, the mid-August weather at these elevations was warm and sunny, only slightly cool in the mornings, making hiking a pleasure.

They reached and celebrated the 1,900-mile mark just before turning on the officially-marked "Mahoosuc Trail" section of the AT, getting Mommy and Uncle Stan excited because that meant Maine was just ahead! Stopping at a shelter right before the state line to camp that night, Mommy held Zoby in her arms while perched on a rock looking out over the view, and she went back through photos and videos of their journey together. Remembering fun moments, and some not-so-fun moments, she teared up, or smiled and laughed, while Zoby licked her hands, kissed her face, and snuggled into her chest as she reminisced.

Finishing, she put her phone down and holding Zoby up, looked into his sweet face, and said, "it's been one heck of an adventure, with more to come in the next few weeks I know … but baby boy, I am *so* proud of you. We did it! Tomorrow, we will be in MAINE!"

****

Hearing celebratory cheers rising up from the trail ahead of them as their fellow thru-hiker friends passed into Maine, Mommy was choked up well before the sign came into view, but soon as it did, the tears flowed. Uncle Stan was ahead of them with some of their extended tramily, TurtleWizard and Sonar, at the line, applauding and calling out, "come join us in Maine!" Mommy had to pause to gather herself, apologizing to the guys for being so emotional while choking out between tears, "I just can't believe I've walked from Georgia to Maine," … then triumphantly crossed the border with Zoby.

"Welcome to Maine!" came the cheers, with high-fives, hugs and fist bumps.

"Zoby! ZOBY! We're in MAINE!" Mommy laughed and cried at the same time. Wagging his tail and happy dancing, the humans – and the woodland trail angels discreetly gathered – cheered his success and this happy occasion with him and Mommy.

Deciding to sit right there in front of the sign for a break, Uncle Stan and Mommy stared at the "Appalachian Trail: New Hampshire - Maine State Line" imprinted on the wood, and "Katahdin, 282 miles" under it with pleased looks on their faces while they snacked.

"282 miles," Mommy said. "What do you think these final miles will bring us?"

Zoby looked up at his woodland friends. Yes, just what indeed, he knew they were all thinking.

****

Stopping at the shelter just before the start of Mahoosuc Notch that night, Zoby checked in with his "Fearsome Foursome" as he had begun referring to them.

"Hey kid, you're doing great!" Chip bounded over and gave Zoby one of his hugs. "Really showing everyone out here how it's done! And we're all so proud of you to officially be in Maine! You really blew up the betting pool this year, you know," he laughed.

Accepting the congratulations but also recognizing what crossing the border meant, he looked at the other three and stated, "tomorrow morning we're in Mahoosuc Notch."

"Yes, and it will benefit you that there are so many hikers in this bubble camping here at the shelter tonight," Sage confirmed. "A couple dozen humans hiking through the Notch surrounding you could dissuade their plans … a bit."

"Right," Marcus chimed in, "I guarantee they're going to look for a way to get your tramily separated for a bit from the other hikers, and then get *you* separated from your Mommy and Uncle Stan. Becca has provided as many details as she can, and we're thankful."

"Zoby," Blaze flew down to look at him directly, "we are going to keep you safe," he repeated that one more time, "and get you through the Notch. We know the bobcat from the other night will be there, and Becca thinks there may be another as well. The good news she gave us is that most larger predators in the Squirrel Mafia refuse to fight in the narrow, boulder-strewn Notch. But the entire community of squirrels living there will be out en force, a true army ready to battle, and Becca is certain Jezebel has contacted a peregrine falcon resource that lives on Old Speck Mountain, just past the Notch."

Seeing Zoby's agitation at the list of expected enemies gathered in one location, Chip climbed on his back and hugged his neck tightly.

Looking at the quartet of friends surrounding him, Zoby was overwhelmed with simultaneous emotions of both gratitude and fear for their safety. Expressing this, he hugged each one, and digging deep to his reserves to lift his head in bravado, he said, "alright Jezebel, bring it!"

From a hole in a dead tree nearby, Ariana watched the scene. That loathsome domestic had destroyed her life, and nearly taken it. For nearly two months she had burrowed in an old, moss-covered log near the river in Harper's Ferry, slowly healing her broken arm and cracked ribs resulting from the river cascades. To remain hidden, she became nocturnal, and as such, nearly fell victim to predators such as that nauseating owl defending the domestic and befriending her mother's former informant. With no connection to Trail Talk or the Mafia, she had to eavesdrop whenever she could, which wasn't often.

Finally, a few weeks ago she was healed enough to begin the trek from Harper's Ferry to Maine. She had to stay off the trail, taking a circuitous route in order to not be recognized, again depriving her of regular Trail Talk updates. Upon arriving in New Hampshire, she had been able to gather enough intel to track down and follow the despicable domestic and his friends the past several days. She knew her mother was simply *letting* them get to Maine and the Notch, she didn't need anyone to tell her that.

Ariana smiled to herself as she settled in for the night … wouldn't mommy dearest be surprised the next day when baby girl returns from the dead and takes out the domestic?

Zoby pranced around with pent-up, nervous energy as he and Mommy waited for Uncle Stan to finish packing up to get on trail. There was a buzz to the air that morning. He was sure even the human hikers felt it, as all were up earlier than normal and several had already left the shelter area to head to the Notch. Remembering Sage's observation that staying within the bubble of human thru-hikers moving through the Notch would benefit them, he mentally urged Mommy and Uncle Stan to get going.

Once on trail, they entered the south end of the Notch solidly intermingled with a tramily they had leapfrogged for several hundred miles, their friends Happy, Cowbell, MilkyMoo, Painkles and her mom, ShadeTree. A few other hikers were scattered just before and just after them as well. Mommy was laughing with others about "these crazy squirrels in Maine," as they heard their screeching loud chatter echoing off the cliff walls on either side of them, along with some throwing nuts at them. Zoby shook his head at how the humans found it amusing.

He knew Sage was protecting Marcus and had to stay out of sight as much as possible, for Marcus would be viewed by the local community as a traitor. With Chip and Blaze near him every step, despite the chatter and angry pairs of eyes he saw frequently, his nerves were somewhat soothed with all the human hikers around, helping one another climb over, around and under the massive boulders and roots.

Zoby allowed Uncle Stan and Mommy to pass him over larger gaps and giant boulders, figuring he was safer with them doing so, even though he knew he could make it through the obstacle course of the Notch without their assistance.

Pausing a few moments to really look around, Zoby understood why larger animals would have trouble traversing the Notch. A giant "V" between two sharply angled cliffs rising steeply on either side, the extremely narrow space at the bottom was congested by a hodgepodge pile of boulders that really were the size of buildings. Between the massive boulders were tightly throttled openings, many partially blocked by smaller boulders and the fairy-tale sized roots Sage had referred to. Then while climbing over, through and around them, one realizes those openings oftentimes led to deep crevices and gaps, which if one were to fall into, would likely not be able to easily climb back out.

Peering into one of those gaps, Zoby knew an entire underground system of tunnels and caves housed a network of sophisticated animals with one goal: get Zoby off trail.

Suddenly he realized a golden pair of eyes was peering back at him from that gap.

Stumbling backwards, he tangled his paw in a root and wound up with his back pressed against a boulder, facing the gap where the eyes had merged with a face.

A bobcat face.

"Hey Zoby!" Chip called out, unaware of the cat, as he scampered toward him, "your Mommy and Uncle Stan are just over the next boulders, stopping for the water source, but the other hikers are moving on..." trailing off as he saw the fear in Zoby's face when he reached him, Chip spun around just as the bobcat swiped a paw at the chipmunk, sending him flying.

"I don't care about your little friend, Zoby. Besides, Jezebel has promised me a never-ending buffet of whatever my heart desires. No more hunting for me." He paused, grinning at Zoby, "That is, so long as I rid the trail of a certain domestic."

"Zoby, run!" a bruised Chip several boulders over yelled, while he heard Blaze sounding the alarm for the hidden Trail Angels to make themselves known.

But Zoby's back paw was still caught in the root, trapping him to the boulder. As Blaze called for the Angels, two chipmunks appeared, with one continuously hurling nuts and seeds in the eyes of the bobcat, temporarily blinding him, while the other quickly and adeptly untangled Zoby with his nimble fingers. Zoby bolted the second he was free while the chipmunks slunk back into the tiny crevice from which they had appeared. The bobcat blinked away the foreign matter and watering eyes, and then roared in anger when he saw nothing but rocks and roots in front of him.

Running back in the direction he had come – away from Mommy in an effort to keep her safe – the Notch around him broke out in an all-out war. Squirrels were screaming, throwing nuts, and battling one another. Where did Chip go? Jumping from boulder to boulder, slipping and catching himself before falling into any gaps, looking back over his shoulder for the bobcat and trying to find Chip in the chaos, Zoby didn't see the group of squirrels. Two flying squirrels lit upon him from out of nowhere, landing on his back and sides, and two red squirrels came at him from the front. As he went down under the weight of their attack, he heard the bobcat scream from far too close.

The cat swiftly closed in as Zoby rolled and attempted to get free from the squirrels covering him, clawing at him through his hiking outfit and trying to get him to fall down a deep crevice.

"He's mine," the cat hissed in anger, swiping the first red squirrel off

Zoby, digging his claws in to the squirrel in a way Zoby knew was lethal and couldn't help but look away. The two flying squirrels took off, leaping and flying to safety from the bobcat, but the second red squirrel didn't fare the same fate, and as the cat ripped it off Zoby, one of the cat's claws swiped across the side of Zoby's face in a shallow cut, but injuring his eye.

Freed of the squirrels but facing off with the bobcat, under the overhang of the boulder above, Zoby tried to focus through his good eye and shrank back as far as he could without falling into the crevice. In pain, and suddenly furious that at the entire situation he hollered at the cat, "go ahead, do what she's manipulated you into doing for no reason! You said yourself you don't care about *hiking* dogs, only *hunting* dogs! *I* didn't do anything to you! This is all about Jezebel and her power over others, and you're Exhibit A! She's *controlling* you!"

With a sly grin, the bobcat only inched closer, enjoying the game. "Finished?" he taunted.

The bobcat let out a roaring scream, intended for Zoby but changing halfway through to shock and anger as he was suddenly lifted in the air … in the talons of Sage.

"Run, Zoby!" she yelled, as she desperately held on to the furiously writhing, howling cat before dropping him a good 100 yards further back along the trail and up in the cliffs. Swooping back down and giving him two more jabs in the face with her talons, she then returned to the bedlam on the trail below.

Not far from where the bobcat had been deposited by the owl, lower on the cliffs toward the trail, Ariana took in the scene, patiently waiting to make her grand entrance. She had spied her mother, a bit below and to her right, also watching the drama play out.

Meanwhile, Zoby was back to fending off squirrels as he ran through the boulder maze, still looking for Chip. Then he saw his friend, two flying squirrels launching themselves on him as they had Zoby previously. Shaking with anger, Zoby screamed, "get off him!" and grabbed one squirrel in his mouth, sending it flying, while Chip went hand-to-hand with the other. Just as he grabbed the second squirrel himself, he heard Marcus yelling from above him.

"Zoby!" he screamed, "Incoming! Take cover, get under something!"

Too late. The peregrine falcon, the fastest-flying bird in the world, zipped through the air, diving straight for Zoby, clutching him in his talons and taking off again all in a matter of seconds.
But as the falcon tried to exit the narrow, steep bottom of the Notch, he flew straight into Sage and her open talons ready to rip into the falcon.

Dropping Zoby, the birds executed a jaw-dropping mid-air battle. Screeching and clawing, they circled through the air in a deadly dance, flying out of sight.

Heart still racing from the flight that was over before he barely realized it had begun, Zoby dropped his eyes, the one still wounded and hurting badly, from the spectacle above him. He fervently prayed Sage - who had now saved his life four times - would be the victor. And boy was he thankful for his hiking outfit that bore the brunt of the falcon's talons, with only minor cuts on his back from them.

Then raising his eyes, he saw the bobcat again. No, wait, was this a different cat?

Didn't matter, Zoby thought as he scrambled over boulders toward the cliff edge, thinking he could get off trail to safety, then circle back around somehow with trail angel help to find Mommy. Trying to steer clear of the gaps and chasms that seemed larger and deeper in this section, he thought maybe it was his imagination but the squirrel combats around him seemed to be lessoning after the shock of the falcon and owl mid-air clash, too.

Then he came to a dead end and realized he had boxed himself in. The boulder he had just jumped down from was too high for him to make the jump back up. The cliffs rose in front of him, and a deep crevice was on the other side. Nowhere to go.

Panicked, he looked up. No Sage. No trail angel he was aware of to swoop in and save him. And as he thought this, he heard the cackle of maniacal laughter from the boulder he had just jumped from. Zoby looked up to see the bobcat literally purring alongside the largest – and most beautiful – fox squirrel he had ever seen.

"Jezebel," he whispered.

CHAPTER 23

The Most Fun Mile Or Most Difficult Mile, Part 2

Ariana pulled up short, ducking behind a massive root and molding herself to it in an effort to blend in to remain hidden, still on the cliff above the trail of boulders below. When she saw the domestic pin himself against the cliff wall, she thought she had the opportunity she'd been waiting for. She could use the element of surprise at him seeing her alive to her advantage and push him into the crevice, where below she and Jezebel would allow the Squirrel Mafia to enact their revenge. And Ariana could shed the humiliation of failed attempts all spring and especially Harper's Ferry, finally winning her mother's favor.

Then her mother showed her face. With a second bobcat she clearly had woven her magic spell around as the feline was literally acting like a housecat rubbing up against Jezebel, and Ariana swore it was purring.

Despite her complicated feelings toward her mother, Ariana was mesmerized by her abilities.

Hearing a sound above her, she looked up and saw the first bobcat, bloodied from the attack by the great-horned owl, seemingly incredulous – or furious? Or both? – as he stared in bewilderment at the second cat and Jezebel, as always flanked by her bodyguards.

And so she waited, and watched.

****

"Hello, Zoby. It's *such* a pleasure meeting you," Jezebel's voice dripped with disdain. "How kind of you to come to my home, as uninvited as you may be."

Where was Chip, Blaze, Marcus ... any trail angel?! Zoby thought.

Lifting his head and looking at Jezebel, her bodyguards, and the bobcat through one good eye, Zoby replied, "too bad I can't repay the compliment, Jezebel, as it is *not* a pleasure to meet you. And thanks for rolling out the welcome mat."

Throwing her head back in delight, Jezebel laughed. "Oh goodness, you *are* a feisty one." Looking down at him as she pet the bobcat beside her, she cocked her head in interest. "I had been so humiliated that my incompetent daughter as usual was incapable of something as simple as removing you from the trail ..."

Above them, Ariana stiffened and did a slow burn at her mother's words, eyes narrowed in anger as she continued observing the enlightening scene.

Below, Jezebel grinned as she continued, "but now I'm thrilled her pathetic attempts failed and I get to have this pleasure. For it is, a *pleasure*. Or rather, my cat friend here will have the pleasure."

From the cliff, a livid voice called out, "*Which* cat friend, Jezebel?" Infuriated, the first cat leapt down ledges until he was directly above Zoby staring across at the grouping on the boulder. "Did she make the same deal with you?" he taunted the second cat.

Zoby pressed himself as flat against a shadowy part of the cliff as he could, desperately trying to figure a way out of this situation that was about to explode.

As the cat taunted above, he heard coming from his side below a whispered, "Zoby! Down here!"

Daring to look away from the drama unfolding above him, he could just make out a squirrel. Then a second popped up beside the first. "It's Marcus. And Becca." He said, then added, "we are working on a distraction up there, so you need jump down here then."

Quickly looking back up, he spoke out of the corner of his mouth back to them, "I think there already *is* a distraction happening up there."

The first bobcat was in a fury and bellowing at Jezebel for double-crossing him. "You're *done*," he growled at her and in an outburst of rage, he leapt across the gap with her in his sights.

The second cat jumped to protect her, but the first was larger, and fueled by passion, easily heaved the other off the boulder back toward the trail, crashing into the rocks below. Turning to Jezebel, the bobcat hissed.

"*Now,* Zoby!"

Closing his eyes, Zoby jumped into the dark abyss.

Above him, as the cat lunged for Jezebel, in a blur and from an angle no one except someone sitting above could clearly see, Jezebel spun and threw one of her bodyguards in the cat's fearsome fangs and claws, as she scrambled down the rock to disappear in a small gap between the boulders.

From her perch above, Ariana saw it all clearly.

And something deep inside her memory started to unlock. Fuzzy images she had forgotten blurred her vision, images she couldn't quite make out, and then just as quickly faded.

Shaking her head to come out of the fog, she realized the scene below her, and indeed the entire trail around her, was now quiet and empty.

Hitting a slippery rock incline not all that far after he jumped, Zoby slid and bumped his way down in the darkness until he hit bottom with an "oomph."

"Hello?" he softly called out.

"Shhh. Over here."

Eyes adjusting to the darkness, and one still watering, Zoby shook his head, "I can't see."

A pretty squirrel appeared in his vision, nose-to-nose with him and whispered. "Then you'll have to feel, and do your best." Taking his paw, she said, "I'm Becca, and we're getting you out of here. No lights, no talking … we're taking the servant's tunnels, and we have to hurry."

With Becca on one side and Marcus on the other, they swiftly and quietly hurried him through a mind-boggling maze of tunnels, with twists and turns and ups and downs he never would have been able to escape from on his own. After several minutes, it got substantially colder, and he heard water running.

"We're almost there," Marcus whispered in his ear, "Chip and Blaze are out there, trying to distract your Mommy, but it isn't working. She's freaking out looking for you."

Zoby's heart hurt. Her face had flashed in his eyes multiple times in this ordeal, wondering if he'd see her again and how much she would suffer and cry for him if he disappeared, and didn't make it. "Please take me to her," he whispered back, "I ran the other direction to keep her safe today. I can't stand it that she's scared something has happened to me."

Coming to the water source, it got loud as water pumped straight from the mountain, ice cold and crystal clear. On the back side of the spring was a very small tunnel. Zoby looked skeptically at the squirrels.

"You can fit," Becca assured him, "and Marcus will lead you." Looking at him, she put her hand on his face, "We didn't get to say good-bye before. I'm thankful we do now." Drawing him close and laying a soft kiss on his lips, she pulled back with eyes full of tears. "Go, hurry. Before anyone sees you."

Marcus said good-bye and turned into the tunnel as Zoby squeezed, barely fitting, after him and headed out to safety.

Becca stood there a moment, her heart breaking, allowing herself to feel the pain. Only for this moment. Straightening her shoulders and wiping her eyes, she turned around to head back.

And nearly collided with Jezebel and her bodyguard.

"He was right behind me, I mean just a step or two behind me, and we got here to the water and I turned around and he was *gone*!" Mommy was crying and talking too fast. "It was only a minute! He had to have fallen into one of these holes. He *had* to have, we've looked and called for him, he *always* comes to me, and he *isn't*! I'll never forgive myself. Never! He's down there somewhere lost and crying without me…" she was working herself into a panic attack, even from within the tunnel Zoby's training kicked in, and he could smell the oxygen level change in her blood as her breath caught and she began hyperventilating.

"Go Marcus, get ahead of me, run out of the tunnel, fast!" Zoby commanded.

With Marcus out, seeing the light and Uncle Stan and another hiker gathered around Mommy, Zoby let out a series of barks and whines and yips, causing Mommy and the hikers to all look up and over toward the source of his noises.

He flew out of the opening into the light and straight to Mommy, going right to work on calming her down. She was all he could think about.

"Zoby!" Mommy and Uncle Stan were crying his name over and over. Mommy just held on to him while Zoby kissed her tears, and Uncle Stan was petting him and choked up, too.

"Baby boy, oh my baby boy. Where were you? I was so scared. We couldn't find you! I thought you were gone, oh my baby boy," Mommy was still too worked up, and her breathing was still funny, but Zoby could sense she was starting to pull out of it. Just a little more time and a lot more love, he thought, giving her both.

As she calmed down, she realized he had wounds, especially that his eye was watering and there was a scratch alongside it. Carefully examining him and trying to flush it out with the clear water from the Notch, she and Uncle Stan agreed they needed to get him to a vet. For once, Zoby didn't mind going to the animal doctor, because he agreed he needed some medicine.

After Mommy was okay again, and they were putting on their packs to continue their way out of the Notch, Chip and Blaze came over to Zoby.

"Hey kid, told ya we'd get you out of here today." Chip punched Zoby lightly on his shoulder, chuckling. Zoby gave him a fake glare in return, "let's not have so many close calls next time if you can swing it?"

Blaze and Marcus looked at each other and agreed, "and there *will* be a next time."

After hiking over Mahoosuc Arm and Old Speck Mountain, they ended their eventful day at Grafton Notch, where Mommy hailed her first hitchhike while holding Zoby. Two ladies, Annaliese and Kim, who recognized Mommy – or more accurately, Zoby – from her vlog and social media, stopped and took them all into Andover, Maine to The Cabin hostel. Run by the sweetest 90-year-old woman and AT legend, "Honey," a dog-lover herself, she immediately took a liking to Zoby, and helped them make a vet appointment for the next day.

As they were claiming their bunks in the private front room, Mommy and Zoby heard familiar voices calling to them … Auntie StickyBuns, her dad Bouncer, and dog Aussie were at the hostel!

After excited hugs and introductions to Uncle Stan, Mommy learned that StickyBuns was now section hiking, and with family in Maine they were up there doing a section.

Aussie was excited to catch up with Zoby, asking where Chip and Blaze were, and how things were going with the Squirrel Mafia. Zoby just chuckled and to answer, led Aussie outside for the nightly recap with his Fearsome Foursome.

"It wasn't all that dramatic after that initial confrontation," Sage was relating to the others the falcon encounter as Zoby and Aussie joined, "he was only after you, Zoby, and wasn't interested in getting hurt or dying over it. I gave him a few jabs just to make it clear he better leave you alone, or he *would* get what he wasn't interested in, and so would his family," Sage winked.

"Everyone kinda scattered after that though," Chip told Sage, "I mean, it was a pretty awesome, and fearsome, sight to see two birds of prey duking it out mid-air." Chip mimicked a boxing match, or some mix of martial arts, as he kicked and punched, yelling, "hi-yah!"

"Everyone scattered except the bobcats and Jezebel," Zoby muttered.

"That bobcat turning on Jezebel was one of the craziest, if not *the* craziest, things I've ever seen. We'll hear from Trail Talk how everything went down after we got you out and back to your Mommy," Marcus said, "and it will probably be a day or two before we hear from Becca directly again. She'll need to lie low." Marcus' voice grew softer as he remembered saying good-bye.

Zoby went over to Marcus and put his nose to his, then lay down beside him. "She is brave, and special, and I am indebted to her as she saved my life today. You both did." Looking at the group, he added, "you all did."

"Zoby, Aussie! Come on in," Mommy and Bouncer were calling.

Looking at his friends, Zoby expressed his gratitude again. "Alright, night guys, get some rest. Got a zero tomorrow and my doctor appointment. Love you all."

"Love you too Zoby, good night," came the responses.

CHAPTER 24

The Notch Fallout

"Well, this little guy here sure is a trooper," the vet exclaimed, giving Zoby love. "What a champ, hiking all these miles from Georgia!" Looking at Mommy and Uncle Stan, she said, "He's got a few small cuts on his body that are already scabbed over and healing, nothing to worry about there. The wound near his eye avoided any serious injury to the eye itself. Just a small scratch on his cornea that is slightly infected, so it's probably painful for him, and he needs to stay off trail several days to ensure no foreign objects get in his eye. Give him these eye drops twice a day, let him rest so his body can heal, and call me if anything comes up. He'll be fine and back to hiking soon!"

Relieved, Mommy held Zoby and kissed him. "You're such a good boy. We're gonna do just what the doctor ordered for you, ok?" Looking into his eyes, she was so thankful he didn't have a serious eye injury, or was blinded by … well, whatever had happened to him.

Zoby on the other hand, was not happy to be told to stay off trail for several days, not when it might make Jezebel think she had won and they got off trail for good. He was going to need to talk to his Fearsome Foursome about this. In the meantime, the treats Mommy and the vet were giving him made up for that news and the never-enjoyable doctor visit.

"So what's the verdict?" Aussie asked as they returned to Bouncer's car, as he had taken them to the vet that day.

"I have to get off trail a few days," Zoby grumbled, "and I don't want that witch thinking she won."

Aussie gave him a sympathetic look, then encouraged him, "she knows she didn't. And you can trust your Fearsome Foursome to let Trail Talk know, so it gets back to her."

That did cheer Zoby up. A little. He *hated* getting off trail now.

Honey had already told them she would allow Zoby to stay behind in their private room if he needed time off trail to heal, then Mommy and Uncle Stan could continue on by slackpacking the next few days, returning to The Cabin each night. Deciding that would be best, they went ahead and booked the hostel. Mommy was trying to figure out if they could slackpack the entire way north to Rangeley, where they had already arranged to meet their friends Mike and Julie, who planned to set up at a road crossing doing trail magic, then take them into town.

Studying her FarOut app and planning routes, Mommy asked Uncle Stan and Bouncer, "four days of slackpacking if we can do it the whole way to Rangeley, plus today's zero. That should be plenty of time for Zoby to heal, don't you think?"

The men agreed, Uncle Stan adding, "I got the impression Mike and Julie were gifting us a night at a hotel in Rangeley. If that's the case, we could add a nero. Stay at the hotel until checkout, then do a short day in the afternoon to start the Saddlebacks."

Touched, Mommy replied, "Julie said something about a hotel but I didn't realize they were gifting it –" she cut herself off as Julie replied to her text, and she laughed, "but what timing. She just sent me a link to a hotel confirmation for us in Rangeley. Ooooh it's on a *lake*! Oh my gosh, how wonderful of them to do this!"

"Well, you guys are certainly platinum blazing southern Maine," Bouncer laughed, "but this terrain is tough, and you've got an injured hiker," he smiled at Zoby, "so if you're gonna do it anywhere on the trail, this is a good section!"

"So five and a half days total then, for Zoby to heal up. That will be good," Mommy said.

Zoby sat up and stared at her. Five and a half days?!

Helplessly he looked at Aussie, who shrugged back. What could they do? Zoby was temporarily off trail.

****

"We haven't heard from Becca, but it's only been a day," Marcus was saying later that afternoon, "but if I know Jezebel, she's going to want to enact her revenge on you sooner rather than later."

"There's already Trail Talk about her 'failure' in the Notch," Blaze added, "and she's not going to care for that. So let's think through how this time off trail will be seen by her, and how we can use that to our advantage..." Blaze trailed off thoughtfully.

From his spot lounging on Zoby's back, Chip was laughing to lighten the mood a bit, "well the kid here is going to get into central Maine without having to hike southern Maine, so that's not a bad thing!"

While the others rolled their eyes, Sage saw the wisdom there. "No wait, you're right. Zoby *will* be in central Maine. We spin it with the focus on not only her failure in the Notch, but that by injuring him, she actually *enabled* him to get further up the trail ... and there's nothing she can do about it. It backs up the Trail Angels objective by showing that needless violence over presumed injustices never wins."

Zoby looked at his friends. "But ... this isn't over. Soon as I'm back on trail, she'll try something else."

"Exactly," Blaze, Sage and Marcus said in unison.

Confused, Zoby looked through the top of his eyes at Chip hanging over his head. The chipmunk shrugged. "Um, enlighten us?" Zoby requested of the trio.

Chuckling, Blaze fluttered down to Zoby's side and jokingly flipped his wing at Chip. "You're slacking, buddy." Looking at Zoby, he said, "momentum shift. Like in sports, when the crowd's energy flips from one side to the other, the team on the field performs the impossible comeback and wins the game. Like that, your Notch victory, plus spinning your injury and time off trail the way Sage suggested, gives us the opportunity to potentially get disenfranchised Squirrel Mafia to flip sides – like the first bobcat clearly did on his own yesterday – and as a bonus, time to rally the local Trail Angels in central Maine."

"When – and I do mean *when*," Sage put in, "she attacks again, we'll be ready."

"Plus, Marcus added, "we have Becca's intel. We'll be prepared. No surprise attacks."

Feeling better, Zoby stretched and sent Chip rolling off his back. "Well then, while you guys are out there fighting a war ... I'll be in the infirmary sleeping for five and a half days." With a laugh, he lightly grabbed Chip in his mouth and returned him to his back. "Come on, slacker, let's go take a nap."

Three days. Judging by the light and looking at the third hash mark she had just drawn on the wall beside her, it had been three whole days now, Becca thought to herself. Since that fateful moment she turned around into Jezebel's murderous glare, Becca knew her sins against her would be punished in malicious and torturous ways.

For three days she had been held in a tiny cell far below the Notch, a crevice barely large enough for her body, sealed off by a heavy stone door. Near the source of the deep mountain spring, it was damp and freezing, and the constant dripping around her being the only sound she heard for days was literally about to drive her mad. She'd been given no food or water, and the lack of sustenance was making her weak and dizzy on top of the constant shivering and numbness from the cold.

Her only visitor had been a bodyguard, coming to do Jezebel's bidding. Through various forms of physical punishment of which she now bore the cuts and bruises, he had been directed to retrieve Trail Angel intel from her.

Becca refused to talk. She hadn't uttered one word. She would die before betraying Marcus, Zoby and the others.

And dying, she knew, was a distinct possibility.

In a secret den of her own, Ariana waged an inner battle each day and night as she fought to either unveil the gray mist to clearly see the images crowding the edges of her mind, or in frustration and slight fear, push them back to remain obscured.

She knew without a doubt seeing her mother push the bodyguard in front of her – straight into the jaws of the bobcat while she fled to safety – had started to unlock something. What, she wasn't so sure she actually wanted to remember. If indeed, there *was* something to remember.

But she couldn't deny Jezebel's clearly stated words about Ariana. She heard them echoing in her mind, *"pathetic, incompetent, humiliated, failure…"* While she had known, deep down, that's how her mother felt, she still suffered the slow shredding of her heart as the truth penetrated. All this time, she had still held hope to find her mother's approval, that child-like desire for her mother to be proud of her. Instead, she had seen the opposite. Ambivalence toward her supposed death. Indifference. If anything, annoyance *she* now had to rid the trail of the domestic due to her "pathetic, incompetent" daughter's failure.

Between the flitting half-memories and the shock of seeing and hearing Jezebel's apathy toward her sinking in as reality, Ariana was torn, undecided how to continue on.

While Mommy and Uncle Stan slackpacked their way through southern Maine, the Trail Angels set about their jobs getting Trail Talk talking. Informing the woodland chain Zoby had a minor injury as a result of

Jezebel's thirst for violence, they assured all that he was healing and more important, would be returning to the trail with his humans in central Maine. Doing this, they rode the momentum shift, convincing those animals already upset violence was becoming the norm on the trail to jump sides. Never before had a domestic divided the forest so deeply, but the stronghold Jezebel held over Maine was slowly starting to release its grip after the Notch.

Their biggest concern was the silence of Becca. She had missed her regularly scheduled meeting with Sage, and had not sent word indirectly otherwise.

Sage had finally been able to hear directly from a reliable source no one had seen her since that morning. Marcus was withdrawn and distant, fearing what Jezebel may have done If she discovered Becca had aided them out of the underground tunnels of the Notch.

Chip largely stayed with Zoby at The Cabin each day, the comical chipmunk keeping Zoby's spirits up while he waited and worried. He hated feeling so useless. He didn't like being away from Mommy and Uncle Stan on trail, and he detested the news that Becca was missing.

Saying as much to Chip, and Blaze who had joined them the morning of the fifth day, Zoby wondered to his friends why Jezebel wasn't making it known what had happened to Becca.

"What do you mean?" Chip asked. "She's not going to publicize it if she's torturing her maidservant."

"Hold on," Blaze said thoughtfully, "you're right, Zoby. Unless Becca *is* actually giving her information about the Trail Angels – which I don't think she is," he quickly added, "Jezebel would deem her useless otherwise. And a traitor. With Mafia detractors on the rise – and Jezebel has to know that – it would make more sense for her to use Becca as an example to the masses. That her own servant, her *friend, her confidante*, has betrayed not only her, but the legacy of her husband and daughter. She would rally the Mafia to get behind punishing Becca, and anyone *else* who is deemed a traitor. 'Betray me, betray all!' And as a result … well, die?"

Zoby and Chip stared at Blaze.

"We can't let that happen!" Zoby shouted, angry for his new friend. "Becca and Marcus saved my life! They should be able to be together, not caught in all of this!"

Blaze gazed sorrowfully at Zoby. "We may be too late."

****

That afternoon, Zoby was taken to Rangeley along with Mommy and Uncle Stan's gear, via Mike and Julie, to the quaint hotel on the lake they had been gifted for a night. Set up at the trailhead doing trail magic, when Mommy and Uncle Stan finished their slackpack and reached Route 4, they happily hugged and reunited with their friends, and of course with Zoby. Dinner in town together followed, and while Zoby had been putting on his happy face for Mommy, he didn't have to pretend when she bought him a burger all his own.

Every night at the end of their hikes, Mommy had curled up with Zoby and her phone, showing him pictures and videos from the day so he could see and "hike" it with her. He loved those moments with Mommy, her exclaiming over the beautiful views from the Baldplates, the rushing waters of Dunn Falls, the terrible climbs and wet river crossings, and then her favorite, popping out from a particularly nasty climb up to Route 17 and the stunning views from an overlook called Height of Land. She had pointed to the lake in the pictures and told him they'd be staying there the following night in a hotel … and now that night was here.

Walking outside while Mommy took pictures, he spent a giddy moment pretending to chase the dozens of ducks lining the lake, then looked around for his Fearsome Foursome. Not seeing anyone, he shrugged it off seeing as how they had to travel to the hotel from the trail via foot or wing, not in a car like he had, he thought with a chuckle.

"Zoby! *Zoby*!" Blaze was practically dive-bombing him as he flew across the lake toward him. Out of breath, the red bird dropped beside him. "It's Becca."

Earlier that morning, just after she weakly scratched her mark for day number five, a sick, shivering and starving Becca had barely been able to hold her head up when the door opened.

There stood Jezebel, petting the bobcat who had fallen under her spell like a kitten.

"Just what *exactly* did you think I meant," she asked in an icy cool voice dripping with disdain, "when I said, 'don't do anything you'll regret?'"

Becca held her gaze but refused to open her mouth.

"What's the matter?" Jezebel softly chuckled as she nudged the bobcat beside her forward, "cat got your tongue?"

With a hiss, the cat walked right up to Becca and stood an inch from her, mouth open, fangs glinting.

"You see, Becca…" Jezebel walked around the cat to put her finger under Becca's chin and lift her face toward her, "you're only useful to me until you're not. And now, you're not. But to complicate matters, you're not only useless, but you betrayed me."

Crouching down to stare eye-to-eye with her, Jezebel leaned in as she said, "and now I have to make an example out of you."

Nodding to her bodyguard, she quietly commanded, "take care of it," as she walked away. The bobcat gave one more hissing half-lunge toward Becca before following her.

Becca had only a fleeting thought of her final moment with Marcus before her world went dark.

"What we know is," Blaze was telling Zoby, "Jezebel called an assembly, just a little bit ago. She did exactly what we predicted. She had a beaten, starving, sick and barely alive Becca on stage with her," Zoby cringed and his heart hurt at that, "and she used Becca as her pawn to rile everyone up due to her betrayal, of course playing the Ariana and Ahab card, but moreso using her to instill fear in anyone who had thoughts of detracting."

"And Becca? What happened to Becca?" Zoby whispered.

"She let the crowd decide," Blaze dropped his head, "and being so misled, they chose her … her … demise," he finally choked out. "The guard took her off stage, and that's all we know."

Zoby hung his head as tears came. This had gone way too far. Looking up at Blaze with steely grit in his eyes behind the tears, he growled, "This. Ends. NOW."

CHAPTER 25

A Savior Moose and "Celebrity" Crush in Central Maine

The following afternoon, a fully healed Zoby returned to the trail with Mommy and Uncle Stan, heading north from Rangeley into the Saddlebacks. Surrounded by his Fearsome Foursome as he hiked, he knew everyone was on high alert following the uproar Jezebel had created with her assembly the night before.

A short while later, they completed their nero by arriving at the campsites around a pond popular with hikers. This set them up to hike across the exposed, above-treeline Saddleback range in the morning, and offered a lovely evening on the pond with sunset mountain views reflecting in its waters.

"Zoby, come here!" he heard Chip whispering, gesturing excitedly for Zoby to join him in the direction where the pond angled away from their site in a small cove. Looking back at Mommy, seeing she was chatting with Uncle Stan and other hikers, he followed.

And widened his eyes in surprise at the largest animal he'd ever seen in real life, an enormous bull moose wading in the small cove where his friends were gathered.

"Zoby, meet Maverick!" Chip was practically doing cartwheels. "One of our favorite Trail Angels that we hardly ever get to see!"

Coming over to the edge of the lake, Maverick lowered his head, and that impressive rack, to the ground near Zoby to meet him at eye level. "Hello, Zoby," his deep voice surprisingly soft and gentle for such a large animal.

His first time seeing a moose in the wild, and not from the car with Mommy, Zoby stared in transfixed wonder at the thick, wide, tree branch-like rack curving up from the bull's head above his powerfully built, muscular body.

Nudging Zoby, Chip giggled, "it's your turn to say hello. Repeat after me, 'Hello, Maverick,'" he said while climbing up onto those branches sprouting from Maverick's head.

Still wide-eyed but smiling, Zoby said, "I am certainly glad you're one of the good guys, Maverick. It's nice to meet you."

"Likewise, it's nice to put a face to your name. You've become a bit of a celebrity, you know, Zoby," he said with a chuckle and twinkle in his eye, "I've been hearing of your exploits for months now, and it's an honor to help keep you safe here in Maine."

"Wow," Zoby was taken aback by the praise, "I really had no idea. I'm grateful for your support."

"Zoby," Blaze flew over and landed beside Chip in the palm of Maverick's antlers, "we don't know exactly where or when, but we can be sure she's going to wage another attack. Whatever it is, Maverick will be there to help, he's following us along the trail now nearly the rest of the way to Katahdin."

"Without Becca," Chip started then cringed as he saw Marcus' face, "sorry. Without a direct source, we just have to be prepared at all times. Between Sage and Maverick, we've got a tough-to-beat lineup!"

Zoby smiled at his friends perched upon the giant moose, and over at the others in the tree beside them. Humbled he wondered, "well what can I say in response to this?"

"How about …" sticking his chest up and throwing his head up, causing Blaze to take wing and sending Chip into the shallows of the pond, Maverick continued, "small dog, big adventures!"

Laughing at a soaked Chip, and with Blaze landing safely on dry ground beside Zoby, he obliged. Puffing out his chest, he struck his infamous pose with his head up, "small dog, big adventures!"

That night and most of the next day it rained, socking in views from the Saddlebacks and making the bouldering descents from peak to peak across the range more dangerous. Their day ended with a treacherous river crossing, the normal stepping stones well under water with the river swollen from all the rain. Mommy put Zoby in his carrier, strapped to her front, and with his head out, he watched the turbulent whitewater of the river pass beneath him while Mommy carefully picked her way across the knee-to-waist high water. Nearly 2,000 miles in, and he was still not a fan of rushing rivers.

Camping beside a waterfall after that crossing, Mommy and Uncle Stan were delighted to be with their thru-hiker friends Detour and Fireball, also setting up camp with them and planning to hike the next couple days together to end that section at The Maine Roadhouse hostel. With the day's rain finally stopped and everyone hanging out gear to dry, the soothing sound of the waterfall nearby and Mommy's laughter with friends ringing through the camp, Zoby felt himself drifting off after his first full day back on trail.

The next couple days were similar, with strong rain showers off and on, making the trail muddy and slick, and rivers high on their banks. Despite the ever-present loud chatter of the crazy squirrels in Maine, and the occasional nut being thrown at them, Zoby felt the comfort of his friends right alongside him on trail, and he saw Maverick one time during the day when he was in a pond they stopped at for lunch. Much to the human's delight, he obligingly posed for photos with the sun streaming through the just-breaking up mist after a rain, the golden rays silhouetted against his muscular body and rugged rack.

They were close to finishing up their final day in this stretch, with Zoby wondering how they had managed to avoid any Mafia confrontations, when it happened.

Mommy was hiking slower than Uncle Stan, Detour and Fireball, especially on a slippery, steep descent at the end of their hike, so the others had gotten a bit further ahead when they reached the river. Bloated well beyond its normal size, the bouldering stepping stones hikers had been using for crossing were literal rapids instead, as the footbridge had been destroyed by beavers that week. Someone had placed a board from the largest boulder on one side to the largest on the other side, creating a makeshift – but dangerous – bridge. One wrong step or loss of balance, and one would be in the rapids beneath, potentially swept downriver.

Looking down at Zoby, Mommy said, "I think I'm gonna need to carry you over this one, baby boy."

Feeling a surge of bravery and wanting to impress her, Zoby held his head high, and started out onto the board ahead of Mommy.

"Oh, really?" Mommy laughed, "that's how it is, huh? You're just going to show me how it's done, aren't you? Look at you, all brave with a river crossing now."

She followed him onto the board.

Ignoring the sound of the crashing water below them and keeping his eyes on the boulder ahead, Zoby and Mommy made it over halfway across when the bobcat appeared.

Mommy had her eyes down on the board, and with the sound of the cascading water, didn't hear the warning growl and hiss the cat emitted from the boulder on the other side. But looking straight ahead, Zoby saw the cat and recognized him as the one with Jezebel in the Notch.

Stopping abruptly, Zoby nearly made Mommy trip over him. Already off-balance, she looked up – and saw why Zoby had stopped. The bobcat had his fangs glistening in the late afternoon sun and was clearly ready to pounce.

Letting out a blood-curdling scream, Mommy tried to catch her balance and pick up Zoby at the same time – causing them both to tumble off the board, just as the cat jumped toward them.

Hitting the water and rocks below, Mommy was able to quickly grab a boulder and pull herself up, able to stand in the waist deep water ... but realized a sharp rock had cut the leash tethering Zoby to her. Screaming his name in search for him, she saw him as the current sucked him past her but she couldn't reach him.

"Zoby! *ZOBY*!" Mommy screamed helplessly in panic and terror.

Meanwhile the bobcat had leapt off the board and across the river, now hopping from boulder to boulder alongside and within the river, following Zoby.

Although not a huge fan of water or swimming, Zoby *could* swim – and he was doggy-paddling for his life now – but he had never been caught in the current of a swiftly flowing river. The rapids near the board had been brief, and although scary, he was now just focusing on keeping his head afloat, while dodging – or hitting – rocks along the way. Out of the corner of his eye, he saw the bobcat ahead of him on a rocky section that was going to turn into a set of rapids that Zoby wasn't sure he could get through as easily as the first set. He could still vaguely hear Mommy screaming up river, and Uncle Stan's voice had joined hers. Her tears ripped at his heart. He *had* to figure out how to get out of this current, and safely away from the cat.

That was solved for him when Maverick appeared, his powerful body charging upstream as if there were no current or rapids whatsoever. Storming forward, he lowered his head to charge the bobcat, who emitted a piercing scream before leaping away at the last second. Reaching Zoby, Maverick lowered his head again while commanding, "grab on," swiftly and adeptly scooping him up in the basin of his rack like a captain scoops fish in a net.

Moving to the edge of the river, Maverick set Zoby on its bank as his Fearsome Foursome surrounded him, all talking at once.

"Where's the cat?" Zoby asked, ignoring them and looking around wildly. "He didn't go for Mommy, did he?" Shivering from more than being wet, he felt his heart stop, thinking about the bobcat hurting Mommy when she was already so upset over Zoby's safety at the moment.

"No, he ran the other way, and you didn't see them, but the beavers who destroyed the footbridge were waiting for you to cross, in case you made it, as well." Blaze answered him. "But right now, we need to get you to her."

"Not for nothing kid, but you're not much bigger than me with all your fluffy hair wet," Chip laughed, in an effort to brighten the mood.

"CHIP!" Blaze, Sage and Marcus admonished him in unison.

Shaking his head, Zoby just looked at Maverick. "Can you take me a bit closer upstream to Mommy? I can hear her, and Uncle Stan and now Detour and Fireball, calling for me and getting closer, they must be walking down the river."

Maverick nodded, "Climb aboard."

Doing so, they headed upstream to where, as they were about to come around a bend, they would have ran into them. Quickly heading to the river's bank, Maverick lowered Zoby, who took off around the bend to Mommy.

"Zoby! Oh my God, you're here, you're safe, you're alive! You got out of the river! How?! Oh I don't care, I just care you're safe and here with me!" Mommy was babbling in her relief, laughing and crying and holding Zoby tight. Uncle Stan even took Zoby from her to hold him tight and did his own babbling bit of hugs and kisses in relief. Detour and Fireball held Mommy and hugged her, wiping her tears away while they reassured her all was well now.

Then Mommy gasped and pointed. "Guys, *look*! Bull moose! Like, right in front of us! And he's *huge*!"

Sending Zoby a wink, Maverick held his head high, then casually walked across the river and disappeared into the woods, as if he just happened upon the scene and hadn't actually been Zoby's savior.

"And we didn't get a picture!" Uncle Stan laughed as he passed Zoby back to Mommy.

Nuzzling Zoby, she counted the blessings down, "I'm taking that as a good sign. The bobcat didn't do anything other than scare us into the river. We're both wet and banged up but otherwise fine. And we got to see a moose. We passed the 2,000-mile mark. We are getting picked up in a half mile by the Maine Roadhouse, where we can dry everything out. We're planning to go into town to have fresh Maine lobster. Yeah, we're good. We're real good."

****

"Oh. My. *Gawwwwd*, it's you. It's really *you*! You're Zoby! You're the dog everyone has been talking about. I can't believe you're actually here, and you're staying with *us*!" If the heart-eyed emoji had a real-life equivalent, the female maltipoo named Bentley belonging to "the Jens" – the Maine Roadhouse owners both named Jen – was it.

Still damp, and sitting on Mommy's lap in the middle backseat of the shuttle, Zoby cautiously returned the starry-eyed Bentley's gaze. "oooh-kaaay," he said, backing up into Mommy's chest as Bentley leaned into him from the console between the front seats, "maybe you can give me a little space here?"

Ignoring him, Bentley gushed, "I've been hearing stories, and saw you on your Mommy's YouTube channel! Did you *really* throw Ariana into the river? And you almost got *eaten* by a bear? And you've dodged coyotes and foxes, and bobcats and fishers and falcons, and –"

Mommy and Jen burst into laughter as Bentley fell off the console into the back as she had been inching closer and closer, completely mesmerized by Zoby. "I think someone has a crush," Mommy giggled as she picked Bentley up and set her back on the console.

Rolling his eyes but being polite, Zoby asked Bentley, "how do you hear all this?"

"Oh I know all about Trail Talk, the Mafia and the Angels! I met Chip and Blaze once, when they were in Maine with another dog they helped. OH, I heard you even have Sage on trail with you now, and that she has saved your life! She is like, the Queen of Maine's Trail Angels. Will they be at my home tonight to talk with you?! Oh my gosh, I can't *wait* to meet Sage! Oh, and I heard the rumor about Becca too –"

At that, Zoby cut her off. "Bentley, stop. Yes to all of the above and I appreciate your support. But you've *got* to be careful what you say about Becca. We don't know anything for sure … and Marcus is with us." Her eyes widened at that. "Yes, so please … be understanding."

"Absolutely, you got it," she said, still fawning over him as she continued, "every hiker gets a polaroid at the hostel and signs it. Will you take a polaroid with me, and sign it for me?" Her eyes riveted on him as, spellbound, she toppled off the console again.

Groaning inwardly, Zoby said, "sure, whatever," while Mommy burst into giggles and helped Bentley up again.

This was going to be one long hostel visit, Zoby thought to himself.

CHAPTER 26

Goshawks and Marching into Monson

"Zoby's got a girlfriend," Chip sang in his high voice, causing the others to break out in giggles.

Scowling, Zoby took a playful swipe at Chip, "knock it off."

"Oh Zoby, Zo-by, will you sign my picture?" Chip impersonated, batting his eyes while pretending to hold something in his paws which he held up to Zoby's face.

Zoby cast a pleading look at Blaze. "Do something?"

The cardinal only laughed and said, "well maybe it would help if you weren't so..." he set his voice to a higher, swooning pitch, "so brave, and so strong and, so, sooo handsome..." Blaze about fell off the rock he was perched on from his own hysterics.

Grumbling under his breath and walking away from them, he moved back over to where Mommy and Uncle Stan were leaned up against some rocks atop Avery Peak on the Bigelows exposed ridgeline, taking in the sweeping 360-views on a break. They had left the Maine Roadhouse that morning, and while he enjoyed the actual hostel, he was more than ready to escape Bentley's fixation. He should have known Chip and Blaze would rib him over it.

Sage had flown back south for the day to glean any new intel following the incident at the river. Zoby looked over at Marcus, seated near Chip and Blaze, staring out over the mountains. He had, understandably, been quiet and withdrawn. Picturing Becca's sweet good-bye in the tunnel, Zoby's heart hurt for him, and made him even more determined to end the pain Jezebel and the Mafia were causing woodland creatures up and down the trail.

In her hidden den in southern Maine, Ariana treated the wounds on the squirrel she was tending to, and noted they were nearly healed after a few days of care. More concerning had been the fever and unresponsiveness of her patient.

Hearing a sound near the entrance of her den, she tensed up, prepared to fight if need be, but it was him. "How is she doing today?"

"Better," Ariana answered, "especially after you were able to swipe some medicine from a human's pack yesterday. That was good thinking, Ryder. What's the latest?"

"She's fuming after the failed attempt at the river," Jezebel's bodyguard replied. "The way she turned on the cat, I don't know how she didn't wind up a special bobcat treat herself. Kitty kitty has been banished."

Ariana shook her head, "unbelievable. The control she gains over woodland creatures that should be her predator is mind-boggling. Like the hawk that day on MacAfee Knob," she added as her eyes went distant. The gray edges of memories had been gaining clarity.

A stirring came from the bed at the edge of the den. As Ariana and the bodyguard looked over, Becca opened her eyes.

Moving north from the Bigelows, Mommy and Uncle Stan were excited about their planned stop at Harrison's Sport Camp, near Pierce Pond. Tim, a very hiker-friendly owner, designed a cluster of primitive rental cabins along a river with no electric, heat or air, but the fully-equipped main house boasts a large, cozy gathering and game room with dining area, where every morning a huge stack of melt-in-your-mouth blueberry pancakes are served to those lucky enough to snag reservations. Uncle Stan had managed to snatch the last available cabin, guaranteeing a spot for both of them at breakfast with the booking. The remaining thru-hikers on the trail camping around Pierce Pond were on a first-come, first-serve basis to get their names in for a spot at breakfast. Therefore, the race was on, and all the hikers were ahead of them on the trail that day.

The night before, his Fearsome Foursome had warned Zoby of a very territorial Northern Goshawk that lives on the AT near Pierce Pond. In spring and early summer while the young are nesting, the hawk annually attacks human hikers, leaving some with nasty wounds. Typically, by late summer and fall – and it was currently the end of August – the attacks stop, but Sage in particular was concerned Jezebel had contacted the ill-tempered bird.

"I'm reversing my nocturnal self to travel along the trail with you today," Sage had informed him in her soothing voice, "and you'll be safe tonight in the cabin at Harrison's."

Chip, from his furry bed on Zoby's back chuckled, "And *we* get to sleep on the cabin's porch. Tell Uncle Stan thanks for giving us a comfy spot too!"

Blaze chuckled and settled in beside Zoby, "I heard your Mommy and Uncle Stan talking about the Goshawk; it's well-documented in FarOut and there are signs posted on the trail. They're ready to defend themselves, even though they're aware it's not the season attacks typically occur. So, you have a lot of protection." Blaze looked into Zoby's eyes as he gave his amused warning, "no unnecessary acts of bravery, got it?"

Zoby nodded, thankful for his friends. What would he have done without them?

****

"Incoming!" Zoby heard Marcus shout from a tree above him, slightly ahead of them on the trail.

With shrieks and screams, the goshawk swooped and dove toward them. Already hiking with their trekking poles up, just in case, Uncle Stan and Mommy – along with their extended tramily they'd been hiking with that day, TurtleWizard and Sonar – started swinging and batting the air over their heads. Mommy scooped Zoby up and stuffed him in his carrier she had out and ready.

"Gotcha!" Uncle Stan yelled as he made contact with the dive-bombing bird, just over Mommy's head while she was getting Zoby in the carrier.

Popping his head back out, against Mommy's yells to stay down, Zoby watched with wide eyes as the humans hollered and four sets of trekking poles zipped through the air, batting away the goshawk.

"I see you in there, you revolting domestic! Humans are loathsome enough on trail, I have no problem getting a trouble-making, killer domestic off trail too!" The goshawk screamed as she circled back and dove toward the group, targeting Mommy, yet again.

Mommy also had her umbrella ready, to add another layer of both physical and visual protection, and she popped it open and crouched low, while the others swung their poles above her like baseball bats, making contact yet again with the hawk, much to her dismay.

And then the group went nearly still in shock as a great-horned owl swept into the scene, talons outstretched and open, as she soared directly into the goshawk's path.

Screeching in pain and disgust, the goshawk fought back against the slightly larger owl. "Sage! I should've known *you'd* be out here, rushing to defend the pitiful domestic."

The humans, and Zoby, watched the birds fight, speechless.

Gaining a position of advantage, Sage got a jab in with her talons, clutching the goshawk with one, and lowered them both to the ground. Hovering over the hawk, Sage stated in an eerily low voice Zoby had never heard from the normally calm and soothing owl, "get out of here. If you touch him or his humans, you won't survive my next attack. You. Have. Been. Warned."

Releasing the goshawk, she flew off, stopping briefly in a nearby tree to shriek back to Zoby, "watch your back, domestic. Jezebel won't let you win ... but *her* victory is not going to come at *my* expense."

In absolute bewilderment, the humans looked at the owl still on the forest floor near the trail, looked off in the direction the goshawk had flown, then looked at each other and Zoby.

Then all began talking at once.

"I *told* you we've had crazy animal experiences!" Uncle Stan was saying to Sonar and TurtleWizard. "No kidding," came their still-stunned reply.

After enjoying the as-delicious-as-promised blueberry pancake breakfast complete with eggs and sausage (which Mommy shared with Zoby), they made the iconic canoe-ferry ride crossing the Kennebec River. Sitting in Mommy's lap in the middle seat of the canoe while she recorded Uncle Stan paddling from the seat in front, and the canoe operator behind, Zoby watched Blaze flying over the river alongside them. The sun sparkled off the water while the mountain peaks rose up behind it, and looking ahead, he saw Chip and Marcus already on the other side, waiting for him, Chip doing cartwheels and other silly antics to celebrate this significant moment on trail. Zoby imprinted the moment on his heart.

A heatwave was hitting Maine, one final blast of scorching weather before summer would release its grip to autumn in this extreme northern area of the country, and the mid-day temperatures were hovering around an unseasonable 90 degrees. As they made their push to Monson, where they would then begin the 100 Mile Wilderness, they stopped frequently for dips in Maine's abundant lakes and river swimming holes.

Their last night before a short nero into Monson, they camped beside one such swimming hole, at the base of flowing cascades. Mommy and

Uncle Stan were talking about meeting up with their human Trail Angel friend, IceMan, in Monson, who would then be helping them through the 100 Mile Wilderness, and how they couldn't believe the thru-hike was coming to an end. In just over a week they would be climbing Katahdin. Zoby sat up in surprise at that – he knew they had been getting close, but didn't realize just *how* close.

Getting up and walking over to where his Fearsome Foursome were perched, he questioned Jezebel and the Mafia still attempting to thwart him, now that he was so close to completing the thru-hike.

"I mean, if there's only a little over a week, and 100-some miles left … every attempt since Georgia has been overcome, and I'm still on trail. At this point, it's making her look ridiculous, don't you think?" Zoby said to them, "maybe she'll just let me finish?" he added hopefully.

"Never gonna happen, kid," Chip said, climbing up onto his back. "I think the goshawk was her last significant resource before Katahdin though, so we may luck out with a quiet hike through the 100 Mile Wilderness."

Blaze agreed, "Trail Talk is still buzzing about the Notch and now two subsequent failed attacks. But the chatter is more subdued now, after what happened to Becca–"

"We still don't know what *actually* happened to Becca," Marcus interjected forcefully, "we only know no one has seen or heard from her since that night."

The rest looked at one another in silence, not daring a glance at Marcus. Eventually, Sage continued, "Jezebel can't stand looking incompetent, so she will literally die trying to get you off this trail, Zoby. She'll show her face again. With not many resources and tamer terrain through the long stretch of the 100 Mile Wilderness, the smart bet is on Katahdin."

"And if that's true," Chip dropped himself upside down over Zoby's face, "she'll have to travel up to Katahdin from southern Maine," he paused, then laughed, "and she hasn't traveled in three years. To go nearly 300 miles, she'll probably make her bodyguards *carry* her!" Chip found his imaginary vision quite amusing, as he fell off Zoby in hysterics.

Laughing more at Chip's antics than anything, Zoby looked around at his friends. "I'm very thankful for all of you. I can't believe we only have about another week together. I want to savor it, and make good, happy memories together, ok? Let's put aside Mafia talk unless it's necessary, and enjoy the 100 Mile Wilderness."

Smiles and nods met his suggestion, and their talk turned lighthearted, sprinkled with laughter, particularly as Zoby hit his now infamous pose with the cascades as his backdrop and exclaimed with exaggerated swagger, "small dog, big adventures!"

****

Monson was a crowded, excited hub of thru-hikers gathered mostly at Shaw's Hiker Hostel and The Lakeshore House hostel. The last trail town before entering the 100 Mile Wilderness, which ends right at the entrance of Baxter State Park and the base of Katahdin, thru-hikers were in celebratory moods. Zoby fed off the joy he felt radiating from Mommy and her interactions with Uncle Stan and their extended tramily of thru-hikers.

Additionally, IceMan surprised them by getting into town earlier than anticipated and was waiting at the trailhead near Monson for them, bringing them into town and helping with resupply. He planned to drive along the trail, slackpacking Mommy and Uncle Stan the first several days through the Wilderness, and camp with them along the road crossings where they would end each day.

The morning they were ready to start the 100 Mile Wilderness, they enjoyed the famous hiker breakfast at Shaw's, along with dozens of their thru-hiker friends. Zoby was passed around and praised for also making it so far on the trail, and many had heard about the "crazy squirrels" and "wild animal encounters" they had experienced, so his bravery was praised along with his stamina. Finally, Zoby thought with a laugh, it only took nearly 2,200 miles but he was finally not being laughed at by humans for being a small dog on a big trail!

And then, just like that, they were being dropped back off at the trailhead from where they had emerged the previous day, and were beginning the final week of their six-month journey.

"Why am I the only one who is competent?" Jezebel snapped to her bodyguards, now a trio for the trip up north to Katahdin.

"It must be exhausting," Ryder, her longest-running guard stated stoically.

Casting him a sideways glare, she contemplated lashing out at him, but instead decided it would be a waste of energy – and she would need it for the dreadful trip. Instead, she merely muttered in response, "indeed, it is," as she glowered at him through her mirror.

Continuing her original thought process, she nearly shimmered with the pent-up rage she was holding. "For nearly 1,100 miles that worthless daughter of mine couldn't get the job done, then every resource we've used since has been dimwitted enough to either get themselves killed, or been too spineless to pursue their victory in the face of a challenger from the other side. And that traitor," her face darkened, "my own maidservant providing intel. Well," she huffed, "it's true what they say, if you want something done right…"

"…do it yourself," Ryder coolly stated in what could have been mistaken for a flippant, disrespectful tone.

But, of course, that couldn't be what her longtime guard meant, right? Jezebel narrowed her eyes at him as she turned to face him.

"Yeessss," she drew out in a hiss under her breath. Walking up to him she stared him dead in the eye. "Exactly."

And with that, she marched out of her den, her trio of guards and an army of hand-selected Squirrel Mafia following, as they started their journey from Mahoosuc Notch to Katahdin.

CHAPTER 27

The 100 Mile Wilderness, Baxter State Park, and Summit Day

"There she is. I can't believe it. She's staring right at us," Mommy was choked up as she stared at their first view of Katahdin off the peak of White Cap Mountain.

"Pretty unbelievable," Uncle Stan agreed, "and in a few days we'll be standing in front of that sign on top of her summit."

Taking their lunch break there, with "Mama K" – as the hiking community affectionately referred to Katahdin – staring back at them, Zoby was all smiles. It was their third day in the 100 Mile Wilderness, and it had been glorious.

Perfect weather and beautiful scenery jumped out at them around every bend, from ponds and lakes, to waterfalls and streams, to expansive mountain views. Then there was the added bonus of his Fearsome Foursome feeling extra playful and doing silly things along the route to make him laugh. They had also been bringing him congratulations and encouragement from Trail Talk and Trail Angels he had encountered along the way, from Peyton and Eli, Shelby, Knox, and more woodland friends. Plus, Maverick had made the journey north and accompanied them the first two days, much to Mommy and Uncle Stan's delight at seeing the bull moose in a pond one morning.

All this enabled Zoby to pretty much ignore the squirrel chatter he still heard ringing through the forest as they hiked, and even the occasional nuts being thrown their way. Instead, he had enjoyed their hikes over the Chairback mountains and around all the lakes, and of course, being spoiled by IceMan's trail magic every morning and night as he made breakfast and dinner for Mommy and Uncle Stan ... with some savory items for the smallest hiker of the trio as well.

Continuing north, they said a fond farewell to IceMan the morning of their fifth day in the 100 Mile Wilderness, continuing on from there with only a day and a half left to hike before they had plans to meet Stan's daughters, Courtney and Carissa, at Abol Bridge. The girls had been able to rearrange their schedules to drive up and meet them in Maine, excited to hike Katahdin and celebrate the thru-hike finale together.

That final morning in the 100 Mile Wilderness, Zoby chatted with Chip and Blaze as Mommy and Uncle Stan packed up their tents one last time.

"Guys, this is it. Our final morning in the forest together. We'll be at the Airbnb in Millinocket with the girls after this now. Can you believe it? Who would have thought that first morning on Springer we'd have all these amazing adventures together over the last six months," Zoby reminisced wistfully.

"Awww kid, you're gonna make me cry," Chip threw his tiny arms around Zoby's front legs in a bear hug. Grabbing Zoby's ears, he pulled his face down and smacked a kiss on his muzzle between the eyes. "We're kinda fond of ya, Zobes."

In a rare show of outward emotion, Blaze allowed his teary eyes to be seen as he softly landed beside Chip and wrapped his wings around both the chipmunk and dog. "You have blessed *us* as well, Zoby. We believe you have, and will continue to, change the way many along the trail view domestics, and the Squirrel Mafia."

"Aww you guys…" Zoby was humbled, and beyond words.

Jumping up on Zoby's back, Chip stood on his back legs, puffed his chest out and raised his head, then bellowed as loud as possible in his high-pitched voice, "small dog, big adventures!"

****

Just a few hours later, in the early afternoon sun, they emerged from the 100 Mile Wilderness onto Abol Bridge. Flowing over the Penobscot River and offering an iconic photograph of Katahdin in all her glory towering over the river, Abol Bridge is a major milestone to reach – the northern end of the Wilderness and the southern border of Baxter State Park, wherein lies the final 15 miles of the AT and its northern terminus on Katahdin.

Hearing cheers and familiar voices as they walked over the bridge, they saw Courtney and Carissa in the Abol Bridge General Store parking lot wearing party hats and holding small bottles of champagne and sparkling cider. Several of their thru-hiker friends surrounded them, all cheering and joining the mini celebration. Popping them open with foamy sprays, the girls poured small glasses for all and toasted to finishing the Wilderness and the imminent summit that would complete the entire trail. Getting into the celebratory spirit, Zoby even sampled the sparkling cider, but the fizzy bubbles tasted funny, and the giant Slim Jim the girls had for him was a *way* better treat anyway, to his thinking.

Blaze and Sage followed the car during its 40-minute drive into Millinocket to establish the bird's home base in a tree at the Airbnb rental, while Chip and Marcus stayed at Abol Bridge. Chip set about chatting up the local Trail Angel woodland creatures to see if there had been any signs of Jezebel in the area. Trail Talk had already confirmed her moving along the trail just a bit south of them a few days ago, accompanied by a legion of Squirrel Mafia, but intel hadn't verified her in Baxter State Park as of yet.

After enjoying a lobster dinner in nearby Bangor and a good night's sleep in the rental, the tramily enjoyed a stunning 10-mile hike through Baxter right up to the base of Mama K at Katahdin Stream Campground. The magnificence of Maine was on full display as they hiked along the Penobscot River and Katahdin Stream, passing cascade after cascade and the stunning waterfalls at Big and Little Niagara Falls along the AT. Mirror-like turquoise alpine ponds reflected the mountains around them, in particular Katahdin herself, and their anticipation grew with every step bringing them closer to completing the trail.

Obtaining their thru-hiker permits from the Ranger Station at the campground, they left Baxter with all the proper passes and permits in hand to return the next morning to climb the final miles up Katahdin to her iconic sign awaiting them at the summit.

From a den deeply hidden near Katahdin Stream Campground, Becca could scarcely believe the turn of events of the past couple weeks since the scene at Mahoosuc Notch. Ariana had explained that witnessing Jezebel shove one of her bodyguards into the jaws of a bobcat that day had unlocked some memories, ones she had been vague in discussing, but Becca understood focused on the death of her father, and the surrounding events that unfolded three years ago on MacAfee Knob.

Ariana took a huge risk by revealing herself to Ryder, her mother's long-time bodyguard whom had suspected foul play by Jezebel both on MacAfee Knob and with his partner's death in the grips of the bobcat in Mahoosuc Notch. Seeing Ariana alive and hearing her recount what she witnessed in the Notch, as well as the fuzzy MacAfee memories coming clearer, had been the catalyst for Ryder to secretly join forces with Ariana. When Jezebel assembled the masses and rallied them to call for Becca's death, he seized the opportunity to save her instead, and without asking Ariana, brought Becca to her.

At first, Ariana had been resistant, but compassion won in the end. Seeing the injuries inflicted upon the poor girl, and her delirious state from hypothermia and malnourishment, she just couldn't stand by and let her mother claim another innocent life.

And so now, a healed and recovered Becca had joined Ariana on a stealthy, nocturnal voyage north to Katahdin. Ryder, of course, had traveled with Jezebel, but had met them a couple times in the middle of the night as the girls traveled through the areas near where Jezebel had camped.

It destroyed Becca that she couldn't get a message to Marcus she was alive, but she had managed to convince Ryder to simply not confirm her death via Trail Talk, to make just vague enough statements to keep tongues wagging as to her possible survival.

As for Ariana, she was utterly determined to clear the fog of her memories, right the wrongs of her mother's reign of terror, and avenge her father's death.

She only knew somehow deep down that Zoby, and her mother's plans on Katahdin, would be her key to that. What those plans were, and how she would stop them, she didn't know.

September 8, 2022 – Summit Day

"Summit Day!" Mommy excitedly grabbed Zoby, spinning around in circles. "We did it, baby boy! We walked through snow and rain and heat and bugs, we've survived crazy squirrels and animal encounters, and *we did it*! Today we summit Katahdin and complete this amazing journey … oh my goodness Zobes, we hiked the *entire* Appalachian Trail!"

Courtney, Carissa and Uncle Stan were laughing at her boundless energy at 4:00 a.m., but also understood and shared it. However, they demanded a stop at a coffee shop before heading into Baxter. "I mean, but first – *coffee*," Carissa and Courtney laughed.

After waiting in line to enter the Park, they finally arrived back at Katahdin Stream Campground a little after 7:00 a.m. Only five miles remained, but they knew the climb up to the summit may be the most challenging miles of the entire trail. With over 4,000 feet of elevation gain in those five miles, most of them in the first 4 miles, it is steep and filled with large boulders, starting even below treeline. Once above treeline, the scrambling becomes more like actual rock climbing in several areas, some with rebar grips to assist, where near-vertical boulders create the steep trail along the ridgeline's spine to the summit. In several areas, the boulders have abrupt drop-offs on either side, until hikers pass "the Gateway," where the vertical ascent ends and a gentler walk across the ridgeline ends at the infamous Katahdin sign.

Zoby saw Chip and Marcus near the trailhead as they prepared to start the hike, and Chip called out to let him know Sage and Blaze were working Trail Talk intel, but would be around during the day. As excited as he was, Zoby still had a gnawing pit in his stomach, knowing Jezebel was certainly there as well, and would inevitably launch a final attack.

Just over one mile into their hike, the tramily stopped for photos and snacks beside the resplendent layers of tall cascades making up Katahdin Stream Falls. Mommy teared up seeing the Falls in reality, a landmark she had seen online in so many summit videos, now no longer a dream but in living color before her eyes. Kissing Zoby, she whispered into his face as she nuzzled him how much it meant to share this journey, these moments, with him.

Onward they hiked, stopping to sample blueberries or turn to catch the views beginning to stretch out before them as they gained elevation. The gaps in the forest became more frequent as trees were beginning to become shrubs as they approached the alpine zone.

At one point, Mommy laughed with Carissa and Courtney as the girls exclaimed over the crazy loud chattering of the squirrels echoing through the forest. "I'm telling ya, the squirrels in Maine are *crazy*! And sometimes they even throw nuts at us!" Mommy told them, as they all laughed.

Zoby cast a look at Chip, Marcus and Blaze who were alongside them at that point, knowing the chatter was coming from the Squirrel Mafia who had made their way up the trail with Jezebel. His friends nodded, Blaze adding that he had heard they were positioned above treeline, so that's where Sage was waiting as well.

The bouldering climbs began well below treeline, nothing they hadn't encountered along the trail before, so Zoby easily scampered up them. Mommy and Uncle Stan laughed with the girls about how Zoby always showed them up with his "mountain goat" rock scrambling skills.

On high alert, Zoby reached the point where they were in the alpine zone, fully above treeline, and looked back down at his tramily helping one another up the boulders. Taking the opportunity, he walked over to Chip and Marcus to ask, "any signs of her yet?"

Shaking their heads, Chip hugged Zoby's front paws as he said, "the boulders get even steeper closer to the Gateway, with more cliff exposure, as well as more nooks and crannies for squirrels to hide. If I were a betting chipmunk, that's where I'd say she is. They probably got in position last night or early morning before light."

Marcus nodded in agreement, "from my time with her, I can affirm Jezebel's scouts would have certainly reported that as being the prime location to launch an attack. We're on alert, but my money is also on that final ascent prior to the Gateway."

Taking a deep breath to control both his accelerated pulse and thoughts,

Zoby accepted his friend's experience and opinions, and thanking them, headed over to where Mommy was now climbing up the last boulder to be level with him. As she petted and praised him for climbing so well, he rolled his head against her hand and thought to himself that no matter what, he was *absolutely* going to keep her safe.

****

Zoby looked up. Straight up. As did Uncle Stan, Mommy and the girls. The final, steepest ascent loomed before them. Seeing two large, flat rocks just off to the side creating a chair-like structure along a ledge, Mommy told the others to go on ahead and she would catch up. She wanted to take a breather and needed a snack to fuel the final climb.

Agreeing, the father-daughters trio continued on while Mommy and Zoby cuddled together on the granite outcropping of a seat. Enjoying the breathtaking views laid out in nearly all directions around her, Mommy kept snapping photos while she fed Zoby and ate her own snack. Finally deciding it was time to move on and catch up to the others, Mommy stood up on the rock ledge with the intent of leashing Zoby and putting her pack on.

Instead, in the blink of an eye, a dozen squirrels launched themselves at her, and at Zoby. Three flying squirrels hit Mommy first, one landing on her head near her face, causing her to close her eyes and throw her hands up while yelling in surprise, trying to remove it, as the others simultaneously clung to her chest and leg. Meanwhile an army of other large fox squirrels climbed up her and grabbed onto Zoby, rendering him stationary and covering his mouth.

So Zoby could only watch helplessly as, in a matter of seconds, the squirrel attack and momentum of throwing her hands up with her eyes closed caused Mommy to tumble backwards off the ledge, down the rocky cliff.

CHAPTER 28

Katahdin

From atop the boulders near the Gateway sign, Ariana and Becca watched the attack and gasped as they saw Mommy tumble down the rocks.

"We have to do something!" Becca yelled, clutching Ariana's arm as she jumped up.

"Wait a second," Ariana whispered, pulling Becca back down beside her, "where is she? She's gonna show her face, I can feel it. She wants the credit for this. We move then."

And then, Ariana saw it. And her world stopped, as the memories flooded in with clarity, in bold, vivid color rather than blurry gray edges.

Jezebel appeared and stood on the far end of the ledge across from where Mommy had fallen, just enough under the overhang of the rock above her to remain safe from flying predators, taunting Zoby as she waved the black hat with an embroidered white cross on it his Mommy wore every single day of their hike.

Ariana's mind went to a different ledge, on a different day. As a child just waking up from her nap, she saw through sleepy eyes her mother standing on the MacAfee Knob ledge, waving a different black object. The hiking buff that belonged to another domestic's owner, taunting the dog with his human's scent in the air, and the sight of the buff flapping in the paws of Jezebel.

The domestic hadn't attacked for no reason, the realization slammed into Ariana. Her mother had *provoked* him!

And then her mind's eye clearly saw her mother – her *mother!* – tossing the buff onto Ariana, not realizing her daughter was now awake.

But the dog was quicker than she anticipated, and latched on to Jezebel, just as she was tossing the buff onto Ariana.

Then Ariana saw Ahab, her father, racing toward them – toward *her*, she realized. Yelling *her* name, not her mother's. And Ariana's blocked memory unlocked, revealing the image of the dog releasing her mother, and then …

… her mother pushing her father on top of the buff, literally into the jaws of the dog as he grabbed his human's article of clothing.

Her mother had killed her father. And tried to kill *her*.

Ariana's memories continued to tumble out, fresh, clear and vibrant. The hawk swooping down, going for the dog, who would have released her father in the talons of a hawk, but Jezebel screeching at the hawk to save her instead. *Her, not them*, Ariana recalled with clear distinction. But the hawk grabbed both Jezebel and Ariana.

From the tree the hawk placed them in, she heard her mother hollering after it *not* to go back for Ahab, but the hawk was already returning for the domestic as originally planned.

Then the hawk stopping short as the dog's humans swung trekking poles at it.

And the domestic, swinging his head upward and toward the side of the cliff's edge, to see the hawk, dropping her father as he did so.

Her father, landing on the stony ledge of the rock outcropping, but the inertia of the throw fatally rolling him over the edge.

She remembered the look of surprise in the domestic's eyes.

She remembered the hawk being berated by her mother, and then promising her to never speak the truth of that evening.

And finally, her mother's voice in her own ear, twisting her memories over the years.

"Ariana, we have to *do* something!" Snapping out of her reverie and back to the present, Ariana felt Becca pulling on her as she gestured wildly at the scene below them.

In the minute Ariana had gone back to another time and place, Zoby had managed to get out of their grip and toss aside two of the squirrels that had a hold of him. With his front paws now free and Marcus and Chip jumping in to assist with the fight, it was clear Zoby was falling into Jezebel's trap to go after her, and to retrieve his human's hat. By doing so, he would go tumbling down the cliff in a different section from where Mommy had fallen, where she was lying still on a rock. Zoby would fall into an area where, from Ariana and Becca's higher advantage point, they could see the trio of Squirrel Mafia coywolves waiting.

Something broke, shattering deep inside Ariana, and she was filled with righteous fury toward her mother.

"Noooooooooooo!" Ariana screamed as she leapt into action, zooming past stunned Mafia squirrels dotting the steep line of boulders as she flew down the mountain full speed toward her mother. One final dive from the boulder above Zoby and she was on top of Jezebel, rolling with both of them precariously perched on the edge.

"Ariana?!" came the disbelieving cries from squirrels along the boulder ridge.

"*Ariana*?!" a stunned Zoby, Chip, Marcus and Blaze cried out, momentarily frozen in their acts of freeing Zoby from the squirrels holding him.

"*Ariana*?!" a swooping Sage, determined on trying to get to Jezebel around the cover of the rock she was under, hooted as she halted in mid-air.

"Yes, it's her," came the firm, strong voice from the rock above Zoby.

"*Becca*?!" came more astonished cries from all as they turned to see her.

"*BECCA*!" came the strangled and relieved cry of Marcus, as he abandoned Zoby to scramble up the rock and embrace his love, whom he had never really believed was gone forever.

Returning their gazes upon the scene unfolding as Jezebel tried to fight off her own returned-from-the-dead daughter, all witnesses gasped as her bodyguard pulled Ariana off her, but then turned and locked Jezebel within his iron grasp.

"Let her speak. Or I'll throw *you* to the coywolves instead," Ryder steely commanded Jezebel. With a deadly glare to her other guards cautiously approaching, he said to them, "I've witnessed her toss *us* – her guards, servants – and even her own family aside to their deaths. Don't think she won't do the same for you. Let Ariana speak."

All eyes turned to Ariana.

Fighting for calm, taking deep breaths, Ariana marched up to Jezebel's face, and hissing low in a voice only those on the ledge could hear, she simply said, "I remember."

She watched her mother's eyes temporarily widen with shock, then quickly recover as they narrowed into her typical angry slits.

Before Jezebel could speak, Ariana rose her voice and addressed the stunned onlookers. "She killed my father. And tried to kill me."

As jaws dropped and gasps rose, Jezebel started to shout but was quickly hushed by another of her guards stepping up and wrapping a bandana as a gag in her mouth. "Ahab was my dad's best friend," he spit out at her, "I want to hear this."

Quickly, Ariana described the memories that had come flooding back, describing how Jezebel had provoked the domestic and then saved herself while attempting to kill both members of her family. "Thanks to *this*," she said as she grabbed the black hat with a cross on it, "I remembered it all clearly."

The squirrels holding Zoby had relinquished their grip while Ariana spoke. Looking up at Sage, Zoby passed a knowing look to her, guaranteeing she had his back. He walked over to the ledge and saw Mommy had stopped her fall only a few rocks down, much to his relief. She had a few bloody wounds, and was beginning to stir.

Looking up at Becca, he asked her, "how did you survive? Ariana?"

Becca nodded and exchanged looks with Ryder and Ariana, who nodded their assent for her to share. "Ryder took me to Ariana. When Jezebel pushed the other bodyguard into the mouth of the bobcat in Mahoosuc Notch–" At this, Jezebel began shouting against her gag, to which Ryder and the other bodyguard shut her up again, then Becca continued, "Ariana began remembering what happened that day on MacAfee Knob. She and Ryder saved my life, and they came here today to save yours."

At that, a fury-fueled, irate Jezebel gathered all her strength and managed to free herself from Ryder's grasp. Still gagged, she shrieked unintelligible garble as she violently tackled her daughter, sending them both quickly rolling toward the edge.

Vaulting himself toward them, Zoby grabbed Ariana in his mouth, but the momentum of his leap had all of them skidding toward the edge of the cliff drop-off too fast to stop. Tossing Ariana backwards onto the ledge, he spun himself around just as he was dropping over the edge, clinging to the rock.

And he heard Jezebel's strangled screams as she dropped below, into the jaws of the waiting coywolves.

Clutching the edge of the rock, he didn't panic, because he knew, as he looked up, he could trust that Sage was swooping down to lift him up, while simultaneously, Ryder, Ariana, Becca and Marcus were grabbing his paws to help hoist him over the ledge.

Once back on the rock, they all turned around and peered over the ledge to the sound of the dogs, and Jezebel's demise, below.

Looking at Ariana, Zoby said, "I'm so sorry Ariana. For what you've endured all these years, and for my own part in this Mafia mess that hurt you." With a chuckle, he added, "but I sure am glad you made it out of that river to be here today."

Ariana grinned, "No kidding. But thank you, and for saving my life just now. I would have gone tumbling over that edge with her into the trap with the coywolves too. You have shown me before, and showed it again today, you are one brave dog." Putting her paw on his, she apologized, "I'm sorry, *so* sorry, for all the attacks on you and your tramily, simply because you're a small, white dog. You, nor *any* non-aggressive domestic, deserve that."

At her words, Zoby's eyes teared up, "thank you, Ariana," he replied, as he turned to the other side of the ledge, "my Mommy, how do we get to her?"

Sage flew over and said, "Zoby, Uncle Stan and the girls were waiting at the Gateway sign, and when you and your Mommy didn't come, they turned around. They're climbing back down and are almost here. Let me get you over with her, and they'll help you both climb up from where she landed. She's okay, I promise, just banged up."

Nodding, Zoby agreed and let Sage gently grip his hiking outfit in her talons. Before taking off, he looked back at Ariana. "You're in charge now. Peace on the trail is within your power. Right the wrongs." And with that, Sage lifted him off the ledge and flew the short distance over and down to where his Mommy was waking up from her fall.

Jumping up on her, putting his paws on her chest and licking her face, giving her happy yips, he went to work to calm her down, as he knew she could easily slide into a panic attack when she realized what had happened. Disoriented, with a large cut on her temple, she held Zoby tight and looked around in confusion. Realizing she had fallen off the ledge and down a series of rocks to the one she was now perched on, her eyes got wide and she shakily pulled herself up into standing position.

Just then, Zoby heard Uncle Stan and the girls shouting for them. Barking in response, he heard Mommy joining in yelling, "over here!" and then Uncle Stan's face peered over the ledge.

"What on earth happened?! Are you okay?" he yelled down.

"I'm not sure actually," Mommy answered, still dazed, "but I think I'm okay. Cuts and bruises, and boy am I going to have a headache."

"I'll check you out when we get you up here," Courtney, a nurse, called down to her. "Look to your right, there's another ledge, if you can make it to that one…"

And with them calling out the route and Uncle Stan scrambling down to get Zoby and offer a hand here and there, Mommy managed to climb back up to the trail and ledge.

"How did you fall?" Uncle Stan asked in bewilderment while Courtney looked her over and bandaged up her wounds, "did you just lose your balance?"

"I blacked out from the fall," Mommy answered, "and I think I dreamt about squirrels attacking me, and I think there was an owl … and coywolves? …" she shook her head and laughed. "I know I sound crazy."

Zoby looked over at the many squirrels, a chipmunk, a cardinal and an owl, discreetly hiding amongst the boulders and small shrubs dotting the trail. No, not so crazy, he thought.

****

A short while later, Mommy rode the tidal wave of emotion that washed over her as they caught their first glimpse of, then approached, the iconic Katahdin sign. Waiting back a moment for Uncle Stan to reach it first with his daughters, Mommy held tight to Zoby as tears flooded her vision and fell down her face.

"Now it's our turn," she whispered to him.

As they took their final steps on the Appalachian Trail, passing the last white blaze, both Mommy and Zoby remembered the good and the bad on their journey. Their silly moments together, the initial tramily of ladies, Uncles Stan and Steps, the snow, rain, heat, bugs, their illness, the poison ivy, and the pain. Zoby thought of Eli and Tinkerbell in their secret trip out of the kennel in the Smokies, his evenings chatting around camp with Chip and Blaze, and later Marcus and Sage, his close calls with coyotes, foxes, bears, snakes, and more. And both remembered all the Trail Angels, human and wildlife, who had made their epic journey possible.

All around them, human thru-hiker friends and not-so-hidden woodland creature friends broke out in roaring cheers and applause as they approached, and then touched, the sign.

Their thru-hike was complete. They had done it.

Breaking into sobs, Mommy held Zoby in one arm and clutched the sign with the other while laying her head on it. After a moment, wiping her eyes and smothering Zoby in kisses, she laughed and cried, praising him for his strength and courage on the trail with her, and accepting the congratulations from those around her. Uncle Stan came over and wrapped them both in a giant, tearful hug while Carissa and Courtney cried and recorded the memories.

Zoby proudly held his head high in her arms and sent his huge, gaping mouth, tongue-wagging grin toward Chip and Blaze, Becca and Marcus, Ariana, Ryder and Sage, and all the others gathered around, as well as his human thru-hiker friends loving on him as well.

Following thru-hiker tradition by climbing onto the back legs of the A-frame Katahdin sign, Mommy lightly placed Zoby's paws on the top edge of the sign, holding him with one hand and her trekking poles in the other. "Ready?" she whispered to him.

Triumphantly throwing her trekking poles up while Zoby puffed out his chest and tossed up his head, humans and animals alike yelled in unison ...

"Small dog, big adventures!"

Epilogue

Ariana looked out over the woodland creatures gathered and smiled. This was a day of celebration, a day that almost didn't happen.

Today was Marcus and Becca's wedding day.

Presiding over the ceremony, Ariana took a moment before beginning to reflect upon the last few weeks after their return to Mahoosuc Notch. Ariana had declared an official end to what had formerly been known as "the Squirrel Mafia," and instituted new repercussions toward any woodland creature attacking a domestic or its humans without cause. She appointed Ryder, Becca and Marcus new positions in leadership within the Notch clan that were to be recognized along the trail, and instituted new educational programs for woodland creatures young and old to understand the necessity of sharing the trail in peace.

Looking at the glowing, happy couple in front of her, she thought how differently it could have ended for them. How her mother had tried to ruin their love, their joy, even their lives.

Turning to Ryder beside her, she smiled. Maybe it was just her, but she thought he was looking at her a little differently – she blushed as he caught her looking – these days too.

And as members of the wedding party, Chip, Blaze and Sage were happily lined up, ready for the ceremony to begin. Chip, of course, theatrically wiping tears from his eyes and loudly blowing his nose into a handkerchief.

And with one last look out to the variety of animals, big and small, gathered to celebrate, she was simultaneously grateful her mother's reign had ended, while wishing her father could see the legacy she was building now.

"Thank you, Zoby," she whispered under her breath, "for saving us all."

And somewhere back in Georgia as they returned to their RV, Zoby smiled as he curled up in Mommy's lap and wondered what their next big adventure would hold.

Tonya "Monarch" Lonsbury

Walking away from a lucrative full time - but anxiety-producing - real estate career, Tonya sold everything to travel the country in an RV with her dog, Zoby. Hiking, biking, kayaking, climbing mountaintops or scuba diving the depths of the sea, adventure in God's Creation has started to heal the scars of both professional burnout and personal traumas. Returning to her roots, she is now pursuing her passions – and her degree – by sharing her adventures through art and writing, as well as online in social media, blogging and vlogging.

Silly or serious, her prayer is to share her physical and spiritual journeys, bringing the beauty of God's Creation to others who are unable to experience it in person, and perhaps help someone else take steps toward healing, or provide encouragement and joy in a sometimes dark world. Join Tonya and Zoby as they explore new places and a new lifestyle one day at a time, in faith allowing God to write the next chapter of life - the greatest adventure!

****

Love reading Zoby's adventures?

You can watch his *real-life* AT thru-hike, and other adventures, on Mommy's YouTube channel and social media!

Subscribe, like and follow **@TravelingWithTonya** on YouTube and all social networks!

Plus, get the inside scoop, special discounts and pre-sales on upcoming "Zoby" releases Mommy has planned, as well!

AUTHOR ACKNOWLEDGEMENTS

To the One who consistently renders me speechless with His unfathomable love and grace bestowed upon *me* – a mere ragamuffin – daily, my praises are unending of your work within me. How such a fallen being as myself can be the recipient of ceaseless mercy; how I am deserving of Your blessings sending me on journeys into Your Creation, to draw nearer to You, as You fulfill your promise to draw near to me … to be healed and transformed on these journeys … Lord, I am awestruck. I pray my words, my art, and my life can bring You honor, and reveal even a fraction of your glory. Thank you for the metamorphosis of "Monarch," on the Appalachian Trail and beyond.

To my four-legged best friend from whom I have learned strength and courage beyond measure … Zoby, you are the greatest earthly gift. They say "dog" is "God" spelled backward, and you embody that for me. Your unconditional love is as inspiring as your bravery. My greatest adventure buddy, from hiking to kayaking to RV life and trail life and beyond, I can't imagine not sharing my life with you by my side in all of it. I promised you your best dog life if you came back to me after your surgery … but *you* have given *me* the best life I could have ever imagined.

To "Uncle Stan," without whom Zoby and I may not have survived the Appalachian Trail … before getting on trail, I prayed that if in His Will, God would bring me someone to experience this journey with, someone who would also love Zoby, and if possible, also love the Lord and share my faith. He brought me all of that and more, a friend not only for the trail, but a friend for life. Thank you for bringing me not just tramily but real family by sharing yours with me. I love our continued adventures and the bond we share … even if you did steal my dog.

To Carissa, Courtney and Dave, Careis, Sue and Mark, Marietta and Jean … Mine and Zoby's AT journey would have been incomplete without you all a part of it. Your kindness to a stranger who was hiking with your dad/brother/son, etc is unparalleled. You are all family of the heart now.

To "Uncle Steps" and "Aunties PotatoChip, Brazil and StickyBuns" … tramily for life. Thank you, all of you, for *so much* for laughter on trail, for loving me and Zoby, for being an indelible part of our journey, and our lives. I pray to have future adventures with each of you. Oh and Steps, my feet need massaged, where are you?

To Adam and Lou Ann … you have both been a part of my life for most of my life, and shown me that family is not in blood or on paper, but in heart and friendship. Thank you both for being a pillar of undying support for me and Zoby, always.

To Joyce … there's no way to appropriately thank you for your strength in comfort, assistance and encouragement over the years. You have been there through many of my hardest life moments, and I will never forget that.

To Michelle, Hannah, Shannon, Erica, Holly & Eric, Oscar & Rebecca ... my support group on trail of friends and family. Most of you I have known all, or for the majority of, my life. Your encouragement via text messages, phone calls, social media posts and comments, even sending money, and truly most of all your *prayers* – you got me through it all. You really did – I hiked that trail "with" all of you, and my gratitude is immeasurable.

To all the Trail Angels ... I tried to mention and incorporate into this book all the real-life Trail Angels whom, through your selfless acts of kindness, bolstered and carried us through parts of the journey to find our way to its completion. Without you, our thru-hikes would not have been the same, so without you, this book would have been incomplete. I give praises that due to your generosity, new friendships were made that endure after trail life ends.

To the AT Class of 2022 ... thank you. Thank you for loving Zoby, for making him the darling of the trail, for the shared laughs and tears, for the pain and the joy ... for the memories of a lifetime.

Made in the USA
Coppell, TX
10 May 2023

16629358R00125